REMEMBER THE STARS

THE TALES OF THE SELYENTO: BOOK ONE

ERIS MARRIOTT

ISBN Ebook: 978-1-7372711-2-3

ISBN Paperback: 978-1-7372711-0-9

Editor:

Marissa Gramoll - marissagramoll@gmail.com

Proofreader:

Beth Swicker - ricknbeth529@sbcglobal.net

Formatter:

Liz Steinworth - www.theartofliz.com

Cover Designer:

Lilia Dormisheva - www.ldormishev.com

Logo Artist:

Joy Noakes - thisjoyouslife@gmail.com

*This book is dedicated to my mother,
who has read every draft, listened to every story, and held my hand through every
meltdown.*

Mom, if you're reading this, you're the best a daughter could ever ask for.

AUTHOR BIOGRAPHY

Eris Marriott is a graduate student working to pursue her Ph.D. in economics. When not contemplating the quandaries of supply and demand, she spends her time riding her horse, Andy, playing with her dog, Cuddles, and writing.

Her love of writing stems from her love of reading, naturally. Her favorite genres are fantasy, horror, and mystery, all of which she draws inspiration from when she crafts her own worlds and characters.

She likes her coffee black and her days warm and sunny. Nothing makes her happier than to get outside and enjoy life while it lasts.

~

CONTENTS

1

LIGHTS CALLING

Clarisse

A ball of light flicks to life in Clarisse's hand. She hears it call to her every night; tonight is a night she decides to answer. Answering is always fun. Laughter fills the air of the once dark room. A symphony of colors—red, blue, green, white—all crash through the night. More lights tug at the edge of Clarisse's mind. With little more than a wish they, too, join in on the fun.

All about her bedroom they dance with her. Clarisse swears they make music with the way they move. Her little feet become warm against the cold floorboards and a small array of constellations wink and blink all around her.

She hears running. Something tells her she'll be in trouble for this, but she keeps going. That's when Mom and Dad break through the door. Mom screams and Dad jams a hand in his jean pocket. He rips out a lighter and runs over to stick it in Clarisse's face. *Daddy, what are you doing?* Clarisse squirms, the flame getting closer and her pulse getting quicker. He's shouting something, but Clarisse is too dazed to understand him. Her lip puckers. She starts to cry and all around her the little lights crash to Earth and shatter. Now the only light is coming from the flame Dad is waving in her face.

"A witch should burn!" His voice reeks with some horrible smell. It always smells like that when he shouts. The lighter starts to singe her skin when Mom comes running over and she rips Dad off her and plucks the lighter from his grasp. She hurls it into the hallway. "Arthur! Stop it! You're scaring her!"

Dad stumbles back. He blinks slowly, leaning against the wall. His breathing is labored. For now, he's defeated. Clarisse's heart feels like it might leap out of her chest. She rubs her nose where the lighter almost burned her.

A witch should burn?

Mom flips on the lights to Clarisse's room and motions for her to sit on the bed. Clarisse, still crying, nods and joins her.

"Clarisse, what were you doing?" Mom's breath is calm, but something else flickers in her eyes. They look glassy. "You need to tell Mommy."

Words try to find their way from Clarisse's lips, but they never make it. Her breath comes in desperate gasps and she reaches for a hug. Mom pulls back, putting a hand out to push her away. *It's so cold.*

"Listen to me," Mom slurs, "you need to tell me what's going on. This is the second time this week." The smell is on Mom's voice, too. Clarisse crinkles her nose to try and block it out.

"I—" Clarisse sucks in another breath, "I answered them. They talk to me. They tell me to let them out to play."

"Witch!" Dad starts yelling again. Clarisse claps her hands over her ears. This is too much. She just wanted to play. *What's wrong with the lights?* A desperate look at Mom yields nothing. Mom is busy focusing on the wall across from them, murmuring things Clarisse doesn't understand.

Dad starts to move toward Clarisse. She shrieks, covering her face. Dad has hit her before and she doesn't want him to get her on the face again. Mom gets up and stands in the way again. "Arthur, do not test me. We will fix this. I've already found a place." The edge in Mom's voice makes Clarisse scoot even farther back on the bed. Mom isn't kind, but she doesn't let Dad hit her too much, either.

"If she goes to school or is seen in public with bruises, you'll be locked up and I'll be *left* with her. And you'll be bankrupt and stuck with a record. Think with your brain and not the alcohol, stupid." Mom's voice is as icy as the bedroom itself. *Left with me? Does Mommy not like me?*

Clarisse reaches for the little stuffed wolf on her bed. Clutching it to her chest, she closes her eyes. Wishing for everything to disappear is stupid; of course, it doesn't work. It's not like asking for the little lights to come and play. But wishing is all she has. Mom comes back to sit with her on the bed.

"Clarisse, you are *not* going to play with the lights anymore. Do you understand? If I catch you doing that again, Dad and I both will give you the whipping of a lifetime. Do you understand?" The way Mom's eyes gleam makes Clarisse shiver. She whimpers a soft 'yes' and stays as far away from Mom as she can. *Who will save me from her?*

"Tomorrow, I'm going to take you to the Church of the Light. There's a priest there. You will behave and do everything he says. Is that clear?"

Clarisse gives Mom another nod. While she's not sure what the Church of Light is, she knows it doesn't sound good. The look on Mom's face is a lot more dangerous than Dad's right now.

"Then that's the end of that." Mom stands up, wobbling a bit. It's the only sign that she's probably had adult juice just like Dad. *They're always drinking that stuff.* When Mom leaves, Clarisse listens for the sound of their footsteps. When she's sure they're gone, she lets herself cry.

Tucking the plushy even closer, she lets the sadness wrack through her chest. *What's wrong with me? Am I a witch?* Clarisse remembers all the pictures of the strange women on broomsticks from her storybooks. They look like fun! So why is being one bad? Why is magic bad?

Nothing makes sense, except for the sound of her breathing. She wishes she could bring the lights back, but she knows Mom would make good on her promise to hurt her. Her nose wiggles again, the skin still stinging from the flame of Dad's lighter.

Clarisse yanks the blankets as far as they will go over her head. Sometimes, she'll sneak the lights out under the covers. But tonight, that seems like a bad idea. Mom and Dad might be waiting for her to disobey, even if she did hear them walk away. *What if they come back?*

Eventually, Clarisse stops crying. Her breath slows and her eyes fall shut. She sleeps.

THE CHURCH OF LIGHT

Clarisse

Clarisse is right. The Church of Light is the most terrible place on Earth. They arrive in the nighttime. The moon whispers to her like it always does. *Run,* it says. Mom says it's Clarisse's imagination that she hears things, but she knows it's real.

She takes her plushy with her, holding onto it for dear life. It's her only friend. It drips with her sweat the harder she holds it. A mass of people in dark hoods waits on the inside of the strange white building. Clarisse swallows a lump in her throat and feels her temperature rise. *I feel sick and scared.*

They're pointless thoughts—pointless feelings. It's not like they'll help. At the head of this group of people is a man clad in a white robe. He doesn't look like any priest Clarisse has seen before. Mom and Dad have taken her to churches before to try to solve her "problem," but none have been able to fix her. Everyone else says she's fine. Of course, they've never seen Clarisse's lights.

Mom holds Clarisse's free hand so tight that she wonders if she might squeeze it off. The people in robes all step away and Mom lets go when the priest approaches. *What is he going to do? No one can help me, and I don't want to say goodbye to my lights.*

"Clarisse Monroe, please step forward," the priest orders. Clarisse can't see his face. *Is that a mask?* Her feet are like jello when she tries to do what he says. She knows Mom and Dad will be angry if she resists.

The man takes her by the hand. Clarisse stares up at him—the mask he wears is black with gold swirls and markings. It's hard to breathe with all the candles everywhere; the whole world is choked out by the heavy scent of smoke and... *something sweet.* Not like cookies, though. Her stomach rumbles. She wishes Mom and Dad would have let her have food before coming here. No food was offered *all* day. Clarisse knows it's probably because she misbehaved.

"Please show us, the Enlightened Ones, your power."

Clarisse gulps. *They want to see the lights?* She stretches out her hands, doing her best to try and do as the man says. It's hard. The lights aren't calling right now. Her ears strain to listen. They have to come. Maybe once everyone sees them, they'll know that they aren't bad at all.

When she opens her eyes, she smiles. Sitting in her palms is a glowing butterfly. Sometimes they take on fun shapes. Clarisse loves the fun shapes. All around her, she hears gasping. Someone even screams. The priest puts out his hands, demanding calm.

"Thank you, Clarisse. Arthur, Deborah, it is clear here that your daughter needs immediate spiritual attention. I have never, in my life, seen a person so riddled with *demons.*"

Demons? What are those?

Before she can open her mouth to ask any further questions, the priest grabs her and thrusts her into a wooden chair. *Where was that before?* She sees some robed men walking away from it. They must have brought it. Leather straps are forced over her wrists and ankles. She kicks and starts to yell. "Stop! What are you doing?"

"They have her entranced, my friends! What you're seeing is their resistance!"

Clarisse scrunches up her face, wailing even louder. *What are they doing?* Her legs flail as the man has some of his weird friends join him to hold her down. Mom steps forward, her face full of anger. "Clarisse, you sit still for Father Simmons right now or I'll whip the demons out of you myself!" Her voice is so loud—it crashes over the room like an angry sea. No one says anything to her. Clarisse stops fighting.

While she's held against her will, she glares at her Mom. Something stirs in her stomach... something dark. *You're mean, Mommy. I'll get you back for this, someday.* It's a blip in her thoughts. She doesn't know why she would think something so *awful*. But that regret is soon cut out by the feeling of something hot touching her flesh. Turning her neck as best as she can, she sees a hot, iron stick being pressed against her legs. Screaming isn't enough to drown out the pain.

"Great Light, free this child of her demons!" The man, Father Simmons, shouts to drown out Clarisse's groaning and shrieking.

"Great Light, free this child of her demons!" The crowd copies Father Simmons word-for-word. *Please, stop!* Clarisse can only cry out in her head now. Speaking is too hard. Everything hurts and she wants nothing more than to break free of this chair. Squirming can't be helped. *Mommy, I'm sorry. Daddy, I'm sorry. Please, make it stop!*

"Let her be cleansed of her sins!"

This time, the crowd *and* Mom and Dad repeat him. The iron continues to be jammed up against her skin. Anywhere that there's clothing is seared away by the fiery metal. What seems like hours of agony tick by as Father Simmons continues to scream things to this "Great Light." To her relief, Father Simmons sets it aside after almost all of her pants have been burned off. Her legs are covered in horrible burn marks.

Mom's going to make me wear long pants again. Mom does that every time Dad hurts her—or even when she hurts her on occasion. Mom prefers to hurt Clarisse with words, though. Father Simmons steps back. "Do you repent of your sins?"

Repent? What does that mean? Clarisse nods her head as fast as possible. She doesn't need to know what it means right now, though she does wish someone would say. A few of the people in robes step forward and unclasp her from her chair. Her legs give out when she tries to stand. She topples to the floor, weeping. At some point, her plushy dropped from her arms. It lays in front of her, waiting. Reaching for it, she finds that it's hard to even move her upper body. The feeling of its fabric is soft against her aching skin. Her tears stain the fabric as she crushes it against her. Clarisse refuses to look up, or listen. Father Simmons is saying something to the weird people standing around.

Rolling over, Clarisse's eyes widen. Just outside the window sits a wolf made of stars. *What is that thing?* She blinks; it disappears, leaving her alone again. Closing her eyes, she lets her body give out. Sleep finds her, somehow. When she wakes, she's back at home in bed with a book about prayers and fighting off *demons*.

"Make sure you read it."

Clarisse, of course, can only read but so much. She doesn't understand half the big words she's looking at. Holding it in her lap hurts worse than anything Mom or Dad have ever done. It hurts to roll over and set it on either side of her either. Eventually, she lets it slide to the floor. All night, she tosses and turns, whimpering. *What did I do wrong?*

3

THE CON

Father Simmons

Hours pass from the time of the exorcism. Anthony Simmons sits in his dark office, fingers clasped together, his eyebrows knit in deep thought. It's been two years since he arrived in Ashville, a grand plot in his mind to start the Church of Light.

Gathering members was hard. In a mostly devout Bible belt county, convincing people that a different god—a "Great Light" existed and that *he* was the path to true enlightenment was like no challenge he ever faced before. But Father Simmons relished in challenges.

His phone rings.

"Hello?"

"We've put her to bed like you told us. What now?" From the sound of her voice, Deborah Monroe is already a bit tipsy. *Much easier to manipulate.*

"Let her rest. Bring her to the school tomorrow. It'll be a bit before she trusts me, but I'll lead her around and let her get used to things. She'll need to enroll immediately so that I can keep an eye on her and ensure that the demons are completely gone. A few more exorcisms may be in order, if not at least some lashings."

Father Simmons licks his lips as the silence between them continues. Something crashes on the other end of the phone. "Deborah, we are not paying any more money to that man!"

Arthur's slurred voice grates his ears. *We can't afford to have him drunk, now can we?*

"Listen, you both need to abstain from the consumption of alcohol. It offends the Great Light. So does greed. Do you want to be free of these demons? Do you want your daughter to heal?"

Deborah sighs.

"I do. I'll... talk to him. When he's sober. We have more than enough money to enroll her. How much will it take before we're free of her problem? This... this doesn't look good for us."

"Trust in me, Mrs. Monroe. Your daughter's plague will not last you forever."

The phone clicks, but Father Simmons smiles with satisfaction. All afternoon, his wheels have been turning. Burning the child had been... *interesting.* Something he'd never considered before. But when her parents called and spoke of strange lights erupting from her hands and being worried that something was wrong with her soul, he knew that she presented herself as the perfect sacrificial lamb.

Word would spread like wildfire; more would come to his flock. Whispers that other churches turned them away—that he had been the only one *kind* enough to save her would fester.

Of course, someday, the child would grow up and begin to think for herself.

Father Simmons frowns. Though he never saw those lights she made, he knows that such descriptions *have* to mean that she's a fiery spirit. She won't be doused.

"No..."

Then his scheme turns in a delightful direction—one so simple he never thought of. *Why not be a sacrificial lamb that keeps on giving? Giving until I've wrung her dry?*

It'll take time, but he'll win her over. She'll fear him, but know him as the person who can save her. She'll come to him with his ideas. If there are problems, he'll take care of them. He'll be the one to stop her parents from drinking. He'll be there when she's ready to run off on her own. Of course, there will come a day when she realizes that he's built this church from scratch. She may even know that it's a cult. That child's eyes hid true, working brain cells— unlike her parents. He would continue the exorcisms as needed until she became smart enough to question him. Then he'll sow the seeds of hatred between her and her parents and let the consequences grow on their own. Siphoning money from Arthur and Deborah would be easy.

By then, they'll hate her and she'll hate them. It'll be easy to convince them that they're ridding the world of evil. He already has them in his grasp. Convincing them of this religion bullshit he came up with would be even easier. With her father's greed and her mother's vanity, Clarisse's parents would be easy to convince that death is the only way to cure her.

"I'll put it into a trust… make her parents the beneficiary and let them in on the plan when it's time…" Father Simmons chuckles. "Elementary, really."

But right now, his wine store and ledgers are waiting for him. A gleam shines in his wild gray eyes, his ruffled black hair beginning to gray, too. He sighs with a bit of glee in his lungs.

"Give it thirteen years or so and the money I get from her will have accrued me the wealth and power I desire. Her parents will be free and the kid will be forever a symbol that I can cast out demons."

At any cost.

"Everyone will believe in me. And she'll never live long enough to tell anyone any different." Grinning, he leaves his desk and flips out the lights, leaving darkness and murder in his wake.

4

GRADUATION DAY

Clarisse (13 Years Later)

Sweat breaks out on Clarisse's forehead. A pounding starts, making her squint her eyes to shield them from the sun. Growing up in the Church of Light and the associated School of Light isn't something she wants to remember. But that's hard on a day committed to memories. Father Simmons climbs the stage that sits behind the church. It's a sweltering day in June. Clarisse wonders why they didn't hold this stupid ceremony inside. It's not like a ton of kids go to this weird place, anyway.

The sight of Father Simmons' graying hair and stark-white smile makes Clarisse shiver. It's enough to make her want to turn and run. Sure, the guy likes her and all, but she knows his game. It didn't take long before Clarisse realized that the Church of Light is a cult. She figured it out in seventh grade while reading a book she borrowed from the local library. Father Simmons made a point of letting the children go and pick out books once a week from Ashville Public Library. Of course, books on cults weren't permitted, though most kids didn't even know what cults *were* or where to look. Clarisse got good at hiding the forbidden books beneath more benign books on knitting or sewing. Something more believable.

She shakes her head at the memory. Years later, Clarisse hinted at knowing about Father Simmons' truth and what the Church of Light was. An oath of silence was declared between them. Father Simmons wouldn't perform anymore "exorcisms" and Clarisse wouldn't rat him out to the police. Clarisse considered running away many times before striking that bargain, but being a cult kid in a small town has its downsides. *How do you tell someone you're running away from home because your parents are trying to cleanse you of your demons?*

Everyone in Ashville had at least heard rumors about the place. Hearing the librarians chatter about the strange students clad in white and black uniforms was enough for Clarisse to figure out that their backwards religion wasn't a *secret*. It makes her blood boil while Father Simmons drones on, giving a sermon about abstaining from the evils of alcohol, drugs, and sex. The things that would be available to them once they went out into the real world.

"The School of Light cannot protect you, now. You are responsible for your *own* choices, so make them wisely!" He lets that last sentence bounce a bit, a menacing glitter in his eyes. Father Simmons is a stickler for the rules. Clarisse can tell it's killing him that these kids will actually get to walk out today, some of them leaving home forever. While not all the kids know they're in a cult, the rules alone are enough to make most of them want to barf. Clarisse is extra-sure to toe the line only because of her parents.

Thanks to Father Simmons and his crazy followers, Mom and Dad *did* stop drinking. And after a few exorcisms, they stopped beating her altogether. Scars still litter Clarisse's skin. They've whitened with age, but she never lets herself forget. What they've done to her is unforgivable. Despite keeping a calm demeanor all these years, Clarisse hates her parents. She curses the ground they walk on, hoping at any minute that *one* of them might drop dead. It's a horrible sentiment, but she can't help it. How can she?

The only thing stopping her from reporting them is the fear that she might be found out. *What if I can still make those stars? What if they never left? And where would I go?* These thoughts dart about in her mind. She's only brought back to the present by the sound of quiet applause.

"So I offer my sincerest congratulations to the newest graduates of the School of Light. Go forth, and make the Great Light proud!"

That's Clarisse's cue. She throws her graduation cap off her head so fast that it boomerangs, almost smacking someone in the back of the head. Clarisse covers her mouth to stifle a laugh. None of the kids here are friendly to her. She's the *demon kid*, after all. Even if they don't believe in the Great Light, they've seen the exorcisms. All members of the Church of Light are "encouraged" to attend after they turn thirteen. Of course, all the most devoted parents drag their kids along to watch. It's a way of warning them. *Do what she does. Defy me. You'll end up like her.*

Mom and Dad find her in the crowd, Dad looking especially proud. *Jackass.*

"Congratulations, sweetie!" Mom's voice is laced with honey. Clarisse knows it's really vinegar. She chooses not to answer, just smiling at them both instead. Silent tension weighs between them until Dad decides to break it.

"We've managed to get a cake for you! It's at home," Dad exclaims. "Took some saving up, but this is a day worth celebrating, eh?" Dad claps an arm around Clarisse's shoulders. She stiffens up, holding in every urge to slap it off. Barely. It gets harder every day to do what they say. Clarisse is a person, not a *pet*.

Even pets get treated better than this.

Why she keeps complying, she doesn't understand. They get to the house and she eats her cake. It tastes like shit. The icing is melted and it looks like they bought it on the "sell-by" date. It hurts her heart to know they can't afford anything because of her. What sucks the most is deep down, Clarisse *knows* that it's her fault she's in this mess. If she could just control her powers which, as she's found out over the years, are directly tied to her unruly emotions, they would be fine. The thoughts she's allowed herself to think today are dangerous.

Mentally, she chastises herself. She reaches beneath the table and pinches her skin—hard. It whitens under her grip and she holds it. Pain is one of the few things that will stop an inevitable outbreak of lights and trips to see Father Simmons. An exorcism isn't something she's had in years. She doesn't want to test Father Simmons on that deal they made. Sometimes, she wonders if they might actually try to kill her one day.

I hope to the Great Light not. It's a stupid thought. Clarisse knows there's no "Great Light," but sometimes it's just something she thinks. Hearing it all the time makes it almost mechanical. Some god or goddess sits somewhere and judges the "Enlightened Ones" that Father Simmons leads around like sheep.

The last of the grimy cake on her plate slides down her throat. Regret swirls up, threatening to send it spewing into the air along with tears for all the pain and misery she's caused over the years. For all the hiding she's had to do.

"Are you ready to start at the firm tomorrow?" Dad interrupts her thoughts without skipping a beat. He's more bearable now that he's not drunk, but that doesn't change the resentment she holds in her heart for him. *Yet another flaw of mine. If they didn't work so hard to keep me secret, then what would have happened to me?*

Clarisse nods. Words don't come to her all the time—her mind kind of just freezes up, leaving her scrambling about to try and have a normal conversation. Her fingers grasp at her greasy, brown hair and start to wrap them in anxious coils.

"Stop that," Mom slaps at her hand. It stings, but Clarisse is used to it. Mom hates it when she fidgets.

"Deborah, darling, she's nervous! Let her be. She only wants the best for her old man. Isn't that right, Clarisse?" Dad winks. He thinks he's doing her a favor, but in reality, Clarisse just wishes she could disappear from the table altogether. Nothing she does is ever the right choice. She feels a giant anchor start to tug on her heart. It always shows up in moments like this, threatening to drag her below the surface of her misery and drown her.

"Are you sure you want me to work for you?" Clarisse manages to stammer the question before lowering her eyes.

"Absolutely!" Dad's voice is heavy with fake excitement. *How can he possibly be excited to bring his freak of a daughter to work? I'm a walking liability.*

But that's that. Clarisse doesn't dare to ask anything more about going to work at Monroe Accounting. Her fate is determined by other people, as always. She's eighteen, sure, but where is she going to go? Clarisse has no money, no experience, and she has the weight of a cult's reputation hanging around her neck and shoulders. And *threats.* So many threats. It's occurred to her that going to the police might help. *But what good would they do? Where would they send me?*

There aren't many resources in Ashville. No one offers her jobs when she leaves. The only reason Dad has any income flow is because he's the only game in town when it comes to accountants.

Sometimes, though, Clarisse wonders if it would be worth it just to slam that dumb front door behind her and take herself out of here. *As if I have the nerve.*

Her celebration ends with no fanfare. Clarisse offers to clean up, which is really her way of showing that she's still under their thumb —nothing for them to be afraid of. When she finishes dishes, she goes to her room to find a pile of Dad's ripped jeans waiting for her. Sighing, she grabs her sewing kit and patches and gets to work. Clarisse prides herself on being something of a seamstress, despite having never been formally trained.

Within an hour, she has them all repaired and sets them on the kitchen table, good as new. *Well, as close to new as I can get.* Material is hard to come by with how little money they have. Clarisse wonders why Dad doesn't make more at his job. Or why Mom doesn't get one. It has never made sense to her, but she doesn't dare ask. Any struggles this family faces are her fault. *Simple.*

She's grabbing a glass of water from the kitchen when Mom walks in. "Clarisse? I think Father Simmons is going to call you today. He spoke to us before graduation and expressed interest in speaking with you. He said it's *very* important." *In other words, don't embarrass us, you ungrateful screw-up.* Clarisse smiles. "I'll be sure to tell him you said hi."

This seems to appease Mom for now. She leaves the room and

Clarisse lets the icy water clear her throat. When the phone rings, she picks it up without hesitation. It irritates her parents when she doesn't obey right away. *An offense to the Church of Light. Just like my very existence.* Rolling her eyes, she does her best to keep these rebellious thoughts quiet.

"Good afternoon, Father Simmons."

"Good afternoon, Clarisse! Congratulations again on graduating." His smirk is audible; she can picture it just in the way he speaks. "Any plans for after graduation?"

"I'm going to work for Monroe Accounting. Dad needs a secretary." Clarisse keeps her answer short. Father Simmons likes to act like her second Dad. A lot. Sometimes she finds it endearing and, other times, she finds it downright creepy. She's somewhere in the middle today as she hears him whistle with false pride.

"Are you excited?"

Clarisse turns around, staring over her shoulder and listening for anyone that might be standing by. "No," she finally whispers. "No, I'm not."

It's not like this matters to him, anyway. So why not say something? It's the biggest gamble she's taken in her life. The silence is unbearable while she waits for him to respond.

"Why not? That sounds like a very promising job!"

There it is. That subtle hint that she's ungrateful and undeserving—that she should take what's given to her, never asking for more or less. Something in her gut twists about. It doesn't feel right. None of this feels right.

"I know. Don't get me wrong, I love the idea of a steady job and income, but sometimes I just wish I could start something of my own, you know? I've always wanted to start a sewing business. I... I have plans. What materials and training I would need. I just don't know how to get started." Once again, he doesn't answer right away, leaving her to chew on the regret of even speaking in the first place.

"Well, Clarisse, I think that might not be such a bad idea... why don't you see how you do in the *real* world tomorrow? If you don't have any mishaps, then come see me and we can talk this out further."

It's not much, but it's something. Clarisse brightens. "That sounds *awesome*! I won't let you down!" *What are you doing? Stop being so excited!* "Again, Clarisse, this is entirely contingent upon your success." Father Simmons' voice of caution is enough to drag her back to planet Earth. It hurts to crash back so hard.

"Yes, sir. Thank you."

"Any time, Clarisse. I look forward to hearing about your first day." The phone clicks. *He hung up?* She sighs. Everything she's ever wanted is always met with rejection like this. Either silence or outright dismissal. Her feet almost drag her through the floorboards, her sadness so heavy.

Without asking, she steps outside. Her parents never bother to ask where she goes as long as it's in the yard. Granted, it's a big yard —a small farm, rather. It was yet another thing her parents were able to buy before her magic had to go and bother them with its presence. Clarisse's favorite part about it, though, is the abandoned barn toward the tree line. It juts out against the night sky, calling to her.

When she reaches it, she pulls open the all-familiar door and rolls a stone against it to keep it from slamming shut. The wind whips up, tangling her hair and giving her shuddering goosebumps. *Why is it so cold? It's June?*

Stepping inside the barn, she sinks to the floor, pulling her knees under her chin. The sounds of the night slip over her, cloaking her in solitude. Closing her eyes, she listens. Sometimes, she can still hear the moon's whispers. Or even the stars. They aren't hers, but their voices are similar. The language they speak is foreign, but the sentiment hits her just right. Tonight, they're abuzz with conversation. She wishes to stand among them. Her hands stick out in front of her; the stars she creates still call to her. They've never screamed louder.

"You should listen to them."

Clarisse stifles a shriek. Never in her life has she heard a voice in her head that's not her own. *Am I going insane finally?* She stumbles in the dirt, trying to collect herself. *Maybe it was just a fluke.*

"Perhaps. But I highly doubt it. You're far from insane."

Her heart is ready to tear from her ribcage and run a marathon straight out of here. Clarisse shakily stands to her feet, rubbing her temples with her fingers. *This is what I get for being so rebellious today.*

"Yes, so rebellious. How dare you have your own thoughts? Pshh... please. Why do you stay here when they treat you so horribly?"

An icicle lodges itself in her throat.

I need to run away now. If my parents catch wind of this....

"Then what? You strike them down. You walk away. You leave this horrible place and you never return. What do you have to lose?"

Clarisse starts gagging. Her stomach is churning. Before long, she won't be able to keep that nasty cake where it belongs. She regrets having any. The aftertaste is just as putrid as the cake looked.

"That was nasty cake. I can't believe they didn't buy you something nicer."

The voice is decidedly masculine. Deep. Like a booming whisper. As if a shadow came to life and grew a voice to go along with it. The door to the barn slams shut. Clarisse jumps. *There goes my exit!* An uncomfortable realization settles in her bones—she's not alone anymore. The sound of something—someone—moving around makes it hard to breathe. Screaming isn't an option. Her parents won't come for her. *They probably want me dead, anyway!*

"More than you realize."

Please tell me that this voice is attached to the thing or person that's in here right now. Or that all of this is a dream and I went to bed a while ago—that something weird was in the cake.

She's not making sense—she knows that. But how can she? Terror is probably leaking out of her and staining the barn with the smell of her fear.

"You're definitely not dreaming. Whether you want that or not."

Clarisse blinks. A pair of blood-red eyes are staring at her from the darkest corner of the barn. The shadow bleeds closer and closer until she's standing only a few feet away from a wolf made of naught but darkness.

"Hello, my dear."

Clarisse doesn't wait to hear anything else. She takes off running. She wrenches open the barn door and slams it shut behind it, wedging a heavy rock up against it to keep it from reopening.

Anything to buy her time and let her get away. Worry dogs at her heels that she won't make it; when she steps inside the house, she's careful not to let the door slam. *Don't want to upset Mom and Dad.* Checking the locks, she lets out a breath.

She peers out the window, wondering if it followed. *No dice.*

For once, Clarisse wishes for permission to take showers in the evening. But she has an allotted time and graduation day won't be enough to convince her parents to let her indulge. Instead, she rushes to her room, closing the door behind her. Even though it doesn't have a lock, she's grateful for the privacy.

Her breath comes and goes in crashing waves. *What was that thing?*

When she starts to calm, she rubs her eyes. She knows she's tired; she knows she's been letting those awful thoughts get to her too much lately. There's no excuse for the way she's been acting and thinking.

"But there is. You're a victim of abuse, Clarisse."

She throws herself back in a start. Standing outside her window is that same wolf. Everything inside her splits; she's frozen. *Do I tell my parents? That'll land me in the middle of an exorcism for sure, though....*

"Yes, it will. They won't understand what they're seeing. They're too stupid to comprehend things greater than their own pitiful lives." The wolf sneers; it looks more like a snarl, but the tone in its 'voice' is enough to tell Clarisse otherwise. *But how do I know that?*

"You're a gifted woman, Clarisse. You were meant to understand things beyond the world you've grown up in. That's why I've come. I'd like to make a proposition."

Clarisse lets out a small laugh, praying her parents can't hear her.

And you're a figment of my imagination. Probably some manifestation of my powers that's punishment for bothering to think out loud.

She bites her lip, praying it's enough to make the strange wolf go away.

"I see you're not ready to have this conversation. We'll see if you feel differently tomorrow. Meet me after you meet with Father Simmons."

Crossing her arms, Clarisse gives the wolf a glare. Maybe that'll do it. To her relief, it ebbs away with the darkness. For just a moment, she wonders if she made the right choice. Its strange voice echoes in her ears, making for a restless night of no sleep.

5
WORK TO DEATH

Clarisse

The sound of the alarm is anything but welcome, but Clarisse must heed it. Her father expects her to be ready in a timely fashion. She shuffles about her room, selecting a plain, gray dress and a hair-tie to keep her unruly brown mop under control. She makes sure to nab a pair of reading glasses—they're horribly large and make her brown eyes look like they belong on a bullfrog rather than a person when she wears them. She hates them, but they were cheap and her parents insist she keeps them; when she does close-up work with reading for long periods of time, her eyes will stain without them.

She sneers at the sight of them, but stuffs them into an old purse-like object that she's carried with her since the first day of high school. It was a hand-me-down from Mom to hold things like lip balm, mints, tampons... all the things a girl would ever need. But never a phone. Never anything that might be mistaken as *makeup*.

She wishes she could blot out the blemishes on her face with something like foundation, but her parents will never allow her such a luxury.

Something to look forward to if I ever manage to dig myself out of this hole I call a home.

Clarisse is shocked to find herself thinking this way. Usually, it's easy to be complacent. Perhaps the taste of possibility was enough to set her off with some courage—some spitfire notions like the ones she now carries with her as she marches into the kitchen to make herself a quick breakfast.

She peels a grapefruit, carefully placing the slices on a plate and pours herself a glass of water. They're devoured before Dad starts making his own breakfast. The smell of toast fills the room and Clarisse takes the extra time she's bought herself to brush her teeth —she even takes a moment to try and tame her hair a bit more. It's frizzy and gross, thanks to the humidity, but there's no time for a shower.

A dose of some dry shampoo seems to alleviate the problem enough to make herself look much more presentable. It's the only thing Mom and Dad let her have since her hair tends to get greasy. It took years of convincing, but she's grateful to have the bottle today.

She doesn't own any jewelry. A pair of old Mary Janes make their way onto her feet and she meets her father in the living room where he's tapping his foot and looking at his watch.

"Impressive. You finished with five minutes to spare. Come on, let's go."

Clarisse bows her head and smiles while she follows Dad to the car. She suppresses a sigh, knowing full well that it's going to be a long day.

Dad's old SUV sits in the parking lot, the dull gray appropriate for how she feels. She bites her nails when her father gets in; he slaps her hand away from her face. There's no need for him to say anything. *Biting nails is untidy. It's improper. It won't look good at the office.*

The conversation occurs naturally within her head as she focuses her attention on the outside world. A blur of cow pastures, tree-lines, and unknown freedoms pass by. She yearns to open the door and roll out. To just run.

Why am I so out of it lately? Since when have I been filled with so much discontent? I brought this on myself. I'm the reason things have to be this way.

She doesn't know how long she's in the car before it pulls to a halt in the parking lot. It's strange to be there as an employee rather than a visitor. Visits have been restricted to only a few times to bring her father lunch or to sit with him when her mother has errands that are "too stressful" for Clarisse to endure.

She waits for her father to tell her where to go when they step into the lobby. Gray carpet. White walls. The only decoration in sight is a calendar near the desk Clarisse assumes will become her charge until she musters up enough seed money to start her own sewing business.

If that's even really possible, like Father Simmons said.

A kind, elderly woman rounds the corner and smiles.

"Alice, this is my daughter, Clarisse. I have a meeting in ten minutes, so I need you to just jump right into teaching her how to do her job."

Alice nods. By the way her face pulls in something like apprehension, Clarisse knows that she's well-acquainted with her father's temper.

So that's one thing we have in common, then. "Come along, dear. We have a long day ahead of us."

Alice carries a bit of warmth with her that Dad lacks. Clarisse can't get an accurate idea of how old she really is.

"Are you excited to start working at your father's firm?"

Clarisse looks at her fingernails, appearing like they've been through a blender from all the chewing. Her cheeks redden.

"I... I think so. I'm a bit scared of messing up. But I'm a fast learner. I hope I can make Dad proud and do what he needs me to do well. I–"

Alice smiles.

"I'm not here to judge you, dear. I hope I don't sound like I'm belittling you for explaining things you might already know. How much experience do you have with computer software? Word processors? Spreadsheets?"

"I took a computer course in school, so a little. My dad had me take the class so I would be better prepared for when I took this job. I can do most basic functions; I'm sure there's a lot I need to learn, but it shouldn't take me that long."

True to her word, when Clarisse pulls open the different software programs on the computer for Alice to show her the ropes, she's quick to pick up on everything.

An awful program puts her at a loss for words.

"This is the appointment logging system. Here, you'll look at your father's calendar and see what he has going on. The phone to your left will comprise most of your job, along with putting together letters and statements to send out in the mail for less digitally-inclined clients, and putting together more generic emails for your father when he can't respond to a client right away. It's imperative that you memorize your father's schedule. There are certain days he prefers to deal with more recurring clients."

Alice produces a book from the drawer next to her. In it is a nexus of notes far more complicated than Clarisse has ever seen. In them are Dad's *preferences*. When and where he goes to lunch, when he wants to meet with various clients, and what times he's open for new appointments depending on the month.

"This thing changes infrequently; I'm passing it along to you so you don't get slapped with write-ups when you first get started."

"Passing it along?"

"Yes, dear. I've been asked to retire so you can take this job. It's about time I leave. No offense, but I'm rather tired of being told what to do by the likes of your father treating me like I'm dumb since I'm old."

Had Clarisse used such a brazen statement growing up, she would've felt the sting of a belt.

"He's making you retire? Just so I can work here?"

"Yes. But please, don't think that I'm upset over it. I just want to get out of here; when he offered me such a great retirement package in exchange for my quiet departure, I couldn't say no."

Clarisse frowns. "I'm really sorry, Alice. When do you leave?"

"Today is my last day. You'll do great. You learn rather quickly, just as you say. If you follow this book, you'll do incredibly well." As if on cue, the phone rings. "Pick it up, dear."

Clarisse takes careful note of everything the client is asking for. A meeting, of course, and they're a new client. They don't exist in the book. She pulls out a sticky note, knowing full well that she needs to catalog them in her father's personal codex.

Based on the way they talk, she determines them as low-risk and pencils them in for a virtual meeting a week from today. She flags it for her father to see so it will notify him.

"See? You did everything as you were told; twice as fast as me, really."

Clarisse offers a sheepish smile, but the feeling of guilt wallowing in her gut is too much to bear. She looks up at the clock on the wall and realizes that half the day is gone. Her stomach growls, but she knows better than to ask to go eat. The firm doesn't close for lunch.

Dad walks out of his office, a smile beaming on his face. "You're doing great, Clarisse! I got your notification. Well done! Keep up the great work; Alice, you'll be greatly missed when you're gone." He turns on his heel. "I'll be out for lunch. Send me notifications of anyone that tries to give me a call."

Clarisse nods.

"Stupid question: what exactly does my father do? Like, what does he talk about in his meetings?" Clarisse giggles. She can't believe she's asking such a question so late in the day.

"He offers accounting services to larger firms that need things like external auditing, review of expenses for tax purposes, things like that. Since his rates are cheaper, you'll find that firms outside of Ashville reach out to him for assistance, since they can't afford the big-city prices. But your father knows how to hold his own against his competitors out there. He makes quite a lot. It must be nice living in a house with a man who makes the big bucks!"

Clarisse's cheeks burn. She doesn't have the heart to tell Alice that she's forced to live like a damned pauper. She wonders where all the money is going that her father makes. Her mind wanders a million miles from that little office, dozens of questions on her mind. *Why wouldn't he say something? Does Mom know?* Her heart thuds in its cage, blood rushing to Clarisse's ears, threatening to shoot steam from them. Worrying that her emotions will get the best of her, she pushes the thought away for a moment. Another question surfaces.

"Where are his other employees?"

"They come and go. Many of them do work remotely or only work here temporarily. It's hard to work with your father, as I'm sure you've already guessed."

Clarisse laughs for once, giving herself some space to experience raw emotions in the eyes of the public. Well, Alice in this case.

"Did your father give you a cellphone?"

"No?"

"Ah, I see. Unusual, but he did say something about potentially letting you have one. I guess that changed."

Clarisse represses the desire to roll her eyes. It's a daily occurrence where she has to hide how annoying she finds her father.

So he gets a lunch, retires the old lady so I can have a job, and he hides some big bucks somewhere and makes Mom and I live like poor people. I have to go to a cult school to hide my true self so he can have this posh life and not even share? We can't have fun cereal. We can't have nice things. Everything always looks like a mausoleum in the house because we can't afford decorations…. How many field trips did I have to skip because we "didn't have the money?" How much of this money was used to keep my secret "hushed up?"

Clarisse quells anger that moves about, a tsunami of rage building itself up in her core. *It's going to be a long day. I can't afford to blow up now. I just can't.*

She returns to her work, answering phone calls, dancing around Dad's schedule, and accommodating his needs as much as she can. Alice is helpful, but ultimately leaves it up to Clarisse to figure things out. It's for the best. She can't rely on Alice. Alice will be gone soon. *So soon…*

Dad returns to the office. Clarisse makes sure to ignore him to keep that earlier rage from boiling over. She keeps at her work.

Finally, the clock hits five. Clarisse is relieved when her father emerges from his office.

Guilt, anger, sorrow, and a number of other things have built themselves up in her core. Clarisse can't bear to look Dad in the eye knowing his big secret now—that they've had *money* this whole time and he kept it from us. *Or does Mom know, too?* A buzzing starts in her hands. *Control, Clarisse. Control.*

Just as she's shutting down the computer for the day, the lights flicker. Alice looks up and pauses.

"What's the matter, Alice?" Dad asks, as if he actually cares. He's good at feigning things like that.

"I swear I thought the power was about to go out, that's all."

Dad freezes, sending a glare in Clarisse's direction. It's a dare. A *try me* that will end in nothing but pain and sorrow if she doesn't bottle her emotions back up, quickly.

The flickering disappears without a trace. Clarisse returns to blank submission mode, doing her best to make it seem like it really was something to do with the power and not her. *He will punish me in the car.* She shivers, working to keep her body still. *Don't show it. Don't give him anything else to use against me.*

"Never mind. Everything looks fine." Dad, ever the stage master, lets out a boisterous sound. For a short man, he has a big laugh.

The perfect image of a no-good businessman.

Clarisse is shocked at how angry she is. *What is happening to me? First the ambition, now the anger. Such things aren't good. I can't have them. I can't have any feelings.* She wills herself to swallow them down.

"Well, Alice, thank you for your long service with the Monroes." He pulls a card from his briefcase and a check for five-thousand dollars. Clarisse's eyes nearly bug out at the sight of such a large sum. Her father waffles at spending more than five-dollars on a pack of sodas which, in the Monroe house, are a delicacy.

Where are you putting all that money, Dad?

She has half a mind to say something to him but decides against it, just like always.

"Thank you, Mr. Monroe. It's been an honor working with you.

Your daughter will do very well. She did everything perfectly today,"
Alice smiles at Clarisse as they walk out the door together.

It's the last Clarisse will see of the woman. *I can't imagine working
for Dad that long.* It makes her sick to her stomach.

Is this what my life is going to be like? She shudders.

"Are you alright?" The question comes from Dad.

As if you care.

"Yeah, just got a bit of a chill."

6

FATHER SIMMONS

Clarisse

"What were you thinking?" Dad fumes. "You almost threw a whole day of progress away! Are you insane?"

Clarisse stays silent, not finding words to defend herself.

"I don't care what excuses you come up with. I'm taking you to Father Simmons."

"Dad, I was going to go see him today anyway."

He pops her in the face. It's sudden; tears form in her eyes at the violence. She's never been one to fight, get in the way, or tolerate pain very well. But, this time, she doesn't let it phase her. *I can't afford to make him more angry.*

Clarisse cowers, hiding her face from Dad, fearing she might be hit again. She wishes she could be brave. She wishes she could say things like the person she envisions herself to be in her mind. She knows what she would say. *"Dad, what would Father Simmons say about your anger? You know stressful things like that can cause me to become volatile. Listen, I didn't mean to say that out of disrespect. I was going to talk to him today to make sure I have proper practices in place to prevent the lights from flickering anymore. To keep myself on the straight and narrow, just like you want." Like you want... Like you want... what about what I want?*

Arthur lets out a harumph; Clarisse resists the first urge she's ever had to deck him. She hates everything about him. She hates him so much that it starts to boil in her gut. The sight of him makes her want to puke. Being close to him makes her want to jump out of the car. Living in her house anymore is a thought she can't stand.

"Go ahead and drop me off at church. I'll wait for Father Simmons to finish up. We have a meeting scheduled and I don't want to miss it." It comes out harsher than she intended. Something about the way Clarisse's eyes gleam makes Dad pause before throwing another punch. He decides that, despite her tone, his daughter is right. *I scare him... good.* What if lights turn into something far more grotesque?

He gazes at his daughter, a look of pure disgust planted on his face.

I'm a demon.

"Do you want me to come back and get you?"

"No. I'll walk home, too. It's not that far and I could use the space to clear my head. I want to make sure I don't come home with anymore... *burdens*... for you to handle."

It's the first time he's ever heard snark or sarcasm leave my mouth. Any waywardness is met with punishment. Now would be no different, but since she works for him, he doesn't want the volatility to get him killed.

Clarisse makes it inside the church where Father Simmons is waiting. His eyes burst wide when he sees her face. "Clarisse, what happened?"

"Lying is a sin, but for now I'll just tell you I ran into a pole and confess to the truth later. I know the person responsible will never confess, so one of us might as well pay penance."

Father Simmons grimaces. Despite what Clarisse knows, sometimes she likes to think he cares.

"Clarisse, did Arthur do this to you?"

Her silence is enough to answer that question for him. She can tell by the way his face twists up that he's biting back things that he would like to say that he knows he can't.

"Alright, let's get you an ice pack and talk about your business idea over tea, yes?"

Clarisse smiles. "That's the most relieving thing I've heard all day."

They go to the small dining hall adjacent to the church's main foyer. He gets an ice pack—that Clarisse has used more than once—and cups of tea. Father Simmons has admitted to feeling guilty for not calling someone to help Clarisse.

If he called someone to help me, it would risk bad publicity for the church.... *That's always his excuse.* His flock would be subject to so many news reports. Clarisse needs her exorcisms. They keep her safe. The world isn't ready to meet people like her; she can't be subject to living with demons on behalf of becoming the world's spectacle.

His eyes fall to the blood stains on her socks and the horrid shoes she wears on her feet. She squirms, feeling uncomfortable under his gaze.

"How did work go?" Clarisse could hug him for changing the subject.

"Terrible. Dad made some lady, Alice, retire so I could have her job. Then he got mad at me because the lights in the building flickered. Like, it's not even clear that it was me that did it; he immediately accused me of causing the problem. And either way, it didn't last but a second, and if it was me, I clearly had it under control. I wish he would see my progress." She takes a spoon and dumps some sugar into her tea, stirring it around so fast that some of it threatens to splash outside the cup. "I hope he doesn't get too angry at me. You see the bruises. You know. If I mess up, what happens to me?" She swallows a lump in her throat, her hand jerking at the thought of being hurt again, sending tea droplets everywhere on the table.

"Sorry."

"You're fine, Clarisse." Father Simmons hands her a napkin. "It's hardly a spill."

"Thank you, Father."

"I wanted to take the time to talk to you about something before we get into the business idea you mentioned. It's a secret that you have to keep, do you understand?"

Clarisse, though curious, keeps quiet so Father Simmons can continue.

"I set up a trust fund for you. It's got quite a bit of money in it and it's going to start paying out to you here soon. I take it your parents probably haven't set you up a proper bank account yet?"

Clarisse is flustered, but manages to stammer something like a "no," to confirm his suspicions. *This isn't anything at all like the other day! Maybe... he actually liked my idea?*

"Well, I say you take the day off tomorrow and come with me to do so. I'll tell your parents I'm helping you with emotional exercises to help keep the demons at bay. I'm sure your father will have no protests?"

Clarisse tries to answer, but it's futile. Wherever the wind blows, she goes. *That's the story of my life and it's not about to change now.*

"While we're out, I'm getting you a cellphone. You need to be able to contact me at all times if necessary. If something like today happens again where he punches you, I want you to be able to call for help."

Clarisse's mind spins. "Really? Wait, what?"

"Yes, Clarisse. What your father is doing to you is abuse. I'm tired of watching it happen. You need to have an escape. I sense great evil from your parents as of late; I need to make sure you're able to escape."

"Evil?"

"I can't say what, but they have demons of their own that they fight and you can't afford any more than the ones you already bear."

Clarisse heaves, her lungs threatening to burst out of her ribcage. Sweat beads along her forehead and her temperature starts to rise. With great effort in focusing on her chest and heartbeat, she manages to keep herself from making the entire church blow up.

That's a bit dramatic, but whatever.

She feels like she's falling apart. "What about my business?"

"Yes, your business. How much does your father pay you?"

"Uhm, I'm not sure. I know he's paying me cash. He hasn't said how much."

Father Simmons mutters something like "under the table." His brow furrows and something like fire flashes in his eyes. She's not educated enough to know what it is that's making Father Simmons so angry.

"I'm supposed to give him half of my pay as compensation for dealing with the hazard I bring to the workplace. The rest I suppose I'll keep for myself? They'll expect me to put it towards my sewing materials."

His voice rises; Clarisse notices his fists clenching up. "You don't even know how much money you're getting for this?"

"No." Clarisse is ashamed to admit it. She hates talking about it. After reading her contract through and through, there was no information about the amount.

"I won't be surprised if he pays you nothing at all. Listen, here's what you're going to do. This idea of yours is good. You'll need supplies, advertisements, and a place to set up shop. I'd go ahead and establish a clientele if you can. Anyone who needs something mended, you offer. Maybe get some business cards to have on hand to pass out. Wait till prom season next year and offer to make dresses for cheaper than what they go for in stores if you can—or at least price them like the rest of your competition."

He waves his hands frantically, as though putting on a sermon rather than having a regular conversation. "You'll have to make yourself stand out. But I'm confident that you can. The craft fair is this fall, yes?"

"Well, yeah but—"

"Clarisse, this is the rest of your life on the line. You bring business cards. You set up a website. You do everything you can to make this work. I'll let you use the computers here to get this stuff started. Wait a few months so things don't seem suspicious and, by December, I want you out. I want you to have a place of your own that you're renting; I want your business to be started, and I want you to use the money from your trust as wisely as you can."

Clarisse takes a moment to breathe. She's not even the one talking, but she knows if she doesn't pause for a moment, those lights will be the least of their worries.

Just then, she remembers the most important thing.

The wolf! It said to meet tonight in the barn… if it's even real?

She hides the fact that her attention is now a thousand miles away from any sewing shop. *I've got to go see if it's still there! If it's not, maybe there's hope… and if it is?*

"So, do you want me to call your parents or?" Father Simmons interrupts her frantic musings and it takes her a moment to remember what they're talking about.

"I'll make the call. Do you need a lift?"

"No, I'll walk on my own."

She dips her head, gratitude swelling in her soul. "Thank you, Father Simmons. I really appreciate all this. I'm sorry I don't have much to say yet. This is a lot for me to take in."

"No worries, Clarisse."

With that, she hands him her empty cup of tea and runs out the door.

7

WHISPERS OF A SHADOW

Clarisse

Clarisse reaches the barn, panting. At some point, she quit wearing her shoes. Her feet leave vermillion tracks all along the small dirt roads that lead home. Part of her *wants* to see the strange shadow wolf tonight. Playing her conversation with it over and over in her head all the way home is giving her terribly freeing thoughts. Thoughts of leaving. Thoughts of just stepping away from everything that's ever held her captive.

Why do I want to see it so bad though? Why am I not afraid? She feels enchanted. It's as though she can't resist—literally. Her stomach flips and trips over itself, excitement boiling over. The stars and moon are strangely quiet tonight. The whispers are there, but they're... *subdued.* They, too, must be waiting in anticipation of something great.

The door to the barn creaks open. The last of the evening light casts through and leaves the entryway empty of anything. No red-eyed wolves come jumping out. While she thought she'd be relieved, her heart shatters.

I must be truly desperate to imagine something like that. I need to leave this place.

"I agree."

Clarisse gasps, whirling around to find the wolf standing in the doorway. As the last of the sunlight disappears over the horizon, Clarisse finds herself backing into the barn. Right into a corner. Her chest heaves as she waits to be eaten alive. Either by the wolf shadow or her own growing sense of insanity. Either way, she knows it won't end well. Putting her hands over her face, she awaits the inevitable.

But the inevitable never comes.

Clarisse opens her eyes to find the wolf still standing there. He is smiling still. By the way he's acting, she knows he's trying his best to keep her from running away and screaming into the night. Were she not tired and sore from hitting her head and having the most horrible day of her life, she might have done just that. But her legs are lead; they won't let her move. She's *trapped*.

"I'm not an illusion. Keep that silly thought stamped out. And stop hiding your emotions. It's a horrible thing."

Clarisse swallows. "H-how are you reading my thoughts?"

The wolf bows playfully, more like a human than a canine. "Pardon the intrusion. I never go into people's thoughts without permission, but for you, I made an exception. As you can see, this entire meeting is a bit… *strained*. I'm sorry to have frightened you so badly. My name is Terrence."

"Nice to meet you, Terrence," Clarisse grunts, her head pounding.

Terrence glances down at her feet. "I'm sorry your feet have taken such a toll. They've bled horribly. I can heal you if you would like."

"Wait, what?"

Before she can protest, a warmth moves through her feet. In seconds, the pain abates and the blood disappears.

"How did you do that?" Clarisse screeches. "What are you?"

"I'm a Selbena."

Clarisse blinks. "In English?" *Why am I so entranced by this beast? Why do I want to know?*

Terrence laughs. "I'm a god. I've come from the land of Tyrladan to help you. I've watched you struggle for quite some time and have decided that it is best that I step in to help you. I hope you won't mind."

Something tells me that he doesn't care if I do mind. She blinks.

Clarisse starts laughing. She's laughing so hard she's crying. Her body racks with sobs that she can't hold back. Everywhere around them, lights explode into existence. Before long, a miniature night sky erupts, covering the ceiling of the barn. The darkness of the night sets in, making it seem as though they've both stepped inside an entirely different world.

She doesn't fight it, choosing to let the lights shine for the first time since that horrible night. Blue. Green. Red. Yellow. And white-hot. They're beautiful and she can't stop crying at the sight of them.

"I've messed up bad." Her lip quivers; she does her best to try and collect herself.

What will Father Simmons think?

She clutches her arms to her chest, her eyes on Terrence. For a moment, she wonders if he goes by Terry; maybe her mind has brought her little stuffed wolf to life. This is the moment where the demons finally overwhelm her. Right in the moment where she has the most hope. That's when they come to get her. That's when they manage to destroy her and all her precious dreams.

"Clarisse, please. Stop crying." He brushes his head into her, nestling his own into the crook of her neck. It sends waves of relief down her spine. His massive form is awkward as it attempts to lean into her more, offering something like comfort. He's surprisingly hot to the touch. She fears he might burn her like a hot iron if he keeps his presence against her for much longer.

This is the day where everything falls apart. She's so upset she can't fathom how to gather herself back up again. How she can possibly manage to be strong in a time like this?

"Clarisse, what you have here is a gift. I want you to look at those little lights. How many of them there are. What do they look like to you?"

Clarisse can't bring herself to look up. It's too much. She's spent her whole life hiding her lights; she's not about to break that trend now. But, something in her tugs at her soul. Something about this moment is too important for her not to at least dare at a peek.

She tilts her head toward the barn ceiling.

What she sees drops her jaw.

The little lights are stars. It's not just how I imagine them, then….

Real. Stars.

At first, she wonders if it's true. She knows stars are really just balls of super-hot gas; different colors are given off based on what chemicals they burn. But they require intense heat. There's no way… there's *no way* that she can have those inside a *barn* without the whole thing catching fire. Not when they hover so close to the walls.

One of them floats down to her. She grabs at it. It's not hot. Rather, it's icy cold. It's blue—a light blue, at that. She examines it. It has no physical substance to it, but it is no simple light. It bears its own. It twinkles and is almost blinding for her to look at for too long.

"What? This isn't how stars work. That's—"

"What's so amazing about you. You've made a new kind of star." Terrence smiles. He's pulled away from her, relieving her of the scorching heat his fur gives off so that he, too, can look at the star more with more attention. He examines it with the diligence of a scientist.

She smiles at him, unsure where she has gotten the gall to do something so reckless and find the ability to smile afterward.

But for the moment, she enjoys being hidden under a darkening night sky of her own creation.

My own.

Her eyes glaze over with their own kind of light. Terrence takes a moment to analyze them. The brown of her eyes is overcome with the blue light, making them seem to glow with the same color. She catches them in the reflection of a broken mirror; she's shocked to see they really *do* look like stars plucked straight from the sky itself.

"Don't you see?"

Clarisse doesn't answer right away. "See what?"

"Your lights aren't evil. They're not even demons. They're your *creations*. They're actually stars. And they're meant to be embraced, not hidden. You've been lied to Clarisse. And it's high time someone told you the truth."

"The truth?" Clarisse shivers, unsure how to process. Everything is going too fast and she's kicking herself mentally for being dragged along so long. She's too accepting of everything—good or bad.

She's gullible. Usable. A piece of *trash. But why should I believe him? Or you... since you can hear....*

Clarisse blushes. Tears start to form and she freezes when Terrence reaches up to brush them away with his paw.

"What are you doing?"

He grimaces. Clarisse finds it incredible that a shadow wolf made with such an inky black coat is capable of doing such a thing. A wolf making facial expressions—it's incredible.

"I don't like seeing you cry. It's unsettling. So, I want to help you any way I can." He sits back and smiles, like that makes everything smooth and understandable and all better. *I'm losing my mind in its entirety!*

"What do you mean about telling me the truth, Terrence? The truth is that I've been cursed with these... *stars*... and I have to spend my whole life trying to keep my powers at bay. I can't let them overtake my life. That means the darkness wins. The *demons* win. The Light won't be pleased."

Terrence laughs.

"What's so funny?"

"Let me ask you something: don't you realize you're in a cult?"

Clarisse shrugs. "So what if I am? The exorcisms work, Father Simmons helps me—"

"Helps you? Or uses you because of your unique condition? Let me ask you something else: don't you think if he *really* cared about you that he would have removed you from your home by now? That bruise on your eye is turning black. I'll heal that, too, but it's beside the point. Your father is a dangerous man, Clarisse. That darkness I sense in him is straight-up homicidal, as you might say."

Clarisse blinks at Terrence. The icy terror that washes over her, making her want to wrap herself up and disappear from existence. "Homicidal? You think he would *murder* me?"

"Perhaps not in a premeditated sense, but I do very much think he would murder you. What do you think he told your mother when he went home? She's going to see that mark. She's not going to do anything about it. Both of them have been bent on keeping you out of the public's eye for as long as possible. Utterly *forgettable*. Right? Wouldn't that make it easier to brush you out of the public's memory if you someday just went... missing?"

Terrence pauses, biting his tongue.

"Besides... I've seen things... Read things. Clarisse, they've got a life insurance policy taken out on you. With a sizable sum.... It only goes into effect if you die of natural causes, but how do we know they won't spin something? What exactly is defined as 'natural'?"

The way that last word rolls off his tongue sends Clarisse down an even deeper spiral. "You're insinuating that my own parents would murder me! Why would they do that? How did you read all of that?"

Terrence huffs. "I've been watching you longer than I care to admit or you would probably want to know... let's just leave it at that." Terrence growls and Clarisse shuts up. He pauses, his eyes glinting.

"Why do you work so hard to keep yourself hidden from the world? Why do you let them tell you what to do like that?"

"What do you mean?"

"I growled; your first instinct was to go completely blank. To hide. Don't you think that's unhealthy? That's a sign that you've been abused. For a *long* time. You've been taught that you're a burden to them—that you have to sacrifice your dreams—your wants and hopes all for the sake of others. For *them*. Why? Because you made stars appear from your hands as a child."

"And how do you know all this?" Clarisse crosses her arms,

feeling uncomfortable that she's not more defensive of herself. *Why does he have to be right?*

"As I said before, I did a bit of research before coming here. As soon as I learned of the nature of your treatment, I realized someone needed to step in. The forces-that-be have ignored you and that is a *grave* injustice. Just yesterday, you needed someone to lean on; I was the only person that was able to give that to you. You *graduated*. Doesn't that warrant some celebration? Some comfort to someone who's never been allowed to truly think for herself without being in fear that it's the wrong thing to do?"

"But—"

"Listen, you can deny what I have to say all you want. But I think you've known for a long time—but *especially* in the last few days—that what you've been through is unacceptable. No one is in your corner, Clarisse. Your family. Your peers. Your authority figures. Not even your godforsaken librarians have bothered to ask you what it is that keeps you from reading without fear of being caught! Shouldn't they have sent someone to look into what it is that has you *that* frightened of *reading*?"

Clarisse buries her head in a sigh. She knows this wolf is right. Granted, it's entirely preposterous that she's talking to one at all. I mean, who said wolves could talk? Or be made of shadows?

"I'm in your corner, Clarisse." Terrence faces her, leaning down to speak. She's almost childlike in this light. In need of a parental figure. *A savior.* It seems like he has every intention of being just that for her. He wants to be her rescuer, and she can tell. His eyes glimmer with the hope and passion of a real life superhero.

"Clarisse, let me help you. These powers don't deserve to be shoved away into a lockbox. You don't deserve to have to live in a place like that damned house at the top of this hill. You don't deserve to be *alone*. You deserve so much more. Even if you weren't powerful, you couldn't deserve this. No one does. Let me help you."

Clarisse cries; she doesn't know how long the tears have been flowing. It's been ages. Her body aches while her head is screaming in silent agony as the bruising on her eye sets in. Terrence presses his nose to the wound and, just like the pain in her head, the pain in her eye ceases.

She throws up her hands, pushing him away. "Why do you care? No one does. I'm not pretty. I'm ugly. I'm awkward. I'm stupid. I've let myself be treated like this. I've never done anything for myself. I'm a total and utter failure who's doomed to being a secretary with dreams of being a seamstress for the rest of her life. What about me screams 'I deserve help,' huh? My powers? Making little stars with my hands isn't anything to be writing home about."

Terrence shakes his head. "That's just the mindset that allows you to stay in this trap forever. Do you understand how dangerous it is to reduce yourself to such little importance? And it's not even your fault. That's the tragedy in all of this. Clarisse, let me help you. I want to help you harness your power. Become the person you're meant to be. You're not ugly. You're not worthless. You're not stupid. You're a victim. I want to help you get out. I was like you once, you know."

Clarisse pauses. "I thought you said you were a 'god' of some kind?"

"Now I am. But I started out as a mortal. I only became a Selbena—or god—when I passed on to Tyrladan."

"What the heck is Tyrladan? Wait... passed on? You mean you *died*? Am I going to die?" Her heart is racing. *I'm not ready to die.* The thought of being buried–before she can even live her life? *I'm not ready to give up yet.*

Terrence laughs. "We all die someday, though I think by using your powers you might not have to. We can talk about my passing later. I just want you to know that I was a mortal once, just like you. I have been in your shoes, in a sense. Not quite like you've worn them, but I'm acquainted with how they fit." He smiles. "Let me help you, please."

"How do I know you're not really just a demon here to lead me astray?"

He hums a bit at this, as if he's not sure of how to answer.

"Let me put it to you this way. A demon would be here to try and set you up. To harm you. To use you for their own nefarious purposes. Gods can do the same, but a demon would be far more vile and treacherous. Have I come across to you that way?"

Clarisse considers this carefully, chewing on the thought as though it were an exam question instead of a real conversation.

"No, but demons are often some of the prettiest things out there. They don't have to look like they're manipulating you. That would mean the jig is up from the beginning. That misses out on the point."

"Sharp observation! I'm glad you're able to identify manipulation when it comes with a smile. I wonder... why not when it comes in the form of your father and mother? Father Simmons? You literally acknowledge you are in a cult. You were immediately frightened at the thought that your parents might murder you. Why? Because it's true. Would a demon come to tell you that? Would a demon offer to help you get out of that for *nothing* in exchange except seeing you flourish?"

This makes Clarisse stop and think. To chew on his words is dangerous, she knows. He could be a trickster, god, demon, or otherwise.

But she has no choice. She needs to get out. She can't be someone's puppet forever. "Okay, what if I agree to let you help me? What exactly are you helping me with? And how?" Terrence grins at her. "You'll see. Right now, let me assure you that I have no intent to harm you. And my first plan is to get you out of this house. That's how I'm going to help you first. Your powers can wait. Right now, your safety is at stake. I'm going to start following you."

Clarisse freezes, realizing the weight of what he just decided.

"Wait, what?"

"Your parents won't see me as anything other than a common house pet."

She's still not processing.

"I'm sorry, but what?"

Before she protests, Terrence's figure catches up in smoke. She coughs, waving away the furling cloud that smells like sulfur and rot. When the dust settles, she finds herself in the presence of a small German Shepherd puppy.

She squeals, picking him up and throwing all of her worries into a mental trash bin somewhere. Puppies are cute. They're safe. They're warm and snuggly and they're everything she's ever wanted. Her parents have always said no. He seems to be enjoying the attention when a dark thought hits her.

They've always said no.

"My parents don't like pets, Terrence. This will never work."

"Hmm… you're right. I have a better idea."

The smoke returns; in its place is a full-grown German Shepherd. The puppy becomes too heavy to carry and Clarisse sadly sets it on the ground.

"How is this any different?"

"I'm your guide dog. I can fake being a 'service dog' since Father Simmons seems to write you so many excuses anyway, right?"

A letter appears from thin air; on it is Father Simmons' writing and stamp of approval for her to have one given her special "condition."

"But, Terrence, this is fraud!" He rolls his eyes—a strange gesture coming from a dog. "Do any of your family members care about the moral strictures of the law? Or the lack thereof? No. And you need protection. They'll be far less likely to murder you if I'm with you. And this way, I can follow you into town tomorrow when you get things. I can stay with you. Keep you company, and the like. Besides, I can't stay in this barn forever. I don't *need* to eat, but I would like to."

Clarisse laughs, though she's put on edge at the thought of someone plotting to murder her—she still doesn't believe everything he said earlier.

"How do you know my parents would want to do such a thing? A life insurance policy is hardly enough to think anything insidious. I mean, people do die, Terrence. I'm sure they have policies on each other, too." It stings to even say it. Something in her gut tells her that Terrence isn't being outlandish with his claims, but how can she possibly believe him?

Why would my parents murder me? I still just—

Terrence fixes her with a stare that screams 'danger.' "I knew everything about you, right? Don't you think I would research your family, too? I've been watching them as much as I have you. I've *heard* them plotting things that just don't sound right, Clarisse. I can't hear everything all the time—my main focus has been you. But believe me, you do not want to trust these people or give them even the slightest bit of the benefit of the doubt. I haven't heard them say it directly, but I promise you that policy is the icing on the cake."

Clarisse swallows. "Fine, fine. You're right."

She shakes herself, wondering when she's going to wake up from this strange dream. She pinches herself until her skin is almost purple. She blinks. She does breathing exercises. But Terrence is still there. Her wounds are still gone.

She knows for sure—this is no dream.

8

BRAVERY

Clarisse

Reaching the house, she's filled with dread. This isn't going to go well. Her hands start sweating, her heart racing in her chest. The world around her seems to grow hot and cold at the same time, threatening to crowd out any air that might have made it to her lungs. Her eyes threaten to go completely focus until a paw reaches up and places itself in her hand. Terrence. Despite looking like a more normal house pet, even as a German Shepherd, Terrence is huge. He reaches almost to her head with his own. It's not exactly blending in like she wants.

"They'll see me more normal-sized, I assure you. You can see through more of my veneers due to your more... magical inclinations. Not all of my illusion sticks."

So, be careful when I go to touch you?

"I would leave contact to a minimum when they're around, or else you'll look like you're petting the air."

She's quite certain that, with her light and gangly body, she could easily ride him like a horse. Her fingers grasp her ribs without a touch of fat on them. *I've been underfed my whole life when Dad has piles of money sitting somewhere.*

Another pang of sorrow passes through her as she realizes just how *right* Terrence is about everything. Father Simmons would never let her be free, like Terrence is talking about. Free to actually express herself in more than just sewing. To be able to smile without being in fear of what follows is all she wants. *It's a concept I've never been allowed to entertain until now.*

Ever so carefully, she opens the door with as little disruption to the quiet as possible. The coast is clear. Mom and Dad must be in their room. *What am I going to do when we get upstairs?* Terrence is too big to hide in the closet. *Perhaps he can hide under the bed.*

Mom's footsteps come down the hall. Clarisse freezes while her heart pounds so hard it hurts. Although she isn't worried about Mom's approval anymore. She's horrified thinking about Terrence's insinuation that they are plotting to murder her. Without thinking, she grips at Terrence's fur which—to her surprise—is no longer scorching. He doesn't flinch. Terrence seems to know that she needs the reassurance, given everything that's going on. Without him speaking, he really does seem like just a friendly dog.

Deborah rounds the corner, almost dropping the food dish she has in her hands.

"Clarisse! What is that?!"

Gripping the fake paper from Father Simmons, she wonders if they'll call him to double-check if it's true. If Father Simmons would actually work to try and get Clarisse something as important and needy as an *animal*. A full-grown *dog*.

The disruption summons Dad to the hallway. When he reaches Mom's side, his cheeks redden. The dark shadow looming over his face makes Clarisse grip Terrence tighter. He doesn't budge. If she didn't know any better, she would think her dog's fur was rising due to a natural instinct to protect. But she knows it's rising for more than that. Terrence understands more than even she does the horrible things her father has planned.

She believes him wholeheartedly. The way the world around her shifts with cold weight–like shackles–is enough to make her want to run. The knife in Dad's pocket seems to glint brighter in the light. Her father is planning to murder her. She can see it in his face. The way his voice shakes when he finally decides to open his mouth just nails the lid on the coffin shut.

"Clarisse, you get this dog out of here right now or I'm calling animal control to come out and shoot it."

This, oddly enough, is what pushes Clarisse a little closer to the edge than she's ever been before.

"You may not see the marks, but I'll have you know that punching me today almost sent me into a relapse, *Father*. It's called abuse." Clarisse stammers. Her anger comes bubbling over even more. She clenches her fists. "And it makes me angry when you talk to me like that. You push me around when all I've ever done is accommodate you and work hard for you, so you can step right off. There will be no calling animal control. If you need proof that I brought Terrence in here for more than just 'having a pet,' here's your proof." She hurls the paper at Dad.

The venom in her voice shakes everyone in the room. A buzz starts up in her veins that she's never felt before. Power. And not the magical kind. The kind that gives her the strength to tell her abusers to get lost. It's enough to make her chest rattle while she tries to breathe. Terrence moves up, steadying her, while she speaks. "For the record, if you ever try to lay hands on me like that again, I will make sure you regret the day you were *born*."

This is an entirely foreign person that's standing in the living room foyer. Her tears are back. They're streaming down her face. She chokes back a sob.

"You *hurt* me today. You hurt me all the time. So Father Simmons thought a service dog would help me, especially during these difficult times, so that I don't relapse. He saw the marks you gave me. He saw the *abuse*. And he gave me this dog so I don't have another magical episode. You make it harder when you subject me to such tension-filled moments and... and I'm tired of it. I've been kissing ass to you for far too long and I won't stand for it anymore. I need help and you're not giving it to me."

"Clarisse! Watch your language!" Of course, Mom finds a way

to interject about being more proper. A well-placed glare puts her to silence again.

Clarisse is fuming. She can't stand her parents at this moment. "I'll say what I please right now. That's why Terrence is here. I lost my footing today because of Dad's inability to stay peaceful. Do you know I can get you both arrested? I can tell them *everything* and you'll go away for good!" Clarisse shakes a fist to try and hide the tears that are now breaking free from her eyes. It's taking everything in her to do this. Terrence remains steadfast at her side. "Do you understand? I've been forced to live in poverty when Dad makes more than enough money to take care of us and have been forced to live in a cult since I was a child because I had light shoot from my hands."

Clarisse sneers at them, still crying. Her emotions are a blur of confusion, fear and anger. Lashing out for the first time in her life is strange and she's not sure what to think of it, but the shaking in her chest pushes her to continue. On she rages like an angry steam engine.

"I don't know what to say anymore. You guys are terrible parents. I don't love you. I only stay here because you've manipulated me all my life and I have nowhere else. As soon as I can, I'm getting out of here. If you put me on the streets in the meantime, I will use my powers and let everyone know what you've done to me. I will make sure you're locked away and they never find the key. Are we clear?"

Clarisse's cheeks are red. The tears won't stop. They never have. They only stop so she can keep her mask on. "I want you to know that what you're doing to me is unacceptable. I've been shown that now. The way you hit me today set it straight for me, *Father*. You have shown me the light."

Clarisse stands up straight, her spine snapping from the sudden pressure of so much self-confidence. She bears the weight of the world. "I won't stand for this anymore. You either start treating me as a person instead of an animal to be kept in a cage, or we start having some real problems around here. I'm more volatile than ever thanks to the setback today. Don't think that volatility won't affect you."

Silence ensues. No one has ever heard Clarisse say more than a few words at a time in her *life*. This is the most she's said. *Ever.*

I can't keep quiet anymore. I have to let them know I'm not going down without a fight. This crap ends here. Now. Today.

"Clarisse, I'm sorry for what I did to you today," Dad starts. "You could have jeopardized the company—"

"See? It's all about your stupid company. Not me. Don't think you're getting out of this. Don't think you can sweet talk me back into being quiet little Clarisse anymore. I won't be. You can't make me. I never will be. I'm not meant to be kept clamped down like this forever." Her teeth grind together, threatening to shatter under the pressure.

She turns to Terrence. "This is my friend, Terrence. He's here to make sure you all don't get *hurt* while I work on getting myself under control so I can operate meaningfully in the adult world. Take the letter or leave it, but he's staying. I don't care what you say because I'm taking care of him with the money I make at my job, since you fired Alice and don't have anyone else willing to put up with your crap at your crap company."

Dad opens his mouth to speak but she points a finger at him to shush him. To her surprise, it works.

"I'm not finished. Now, I'll keep working for you. I'll keep the 'quiet secretary' façade up for as long as I can. I'll give you, at *most*, a month's notice when I know I can get out on my own. I'll sever myself from you forever and leave quietly. If you try to get in the way of that at *all* I *will* make you pay. And I am not giving you half of my paycheck. That half now goes to taking care of Terrence, who, in turn, makes sure that my 'curse' doesn't affect you more harshly than it already has. Are we clear?"

No one dares say anything to her. Clarisse is dangerous. She sees her dark eyes glow amber in the reflection of Dad's glasses. *Demonic. I look demonic.*

"No," Terrence interrupts. *"You look powerful."*

There in the way her hair starts to wave when there's no wind.

She's coming into her own; she's not someone to mess with once she's gotten a hold of that power.

Just wait until you see all that I can be.

The night was restless. Clarisse finally gets up. In her daze, she forgot to tell her father she's taking off for the day. Granted, she never set an alarm and the time is well-past the start of a working day. *He surely got the hint.*

She stares at her hands and remembers the night before. The stars. The wolf—*Terrence.*

He's staring out into space beside the bed, his jet-black fur shimmering in the daylight. His eyes, though brown, still possess a red tint making them look like orbs of cherry cola. She laughs, thinking of how absurd it is to make a connection like that.

I guess I must really want a soda.

"Well, I'll have you know I'm not edible. Consuming me would kill you. Glad to see you're awake," Terrence winks.

"I thought you said intruding into people's thoughts wasn't something you did often," Clarisse crosses her arms, doing her best to stifle a yawn.

Terrence laughs. "Not normally, no. But I can't help it with you. You've got such interesting things to think about. And I wanted to get a bearing on how you're doing after last night. That was quite the shock. Even to you, I assume."

Clarisse dips her head, running her fingers through her greasy hair. To say it's a mess would be a great disservice to the use of the word. Dirt and grime linger on her skin from the night before. She's desperate to take a shower. The rule is that all bathing has to be done before ten in the morning. Dad and Mom like for showers to be short and concise—to cut back on the water bill. If she showers after ten, Mom and Dad are both gone and no one is around to yell at her to hurry up. Today, Clarisse doesn't even care that it's well-near eleven.

Terrence starts to follow her to the shower, but she holds out her hand.

"No, stay here. You're not following me to the bathroom, that's creepy."

If Terrence could blush, he probably would have. "Sorry, you just had to tell me where you were going. I'll wait outside the door."

Clarisse thinks twice about apologizing for assuming that he would be perverted like that; then again, stories of gods would give someone reason to think twice about their intentions and the forms they took. Speaking of forms… why in the *world* does he look like a wolf?

Clarisse can't wrap her head around anything as she slides open her shower curtain and steps inside, turning the water on and letting its icy cold droplets splash all along her skin. *I wish Dad would actually pay for the water to be heated. Cheap, asshole, lying….*

She stops herself, her chest heaving with rage.

If this is a dream, this will definitely wake me up. And I'll be in a heap of trouble.

The memory of last night burns into her brain forever. *Did I say all that?* She shivers, letting the water wash away the pain she feels from all the beatings she would have gotten without Terrence there.

Terrence's words in the barn echoed through her thoughts. It was his doing. Helping her. Getting her on her feet. Teaching her to use her magic. How he had been mortal once, too, and somehow became a god in the afterlife….

Tyrla… tyra…

"Tyrladan," Terrence calls from the hallway. "And I'm happy to answer many of those questions for you later today."

A terrifying thought passes through Clarisse's head. *What if Mom didn't actually leave?* "Terrence, is my mother home?"

"No, she left this morning. She's going to the local country club with some ladies she's friends with."

"Country club? What do you mean country club? Is she a member of one?"

"Yes, apparently it's a regular thing they do. Your mother is known for being quite good at a round of golf, of all things. She goes while you're at school. I've watched her on occasion."

In all her years, Clarisse has never *seen* a golf club. She's never heard of her mother to be of the sporting type, either. Let alone wealthy enough to have entry at a country club. Her curiosity piques. *Terrence, remind me to snoop on Mom and Dad later.* They can't keep getting away with keeping secrets from her.

But right now, she needs to get dressed and go meet Father Simmons. She rushes back to her room, Terrence on her heels. She pauses.

"Uh, Terrence? Can you wait outside again? I need to change my clothes."

Terrence shakes his head. "You're not wearing those rags."

Somewhere in the distance, she hears a snap. She's shocked to find a pair of pants and a t-shirt covering her and *hugging* her lanky frame. She bites back a sob. *Clothes have never fit me right before.*

"Where… where did you… how did you?"

Terrence cuts her off while she stands there, dumbstruck. "I can create clothing with my powers. I can't create big things, but clothing is an easy trick. It's a rudimentary type of magic. Takes nothing from anyone and uses what's available in nature. It just skips the lengthy mortal manufacturing process, really." Terrence rolls his eyes as though machines and technology annoy him. "Why use human tech when magic is infinitely superior? Though, I must say watching television is a pastime that I rather enjoy," he chuckles.

Clarisse is paying him no mind. She pulls at the hem of her shirt and rubs her hand along the softness of her blue jeans. *Clothes that look good on me.* She's gotten accustomed to the feeling of denim as being *scratchy*. Nothing like this. *What else don't I know about?*

She grabs Terrence's massive frame and pulls him into an awkward hug. "Thank you. I have no idea why you're doing all this and I have more questions than answers, but you are absolutely the best thing that's ever happened to me."

She twirls on her heels, noticing for the first time the flip flops on her feet. Shifting them around on her feet, she ponders how to proceed. *How will I explain all of this to Father Simmons? I can't get away with this lie forever. What happens when my parents double check and ask him?*

But consequences be damned, she's enjoying herself and she doesn't intend to stop anytime soon.

Stepping into the hall, she rushes into the kitchen to get breakfast. She rifles around in the pantry and finds a box of cereal that's normally off-limits. She's used to eating standard bran-style cereals. The fun stuff is for Dad which, in itself, is an irony given his bland tastes in everything else.

"Dad will just have to learn to share," Clarisse laughs. "Would you like a bowl?"

Terrence stares at the food as though it might snap him. "What... what is that?"

"Cereal? Wait... you know so much about human technology and life, but you're telling me you've never had, let alone seen, cereal?"

Terrence shakes his head, cringing. Well, curling his snout up into something like a snarl. "It looks like someone packed massive clumps of sugar together in a box and decided to sell it as food. Is that... safe?"

Clarisse holds back a laugh.

Has he really never seen cereal?

This particular variety has marshmallows in it, making it all the more attractive to her palate in the not-so-early morning.

"Here, try a few pieces and see if you like it."

Terrence takes a crunch. His eyes light up at the flavor and he bounces around the kitchen. His massive frame is comical to watch in a state of such juvenile excitement. "What in the world? That is fantastic! May I have a bowl as well? Like, a large bowl? I'll help you find some to replace it while we're out today!"

His pupils dilate, much like a normal dog would in an attempt to beg for food. She laughs at having caught him in the ridiculous act. "This is just as wonderful as discovering *television!*"

Clarisse laughs, pouring him a bowl. He starts to take it when she holds her hand out.

"Terrence... you're supposed to put milk in it."

"Milk? In this? Why, it's perfect already!"

Clarisse narrows her eyes at him. "Here, look, if you don't like it, I'll just give you another bowl of dry. But you have to try cereal the way it's intended to be eaten," she jokes.

Terrence, she swears, puts out a pouty lip.

"Come on, you'll like it! I think you'll like human technology a lot more than you think. You like television? Then this stuff will rock your socks off!"

"Well, those are fantastic! Instantaneous communication with colorful pictures and shows is wonderful!" He pauses. "I suppose I will try it with milk, then."

A few moments pass and both of them are sitting at the kitchen table. Terrence devours his cereal faster than Clarisse can pour it with a spoon he's managed to get to float. Eventually he realizes the spoon won't work and just downs the entire bowl, splashing milk all over his face and the table. It takes everything in her not to stare and *laugh*. She's barely touched her own breakfast; he realizes his greed and stops.

"You need to eat. You're too thin."

Clarisse drops her jaw. "I beg your pardon?"

"You don't eat! Your parents don't feed you! I'm not judging you. I'm observing facts. Please, eat. I've been overstaying my welcome by not allowing you space. I've forgotten my manners." Terrence bows his head and waits.

"Terrence, it's okay, I like watching you have fun. I can't believe you've never even had cereal before," Clarisse giggles as she shakes him out some more. This time, he's much slower to enjoy it, his spoon no longer a frantic silver machine.

Clarisse finishes her first and only bowl. The box of cereal is empty. She'll definitely need to get her father some more while she's out. *Even after last night, I can't afford to rock the boat too much....*

"Okay, let's go see Father Simmons." Clarisse stands, pushing her chair out behind her and, for once, letting the chairs squeak against the floor. It's a relieving experience. She's never done it; despite how irritating the sound might be, it's an important moment for her. Even the smallest movements toward autonomy are everything.

"Alright. Now, we're going to have to explain... me. And we can't use our letter as bait again for obvious reasons."

Clarisse ponders this. "Terrence, are you able to change your appearance just a bit more? I have an idea."

9

LITTLE BIG LIES

Clarisse

C larisse arrives at church at a quarter past noon, after a long walk debriefing Terrence on how they're going to pull of their deceitful plans. She holds her head down, feigning her normal appearance of meekness. *Have to keep up the act.*

Father Simmons opens the door to the church; he smiles. "Running late this morning, huh?"

Clarisse puts on the show of her life. Her lip trembles and she starts to sputter. Tears stream down her face. Father Simmons ushers her inside as fast as he can, peering over his shoulder like he's worried someone will see. "Clarisse, what is the matter?"

He peers over her like he always does; she knows he's checking for black eyes, bruises—anything to hide from the flock or any other signs that might indicate she could relapse or expose the church.

"I almost relapsed…" she gasps, amazed at how well she's holding up this façade.

"And?"

"I met… I met…."

Before she continues, Terrence arrives—right on schedule. His glistening black coat shimmers in the light. She twists her hand, her stars blurring to form a halo around his head and, from his back, he grows a pair of shadowy wings.

Father Simmons stumbles back as Clarisse moves to join Terrence.

"An angel," Father Simmons whispers. "How? How can this be?" He looks like he might collapse, his voice an urgent whisper.

"He came to me last night with a letter from you, saying you'd chosen him as my service dog." Clarisse pauses. She has to make sure everything adds up if he asks her parents later or vice versa. "I didn't believe it until he showed me what he really is. Father Simmons, I think the Great Light sent him to me." She fumbles with her hands, keeping her eyes cast at the ground. Her soul is screaming—lying is not her strong suit and sweat is beginning to bead at her forehead. *He'll know if I look at him.* "Does he have your blessing?"

Father Simmons' eyes drift about as though his brain's been tossed around and left in a spinning flurry inside his head. Clarisse can see the wheels turning. He's questioning everything; she doesn't have to be a mind-reader to know. They've already talked before. The religion thing is a sham for control; to actually see something divine and powerful? A sign of the "Great Light" he likes to talk about so much? It has to be rocking his whole world. She's living for it. Her eyes cast upwards again so she can truly revel in the moment. He shivers with so much violence she wonders if he might blow away in an unseen wind. Maybe, after all this time, the ice in his heart will spread to his veins and leave him a frozen statue—a testament to the lies he's told all his life.

A moment passes between them. For a second, he can't meet her eyes. Never has there been so much resentment in her heart against him as there is now. It threatens to break free of her. She wonders if she'll scream at him, too. He fidgets under her gaze. The energy in the room betrays everything. The lie is working. The seams of their agreements are coming undone in the wake of the angel-wolf.

"Of course, Clarisse." It's more of a gasp than a true response. "W-Where did you find him?"

"He met me on the way home last night. He healed my face and protected me from my parents. I fear you're right. Father Simmons, I think they're plotting something against me. I... I found documents. A life insurance policy with a lot of money taken out on me. Terrence told me where to find it in a vision. He and his letter were enough to protect me last night. I'm sorry I'm late. I was up well into the night trying to understand, but I've come to terms with it. The Great Light has sent Terrence to save me." She bows her head, holding back a smile.

This is the most devious thing I have ever thought of.

"You've learned from the best." Terrence jumps into her thoughts. Somehow, she can feel him glaring at Father Simmons.

She cuts Terrence a look while Father Simmons is distracted by his own thoughts. He's staring into space, muttering things she can't understand. Clarisse wonders if Father Simmons can tell that the "angel" is glaring at him or not, but she can't risk having everything fall to pieces because Terrence won't keep his mouth shut.

"I suppose he can hide those wings? And the halo?"

Clarisse cuts the lights and Terrence puts away his shadow wings. Father Simmons hums with approval.

"He can do all sorts of things, Father Simmons. He stopped the lights from coming on last night. I was so angry. I yelled at my parents for the first time in my life." Clarisse takes a breath. It feels good to start letting some truths back into her story. "I felt my episode coming, but he kept them at bay. It was very... frightening." Clarisse is proving herself to be a master manipulator and she's terrified.

When did I turn into a glorified actress? A fraud? A fake?

"You're not a fake."

It dawns on her that she didn't question at all the fact that Terrence can now answer her *inside* her thoughts. She's wary of the scope of such a power, but she doesn't fight it. The company is more than welcome.

How am I not a fake?

Father Simmons pats her on the back. "Clarisse, it's alright that you stood up for yourself. You sensed a great evil and I think

Terrence here was sent to help you keep calm in a time when you need help the most. I meant what I said about helping you today; I hope you're still ready to go out and get you that phone?"

Clarisse nods. "I'm more than ready. I want to make sure I can contact you or anyone I can for help if something goes wrong. There's great evil in my house, Father Simmons. I can feel it."

Father Simmons raises an eyebrow. Clarisse knows that he's struggling to accept Terrence and all of the things they've just revealed to him. She's sure that questions about how she knew about the life insurance documents and where to look for them are bound to come up—why Terrence chose her... that and a million more questions are already in her mind, so she knows he has to have at least half of them. He's not stupid; she wonders how long she'll be able to keep her little story straight. For now, she accepts the victory she has.

"Wonderful. I'll bring the car around. You and Terrence can wait at the front steps. Here are the keys. Make sure you lock up." Father Simmons would trust no one other than Clarisse herself with keys to the church. She's the last person who would take anything or use them for nefarious purposes. She helped him with quite a lot over the years; in exchange, the church was a safe space for her. She could vent her frustrations, confess her fears, contemplate things her parents wouldn't even *dare* to consider.

A silent ride to the mall ensues. Clarisse has never been to a mall in all her life. She's used to seeing Father Simmons in casual clothes, but this is the first time she'll be gracing any public place so loudly —in jeans and a t-shirt, no less. No sack-like dress. No awkward shoes. She was just... *normal*. Normal in a way her parents would never let her be. The *other* normal she wrote about in her journals.

Her heart lurches. A bucket of ice drops down her throat and into her stomach; for a moment, she can't move.

She left her journal out.

"I've got it."

What?

Terrence slouches across the backseat of the truck, enjoying the ride.

"I put the journal away."

You can do that?

He fixes her with a stare that almost makes her burst out laughing. Were she not an expert in suppressing her emotions, she would have jeopardized their entire mission with a fit of giggles. Father Simmons would know something is up. As it is, the smile she's wearing is cause for great suspicion.

"Clarisse, are you alright?" Father Simmons parks in the lot.

"Yeah, I'm just excited. I've never done anything like this before. I can't thank you enough."

Father Simmons waves. "Anything for you, Clarisse. I know I've never said it out loud, but you're like the daughter I never had. I want you to know I'm always here to help you."

"Thanks, Father Simmons."

"What a load of bull—"

Terrence!

"What?"

"Did you bring a leash for Terrence?"

Before she has time to panic, one appears in the backseat of the truck.

Terrence thinks of everything and, to be frank, it has her a bit worried about her sanity. He's too smart for his own good. *"I can't believe I'm wearing a leash. Like I'm some kind of common dog... if you weren't in so much danger going everywhere...."*

She clips it on him, grimacing. "Sorry, Terrence. We've got to make this work for the time being."

He dips his head, his ears flat on either side of his head, a tell-tale sign that he's not pleased.

"Alright, Clarisse. Let's head to the store and get you your phone. If you want, you can explore and I can just get it set up for you. I suppose you don't have any contacts or anything to transfer to the new one anyway."

Clarisse laughs. "Yeah. If you want, I can start looking into things that might be helpful for my business—see if there are any comparable shops that I can look into and maybe ask the owners for input or advice on becoming a seamstress."

Father Simmons smiles. "That's a great idea. See if any of them are willing to talk to you."

Clarisse smiles, looking down at Terrence who exudes excitement, too. "Alright, where should we meet and what time?"

"I don't see the electronics store taking that long, so why don't we meet at the bank on the second floor in about an hour?"

"Sounds good. I'll see you then." Clarisse takes off at a jog; she hears Father Simmons chuckling at her as she makes her way to the glass doors. He's doing a great job pretending like everything is normal. She's determined to do the same. Ashville's mall has two floors, but the square footage is nothing to be astounded with. The shops are mediocre and are more like a hub for general businesses than clothing stores and knick-knack shops like most malls would be known for.

But to Clarisse, this is as good as being crowned queen of her own kingdom—she's free to roam about her new castle as she wishes. These little stores and glum patrons are part of a fantasy that she's never gotten to see. Not until now. Now, she can run among them without being held back or being in fear of punishment for stepping out of line. The excitement of it all thrums in her ears and twists in her lungs.

She takes a moment to breathe it all in. Her feet have only been to the parking lot of this place twice with Mom to buy Dad gifts. After a near slip-up so many years ago, she's never been allowed back. But today—today, she has a chance to explore all the shops she's wanted to for her whole life. She's able to step *inside*.

Clarisse doesn't know where to start.

"How about we start by looking for a tailor shop? Maybe you can ask for tips and tricks?"

Clarisse smiles. "That's a good idea. But first I need to use the little girl's room."

Terrence rolls his eyes at her. "You know, you can just call it the bathroom. You don't have to be so proper and uptight."

Clarisse laughs. "Fair enough."

It dawns on Clarisse that she's being watched. There aren't

many people there, but she has to be more careful about talking to Terrence.

Just wait outside the bathroom. I'll be right out. Do you have a service dog vest? Or something?

"What? I don't want to wear a dumb vest—come on, they should know that a well-behaved 'dog' in the mall is probably not just a stray pet."

I don't care, the people in this town are too dumb to know this.

Terrence obliges, dipping behind a wall. While no one is looking, he has one appear on his frame and calmly sits outside the bathroom door.

"Just be careful, okay?" Terrence's concern is admirable, but Clarisse can't help but giggle.

It's just the bathroom silly. What could possibly go wrong in the bathroom?

She leaves him sitting just outside, content that he isn't going to follow her. *I'm alright, see?*

He doesn't answer.

The door to the bathroom slams shut. Curls of icy breath spiral from her lips to the ceiling. Her eyes squint from the lack of light; she can hardly figure out where she is. Placing her hands out to reach for something to hold on to yields nothing. Stumbling about, she's certain she's going to run into something. Her hands are clammy and *lost* is an understatement for how she feels. Breathing becomes more and more difficult; a creaking noise tells her that she's not alone.

Terrence? Can you hear me?

She's terrified as the room goes colder, leading her to realize *many* things could go wrong. Breathing becomes a chore; the hairs on her neck are standing on edge and moving becomes more like trudging through molasses. Her eyes dart around in the hopes of finding an exit as the lights start to come on. She tries to call for Terrence in her mind again, but she can't even think hard enough to formulate words. She's trembling so hard that she nearly slips.

"What's going on?" She whispers aloud. "Terrence? If this is some game, stop messing around."

One of the stall doors creaks open and she heaves—her lungs

can't open up fast enough to let in the air she needs. She feels like she's drowning... suffocating.

Somehow, the air seems to lift just enough for her to finally speak again. "Who's there?"

From the bathroom stall comes a wolf—another freaking *wolf*. And, somehow, this one is far more terrifying than Terrence ever was when she met him. *How is that possible?*

His coat isn't solid darkness. Instead, it is filled with glittering constellations. His golden eyes are covered by a skull mask that fits him a bit too well for Clarisse's liking. She backs toward the door, hoping to all hell that Terrence knows something is wrong.

"He can't hear you here." The sound erupting from the wolf's voice is beautiful. It sounds like a chorus of cellos have been strung together in his vocal cords. The music they make is wonderful; Clarisse's body almost goes limp at the sound. Her legs wobble and shake; it takes everything in her to keep herself upright.

"Why... why can't he hear me?" She doesn't know how she manages to get the question out, while her strength is drained.

The wolf laughs. Clarisse wonders if her spine will ever slouch again as it rockets out ramrod straight.

"Because I'm his original master. He's a rogue Reaper, Clarisse. I decide whether or not he is privy to this conversation and I decide whether or not to let you out of this bathroom alive." His threat oozes like honey.

How can something so awful be said so beautifully?

"You've broken the laws of mortality with the magic you've been performing in the last few days. If you don't stop, you will die."

Clarisse scoffs. "And how do you know that?" The question comes out more like a slur than a sentence, her tongue refusing her commands to speak clearly.

"I'm Death."

10

THE GRIM REAPER

Clarisse

Wait, what? That's—that's impossible.

Clarisse trembles, trying to find the strength to move. To run. Anywhere would be better than here.

Death comes closer to her, his expression hidden by the wolf skull he wears over his own face. The only clue to what he's feeling is his eyes. They don't sparkle like Terrence's, despite their haunting color. Who knew eyes could be gold? Like Terrence, they don't even have pupils in their natural state. Or, if they do, they're the exact same color as his irises, making them look more like glowing orbs than eyes. "You heard me. You're meddling with things beyond your comprehension. It's time for you to stop."

Clarisse crosses her arms, determined not to be thrown off by this high and mighty creature. Her breath rolls up to the ceiling in coils of desperation, a sign that she's not breathing like someone *truly* calm. "How do I know you're telling the truth?"

She doesn't feel like a walking jelly creature so much anymore. Instead, she's a frightened young child. This can't be *Death*. This can't be the actual Grim Reaper in the flesh. Or fur.

Why are all these god figures wolves? What is it with that?

"That question is none of your business. And I am Death. Do you want me to summon some souls of the dead to prove it? It's less than appealing, but I can make it happen," he grins.

Cocky much?

His smile chills her to the bone.

"I'll pass."

"Good. I'm glad you've retained at least some of your senses."

Clarisse bristles. "What do you mean? What is that supposed to mean?" She crosses her arms, putting her foot down. Her voice quavers a bit. The subject is more than raw, but she's not going to let this starry wolf tell her how to live her life. That's not even his job. His job is for the part that comes after. *I'm not going to remain a slave to my parents forever. Magic is the key out of here.*

"I'm not going to be insulted for finally deciding to do things that benefit me, Death." She huffs. "I want to be free of suffering and pain. That's what this whole experience has given me in the last few days."

Death sighs. "I don't mean that being abused is sensible. I'll admit, it was very hard for me to leave you in those conditions when I first came to check on you."

Clarisse's eyes widen. "You mean you saw what they did to me?"

All at once, the flashing memory of a starry wolf standing outside the church all those years ago makes sense. *That wasn't a trick of the light?* Her blood boils, her cheeks growing red with rage.

Death pauses, thinking of the best way to respond. Clarisse doesn't let him.

"Listen up, you asshole. You don't even understand the gravity of what I've been through, do you?" She rips up her sleeve. All along her arms are the scars from exorcisms, the belt, and other devices used to punish her whenever she messed up.

"Does this look like 'sensible' to you?" She hardly chokes out the question. Death's presence is still overwhelming. For a moment, she swears Death's eyes soften, but the mask makes it hard to figure if that's just a trick of the light or genuine emotion.

"No, it does not."

"Then why would you leave me there?" She hisses. "I saw you at the exorcism. Isn't that enough to prove to you that I'm living with lunatics? Have you seen anything *else* while we're broaching the subject?"

Death waves her off with an eye roll. "I'm not here to go over the past. I'm here to help you try and salvage your future. You need to cut ties with Terrence immediately."

"And why should I do that?"

"Did you not hear me, you daft mortal? He's a rogue Reaper. He's gone mad for power and wants to take over the world—the Afterlife."

Clarisse finds the statement so frank and lifeless that she laughs. She can't stop laughing for a good few minutes, manic tears washing her cheeks with salt and exasperation. "Way to lay it on thick there, buddy. I'm supposed to believe that? So far, I've only met a friend. Someone who wants to help me just get out."

"And using your powers to trick a priest into thinking he's an angel is a way to do that?"

Clarisse's cheeks redden again.

How does he know?

"I know a lot of things, Clarisse. I'm Death."

Right, mind-reading. Nothing is a secret anymore. She huffs.

"So what if we did that? It's none of your freaking business. I'm trying to get out of here alive. I'm trying to keep my sanity. I'm trying to find people who are genuinely interested in helping me live and be free. To escape being murdered by my parents. I know it's just your job to collect souls. You probably don't care for anything beyond that, but can't you see that what I'm doing is helping me? Terrence has said nothing about taking over the Afterlife. Does he really seem like the type to do that kind of thing to you?"

Death starts to answer, but Clarisse holds up a finger to signal him to keep his mouth shut. "I can't stand the fact that you have the nerve to come in here and tell me that what I'm doing is dangerous and wrong. How can any of this be 'bad' for me?"

"You can die from using magic, Clarisse."

"So? You can die from drinking water, too, you know. Could have poison in it. Everything is a weapon when you're mortal."

Death groans.

"So why try to expose yourself to more weapons if you can avoid them?"

Clarisse laughs. "Cheap talk coming from the freaking *Grim Reaper*."

I'm for sure going insane. This conversation… it's like the person she's talking to can't figure out emotions. "I don't know why I'm even entertaining this. For all I know, you're just an illusion I've created with my stars. I can make night skies, so maybe I made you so I can talk to you and have someone to bounce my fears off of."

Death freezes. "You make stars?"

"I can hear them. The moon, too." Clarisse continues to ramble. "I can make my own. They speak to me just like the rest. They always want out. Watch." She holds out her hands. He starts to say something to stop her, but it's too late. They appear on command and glitter from all corners of the bathroom. They bounce around and make musical noises as they collide with each other and any surface that they come across.

Death is speechless.

After a few minutes, Clarisse calls them back. In seconds, there's no evidence of the astronomical quandaries that filled the entire room.

"Curious," Death whispers. "I've never seen powers like that." For a moment, he remains silent. Suddenly, he blinks. He looks as though he might've forgotten Clarisse is even there. "But they're dangerous. Clarisse. You're taking time out of your life when you do things like that. It's far too dangerous for you to be engaging in behaviors like this."

"What proof do you have?"

Death shakes his head. For a moment, his stars spark a curious green color. "You're not ready for this conversation, I see. I'll leave you to this. But don't think that this is the last you'll hear of me."

Without warning, he disappears.

Clarisse rushes from the bathroom, forgetting that she's yet to do her business. She runs into Terrence, grabbing his leash and moving as fast as her legs will carry her. His eyes are wide with terror.

She's terrified and doesn't know where to stop. The sight of the sign for the tailor slows her up to walk inside without looking like a maniac. Her lungs are out of breath and the shopkeeper seems concerned as he walks to her.

Way to keep a low profile, Clarisse.

She stands back up to her full height to greet the shopkeeper without looking any crazier than she already does.

He's a man in his late fifties from what she can tell. His graying beard and the wrinkles give him away. "Young lady, are you alright?"

Clarisse manages to pull in a breath. "Yeah, I'm fine. I'm sorry, sir." Stopping herself from bending over to heave takes every muscle in her body. "I-I didn't mean to frighten you. I got a strange feeling I was being followed." A quick glance over her shoulder confirms that Death isn't still lurking. "But I believe I was mistaken," Clarisse smooths her shirt, standing taller.

"I'm sorry to hear that. Do you want me to call security and do a sweep?"

Clarisse shakes her head. "No need. I don't want to cry wolf if I can't prove that there was one."

Haha, Clarisse. How funny.

"What do you mean?" Terrence fixes her with a hard stare.

Clarisse runs her hands through Terrence's fur to calm him. He stiffens; she pulls away when she realizes how awkward it might be for him to be pet like that.

Sorry. Look, I'm not talking about you. I'll tell you in a minute.

"Sorry, I should introduce myself. My name is Clarisse. And this is my service dog, Terrence."

"It's a pleasure to meet you both. My name is Mr. Harris. I'm the owner of In Stitches, here. Now, can I help you look around?"

"Actually, I am here to ask you some questions if you don't mind. You see, I'm an aspiring seamstress. I just finished up with high school and I was hoping to interview some people experienced in the tailoring business to figure out how to get started in a field like this," Clarisse smiles.

Mr. Harris looks pleased with this, his blue eyes twinkling now that she's brought up the subject. "I am more than happy to help you with any questions you might have. Please, let me grab you a seat and something to drink. Coffee? Water?"

"You don't have to," Clarisse waves him off. "You've already been more than hospitable."

"No, no, I insist. What will it be?"

"Water, please," Clarisse blushes. She's not used to being treated with any modicum of respect. Her shattered ego makes it so she's never sure if she's holding herself with a proper amount of dignity or not.

"I'll be right out with it." Mr. Harris disappears into the backroom.

"What do you mean, 'cry wolf?' What happened in that bathroom, Clarisse? Did anyone hurt you? I need names. Faces. Descriptions. I can access your memories if you'd like if you don't think you can remember, I just—"

I met Death.

Terrence's eyes grow wide. He quickly assumes his more natural position when Mr. Harris comes walking back out of the backroom with two bottles of water.

"Now, please tell me about your aspirations and what led you to the idea of becoming a seamstress."

The conversation with Terrence will wait. Clarisse explains her experience to Mr. Harris and how she's been sewing since she was only ten. She talks to him about the craft fairs she's been to, how she mends all the clothes in the family and her knowledge of different types of stitching and the type of machine she's used to working with.

He's thoroughly impressed with everything she has to say. "Do you have anything to show as an example of your work?"

Before she can respond, she feels a weight in her pocket. She reaches inside and finds photos of projects she's worked on over the years. Except, she never took photos…

Terrence, really?

"What? I'm helping you get out, just like I said!"

But what am I paying in return? How did you even get these? Why do you care about me so much?

Terrence huffs aloud. Clarisse thanks her stars that it's something a normal dog might do, at least. Mr. Harris seems unbothered by the sound.

"Can't someone just genuinely want to help someone else? And it's called magic, duh."

She can't keep silent like this though. Mr. Harris is waiting, so she hands him the stack of photos.

"Sorry, I don't actually have a cell phone yet. My friend is downstairs getting one for me, as I've never had one. He let me take the opportunity to walk around so I could interview people who might have an idea of how this type of business works."

Mr. Harris peers down at Clarisse through his round-rimmed glasses. "Who is this friend of yours?"

"My... priest. Father Simmons. He's been helping me get on my feet so I can have a chance to start working in the industry and maybe have my own business someday," Clarisse hangs her head. "I know it sounds strange; I promise I'm telling the truth. My situation isn't normal, I know. But I really appreciate you sitting and talking with me about this. I'm very passionate about what I do."

Mr. Harris appears touched. He holds the various photos in his hands and smirks. "You've got beautiful work in your portfolio." He looks them over a second time, with even more attention. "Clarisse, how would you like it if I offered you a job here?"

Clarisse's eyes light up. "Really? You'd hire me?"

He shakes the photographs with genuine vigor; the way his eyes light up reveals his excitement. "Ma'am, with all due respect, I've *never* met someone with this kind of talent before at such a young age. You'll have to take certification classes but I'm happy to include that in your benefits package when you start working with me. There's a local community college that offers the types of classes you'll need to take. I'll make sure to accommodate your schedule around that. When you meet your friend, ask him to bring you back up here so I can get your cell phone number so I can get into contact with you. I'm going out of town this weekend, but I would love it if you could come this next Monday. Would that be alright?"

Clarisse is shaking, unable to contain her excitement. "I would love to! Absolutely!"

Mr. Harris laughs. "That's wonderful, Clarisse! Now, do you have to meet up with your friend at a certain time or do you have time to fill out some paperwork?"

Clarisse glances at the clock. It's been almost an hour, which is hard for her to believe. "I actually need to run downstairs and see him. He and I have to set up my bank account."

"Well, in that case, I'm going to go ahead and give you the paperwork; if you can fill it out, bring it with you Monday and it'll expedite the process of putting you to work. Does that sound fair?"

Clarisse nods vigorously, scared her head might fall off from the excitement.

"More than fair! Thank you so much!" She stands up and shakes his hand; her eyes are alive with more exuberance than they've ever been in her life. The fire in them inspires Terrence to wag his tail.

"Ah, seems like your friend is excited as well! He's very well-behaved, though I know service dogs have to be. What is he like in a working environment?"

Clarisse chuckles. "He's no trouble. You'll find he makes for a very wonderful companion along with doing his job very well. I hope it won't be a burden to bring him with me to work?"

Mr. Harris waves his hands. "Of course not. Bring him on Monday. It'll be nice to have such a friendly face about when we work. Clients will love it just as much as I will. I'm a big sucker for dogs!"

Terrence looks almost annoyed at being called a dog, but Clarisse covers for him by laughing.

"So am I. He's a real life-saver."

Mr. Harris disappears to the backroom again with a twinkle in his eye to grab her paperwork.

Terrence isn't about to let their conversation go just yet. He takes the silent opportunity to keep pressing her with questions.

"Death? What do you mean you met Death? What did he look like?"

Ah… huge dire wolf-like thing… kinda like you but full of stars? Like, is that even possible? I don't know why I even bother asking about possibilities anymore, but, like, he's huge, Terrence. And he had a skull mask. It looked like he'd fused another wolf's skull over his head. And his voice sounded like… music….

Terrence's hackles raise. He quickly puts them down when Mr. Harris returns and Clarisse finishes hiding any signs of Terrence's aggression by running her hand up and down his back in reassurance. She's lucky that the vest does quite a lot of the job for her.

"What breed is he?" Mr. Harris hands Clarisse a thick stack of things to be filled out.

"He's actually a German Shepherd. I know he's huge. I guess we just fed him really well."

Mr. Harris whistles. "That boy could give pony rides at the fair."

"My god, this man. Just get a dog if you love them so much! Stop staring!"

Clarisse can't help but grin; it takes even more effort to stifle giggles.

Terrence, he likes you. You should take that as a compliment.

If looks could kill, Terrence would be a murderer at that moment. His eyes are saying things that Clarisse can't understand and he doesn't elaborate with any thoughts. She dares to reach down and pet him again as a wary sort of thanks.

"You deserve to shine, not be clamped down."

The statement puzzles her, her eyebrows threatening to knot themselves as such.

Wait, what?

"Don't worry about it just yet. I'll explain later."

"Thank you again, Mr. Harris. It was so great to meet you!"

Clarisse stands up, straightening her outfit and doing her best to look 'normal.'

"Of course! You'll find the details of my business and your hourly wages in the documents I've handed you, as well as how the promotion system works here, what benefits you would receive, and how to register at the local college with my business' information.

They're rather familiar with me in the program you're interested in."

"Perks of a small town, right?"

"Yes, indeed," Mr. Harris laughs. "It's been great to meet you. Don't forget to come back up and tell me your new phone number. The shop closes at seven, which is a bit earlier than the rest of the mall. If you don't make it back in time, just slip a piece of paper under the gate and I'll get it in the morning."

"Thank you!" Clarisse waves goodbye to her new boss. She's so excited to be giving her father notice so soon.

"I realize that this is probably the greatest day of your life, but can you please elaborate on what happened with Death?"

Clarisse huffs now that they're out of sight.

Fine.

11

A MAN AND HIS SHADOW

Terrence

Clarisse looks around the bank while Father Simmons helps her open an account. Terrence takes the opportunity to slip away, knowing that Death is still nearby. His presence lingers on the air wherever he goes. *The starry jackass can't help it.* Sadness. Woe. Loss. All of it. Follows him everywhere.

Where are you?

Terrence won't risk speaking aloud in a public place, but he stands behind a pillar to shift into a more 'human' form. Unfortunately, he looks like a literal shadow that's lost its place when he does. *This is the best I can do.* He huffs, wishing he were gifted enough to become a person-incarnate like Death can.

Terrence sticks to the crevices of the hallway so people don't notice a living shadow on the loose. He slips between walls like a ghost, searching everywhere for his former boss. He focuses in on the feeling of dread that Death leaves in his wake. When the temperature drops, he knows he's nearby. It's a telltale sign that Death is angry when the world gets cold like this. Terrence's throat goes dry in anticipation of what's to come. He braces himself for the inevitable.

An olive-skinned man with golden eyes approaches, his hair covered by a black hoodie. Gloved hands clench with rage at the sight of his old employee. *Show off.*

They step into a quiet hallway in the mall. It might look normal for Death to have an argument, but Terrence would cause too much suspicion with his red eyes and evil-looking form. *Although we are at a mall... some weirdos lurk here. Perhaps I am being paranoid.* His thoughts are quickly interrupted.

"What do you think you're doing, you idiot?" Death hisses. "Trying to get the girl killed?"

Terrence laughs, biting back a flurry of insults and a strong desire to fight. "Funny... you're concerned about someone dying? You're not sticking to your script very well, now are you. You left her to *suffer* in the hands of those damned mortals. She's deserving of far more than they've given her. If it weren't for me, she'd be doomed to work at that stupid accounting firm for the rest of her life."

Death buries his face in his left hand and flips Terrence off with his right. "You don't know that. She's doing rather well without interruption as it seems."

Terrence can't believe what he's hearing. His eyes flash, threatening to spill their bright red light everywhere like fire. He throws his hands in the air to keep himself from exploding. "What do you mean? All of this 'good' she's experienced in the last few days is because someone finally stepped in. *I* finally stepped in. You're a raging lunatic if you think that unaltered circumstances would have lent *any* of the opportunities I've provided her."

"And have you told her the costs? Have you explained what it means to start using her powers like you've convinced her?"

Terrence scoffs, burying a tingling sense of fear that threatens to grip at his soul. *The costs won't be the same this time... she's different.*

"You're just scared she'll become immortal. Live forever."

Death's eyes darken. "For the record, I don't recall that working out very well for you. Using magic defies the natural order. People live. They die. They encounter life without paranormal aid for a reason, Terrence. She's not the key you're looking for. And I don't think she'll be pleased if she finds out the truth of why you're being so friendly with her. Tell me, isn't she the slightest bit suspicious as to why you've been so generous with her?"

Terrence grimaces and rolls his eyes. "As she rightfully should be." He waves his shadowy hands in wild exasperation. "She hasn't really had much reason in her life to trust people. *I wonder why.* You don't have an inch of interest in your heart for her. Not an *inch.* So, who are you to be lecturing me?"

Death's patience is being tested now more than ever. Terrence can tell just by the way his posture changes. He stands taller and his teeth grit together. The veins in his arm are starting to protrude; Terrence can feel it in the air even if he can't see it. Working for Death for so many years at such a high level left him with plenty of memories to fill in any visual gaps. Terrence finds Death funny. If he doesn't have a mask, he has something to cover up his emotional giveaways. A hoodie. The shadows. Something. Emotions aren't something he enjoys having. It makes his job all the more difficult. Death told him this plenty of times when Terrence was still a Reaper.

Terrence knows by the strained look on Death's face that he can't keep up this act much longer. Death is still stronger. The only reason he hasn't struck Terrence down is because Clarisse is insurance. *Maybe you do care more than you say.* He stifles a laugh. *That'll come in handy.* She'll be spiraled into a deep depression if Death locks Terrence away in Kohlu or, Tryta forbid, tries to erase him from existence. Clarisse would crumble now that he's intervened. And that could result in quite a few magical outbursts. Terrence knows he has the winning hand, lest Death convinces her that Terrence is *not* out to save her in favor of something else.

Which is not true.

"Keep telling yourself that, sunshine," Death sneers.

"Since when did *you* specialize in sarcasm, you lump of clay," Terrence quips. "I thought you said emotions were for the weak."

"I did. And they are. I just know that you understand them better than facts and logic."

It's Terrence's turn to roll his eyes again. The whole exchange would look terrifying and ridiculous to an outsider. A man speaking with his shadow. Because, of course, Death does *not* have a shadow of his own. "I'm only trying to help her."

"And in doing so, you're going to destroy her. If you were smart, you would finish your business with her, leave on friendly terms so as not to set her off, and get back to being a Reaper instead of going on this damned mission of yours. You really think that highly of yourself—you think that you're helping *her?*" Death scoffs, his breath becoming like little ice crystals now.

"I'm not going to comment on any of that. First of all, you can't fool me. You'll make me pay for any crimes I've committed before you ever let me be a Reaper again; frankly, that's not something I want to strive for anyway. You can't change my mind. And you know what will happen if you try to fight me. You'll have a massive nightmare to clean up. Clarisse will lose control. The mortals will see strange things that will fill the headlines of every newspaper and the subject of every talkshow for miles. People have cameras that are *far* better than ever—in their pockets now, no less. Is any of that worth the risk? Imagine the clean-up costs."

Death grumbles like a petulant child. Anything that doesn't go his way sets him off; Terrence is having a blast watching his rival lose his mind.

"In the end, I will have her. Do you understand? I will take her from you in the night when her last breath comes. Just don't cry to me when you realize it's your fault that she takes it too soon."

Terrence turns away to hide the fact that those words do, in fact, frighten him. Every part of his body is screaming to get back to Clarisse—fast. "Yeah, okay, old man."

Death disappears in a blink. Terrence returns to his dog-like form, sauntering back downstairs into the bank. Clarisse seems happy filling out various files and forms, Father Simmons guiding her where she gets stuck.

Terrence huffs.

Me? Hurting her? No, no. I'm helping her. This is helping her. Death is wrong.

Terrence sits next to her, ignoring the unsettling fear in his gut. *But what if he's right?* She smiles at him, her beaming face the most reassuring thing he's seen all day. All of his doubts subside for the moment.

I'm going to make sure that smile has all the reasons in the world to stick around. You deserve it.

While the process continues, he dozes off, the exhaustion of arguing with Death weighing over him. His adrenaline is still wearing off. It's been a much longer day than he realizes. And it's not even close to being over.

12

ON THE VERGE

Clarisse

That night, Clarisse's mind is abuzz with a million different ideas. She's more than elated at everything that's happened. Her parents aren't home yet. They're undoubtedly out and about talking about how horrible their daughter is. True to her word, she replaced the cereal in the pantry, so they should have no reason to suspect her having fun this morning and actually eating something other than bran for breakfast.

Sitting in her room, she completes the forms that Mr. Harris gave her. She snuck into her mother's room and took her social security card, birth certificate, and all other related documents. *I'm going to get a driver's license...*

Father Simmons stopped by the DMV the other day and gave Clarisse the driver's manual to study; she signed up for a course at the Church of Light to fulfill her required hours so she can finally be street-legal. *Maybe with my job, I could get a car, too!* Shuddering at the thought, she returns to her paperwork.

Father Simmons treated Clarisse to ice cream, gave her the greatest cellphone in the world—in her opinion—and made sure she had a bank account set up and ready to receive money from her trust. Everything was in her name. Her cellphone was a prepaid device, so she didn't have to worry about contracts; her trust was set to start depositing money this week. *This is what I should have had a long time ago.*

Clarisse hears the door open and freezes. Terrence perks up. Clarisse hopes it isn't Death. She's still very shaken up from the exchange at the mall. While it wasn't physically hostile, it could have taken a turn for the worse very quickly. The dark, chilly bathroom still haunts her even though she escaped unscathed.

"No, we're in the clear... for now."

Clarisse's parents' voices echo through the hall. Dad sounds drunk. His voice is slurred. Clarisse frowns.

He's not supposed to drink.

"What do you mean?"

The Church doesn't allow for drinking. It's... it's considered evil.

Terrence rolls his eyes. "Oh what a load of—"

"Clarisse, who is that?"

The question comes from Mom. Both Terrence and Clarisse freeze.

"Oh, dear."

Terrence!

The door opens before Terrence has a chance to shift back to a German Shepherd. Their carelessness is out on display. Deborah screams. She drops the glass of wine she's carrying; it shatters into a thousand pieces, along with any hope Clarisse had from a previously wonderful day.

Deborah stammers. "What are you doing? What is that creature? What?"

"Mom, calm down! It's just Terrence!" Clarisse waves her hands, trying to act like it's not a big deal that she's conversing with a living shadow. *Fat chance.*

Mom's nostrils flare. Her gray hair almost turns white in the light from the hallway. A very drunken Dad follows behind her, enraged at the sight of the wolf sitting with his daughter. He staggers backwards, almost slumping against the wall trying to keep his balance

"Demon!" Dad screams. *"Delayed much? Just how much did he have to drink?"* Clarisse glares at Terrence; he stops speaking in her head anymore. She can't afford distractions.

"No, Dad! Not a demon!"

"Then why does he look... like a shadow! Like darkness come to life!" Dad flails his hands. He's disjointed, looking more like an angry scarecrow than anything threatening.

Clarisse jumps to her feet, a whipping wind rising about her feet. A crackle of electricity pulses through her veins. Her eyes burn and she swears she hears thunder in her voice as she begins to speak. "You are not to harm him. You are not to accuse him of being a demon. He is none of those things." Her voice magnifies from her powers. Her eyes start to glow again; this time, they are full of a cacophony of colors. She can feel them. A halo of stars circles about her head. "I am done with you both. I not put up with either of you. I will not be beholden to your lies and hypocrisy!"

Mom grabs at Dad. "Go! Go get Father Simmons!"

Before he can move, the doors to the house all slam and lock shut. Dad is knocked off his feet, slamming his face against the floor.

"Terrence is an angel sent by the Light. In your drunken foolishness, you have mistaken him for a demon. Father Simmons already knows of his existence—what he is. Of his power. He takes many forms. Angels are not bound by the strictures of flesh and blood. You, of all people, should know this." Clarisse puffs herself out, quietly asking herself: *How on Earth am I doing this?*

But right now, she can't question it. There's too much on the line. If she doesn't play her cards right, she'll end up getting another exorcism or a round of Dad's belt. *They could kick me out of the house.*

This last note gives her a brilliant idea. "I will leave if you continue with your accusations."

Terrence looks at Clarisse like she's lost her mind.

"And where will you go?" Deborah sneers. "We've fed you. Clothed you. You don't even have a job anymore. Your father and I decided it's best to fire you and keep you here. You need protection, Clarisse! We gave up our lives for you!"

Clarisse laughs. "Really? You gave up your lives for me? Tell me, *Deborah*, how was the country club today?"

Mom flinches at both her name and the accusation.

"And, Dad, did you tell Mom that you make the 'big bucks' like Alice said? How you pay for Mom to have a country club membership, or how you have a huge client base and plenty of money to pay for more than the bare minimum that we have had our whole life. Or at least my life. Where does that money go? Father Simmons set me up with a trust fund today. From money that's been siphoned off to the church, no doubt.

Should I tell you that? Probably not, but I want you to know that I *know*. I know that you all have been giving me the short end of the stick my whole life! You haven't fed me enough; you've kept me sheltered from everything. You beat me for Pete's sake! What is wrong with you both? And you don't think I know? This angel came to me because he knows that you all intend to *murder* me. Enough hunting around the house could have you both put away for life!"

"Clarisse, calm down, calm down!"

She's briefly aware of the light that's pouring from her body— the raw power emanating from her existence. The moon and stars are screaming at her from beyond the walls of the house. They've never been so loud. Shaking, she can't control herself or move from her place on the floor.

Her whole body is consumed with the raw fire of her rage. She can't stop.

"I will leave. Do not tell anyone about this. Do not speak of me anymore. Wipe me from your memories. I've had enough; I can't take it anymore." Clarisse snaps her fingers; a suitcase full of luggage fills itself. Clarisse can't handle the pressure any longer. She's snapping. Tears thunder down her cheeks. The world around her is a blur. She's only partly aware of Terrence's existence when the world goes dark.

13

PLOTTING IN THE DARK

Terrence

Terrence springs into action, moving to protect Clarisse from her parents. Before he can even lay a single paw on her, he's hit by a massive blur of stars. It tumbles him out the window, though no glass shatters.

He and Death tumble and snarl at one another. Gold and red blood is spilled everywhere as they rip at each other. Terrence manages to pull back, bouncing away to temporary safety, his breath coming in heaves.

"What the Kohlu? Death!"

Death snarls at him, his hackles raised. His mask is slightly disturbed, but it rights itself as quickly as his wounds seal themselves shut. Terrence is not so lucky with healing. He does his best to keep baring his teeth, keeping himself looking larger than life. *Just a few more minutes and I'll be patched up, too.*

"It's time you stepped out of her life! You've done far too much damage as it is! Let the girl pay for her consequences. Let her parents sort things out one last time. She won't step out of line and she'll run. She'll leave here and you won't do any more damage."

Terrence's eyes burn with rage. He swears he sees steam curl out of his mouth. Taking a breath, he steadies himself. Death already looks as though he's calming down, though they keep eyes locked and circle each other, looking for a vulnerable place to pounce. Terrence knows Death is holding back. If he wanted to take him down now, he could.

So why not?

Death's eyes reveal nothing but contempt. Ice covers the ground, seeping deep into Terrence's soul. He hears Clarisse's parents screaming at her to wake up. Terrence turns to look. It's a horrible mistake.

Death jumps on the opportunity. Terrence writhes and growls, ripping into any inch of Death that he can grab hold. He manages to escape his grasp again.

"If you want to end me," he gasps, "why not do it?"

"You're not a worthy opponent," Death replies. His voice is just as hollow as his presence. It chills Terrence to the bone. *Not worthy?*

"Then why attack me when I'm not facing you?" Terrence scoffs, doing his best to hide the shaking in his voice. "Clearly I must frighten you in some capacity."

Death's eyes flash. He growls, "Let's be clear. I take you down when you're not looking as a subtle reminder that I can strike at any moment. That my Reapers will not be fair to you. That if you keep this foolishness up, you will be called before the Selyento and made to pay for your crimes." Death hums, his eyes glittering. "I'm giving you a warning. You should thank me. I'm breaking quite a lot of my rules by not taking you myself right this moment."

Terrence snarls. "Oh, why, thank you for your benevolence."

A car door slams. *She's getting away!*

"Why are you lying?" Terrence dares himself to take a seat, his legs and body poised to strike if necessary. "You've been hunting me for years." The car takes off. Terrence is back on his feet. "Please. Let me go to her."

The strain in his voice gives Death pause. "You really care for her, don't you?"

"Yes."

"Then let her pay the consequences," Death snarls.

Terrence takes a few seconds.

Why not just take me out of the picture? Isn't he worried that I'll just go hunt her down? Wouldn't it be easier to just make sure I'm not anywhere near her? Unless...

A lightbulb comes on somewhere in Terrence's head. He hides the grin that would normally manifest in his teeth and eyes, letting it swell in his heart instead. It surges through him, keeping him warm.

I've got to play my hand and play it fast. Terrence composes himself. Death's glare never leaves him while he stews in silence for a moment, thinking what to say next. *Come on Terrence, do it.*

"I'll concede."

Swallowing his pride, even if it is for false reasons, makes him want to choke.

Death's eyes widen a bit, revealing his shock. "You're right," Terrence continues. "I'll slip away. Let me go and I'll let this one go." *Please let this work....*

Death grunts. "I'm glad you're choosing to be wise." The cold crackling in the air tells Terrence that he'll be followed closely. Death isn't buying his lies for a second.

Terrence dips his head in mock submission. He takes off running. Death doesn't take off after him. Slipping into the shadows at the edge of the forest, Terrence sits in wait.

What are you hiding, you starry jackass. Keeping as low as he can to prevent his scent from carrying on the wind, he waits to see what Death will do. For a moment, Death just sits, watching for his rival to leave, no doubt. Terrence holds back a few excited swears when Death finally leaves. Right in the direction he expects.

He's going to see Clarisse. That's why he didn't take me and leave!

Finally allowing himself to grin, Terrence takes off after Death, keeping his distance. He can't leave Clarisse. What they'll do to her is unspeakable. *I'm not letting her go that easy.*

∽

Death

H is heart is thudding when he arrives at the church. It seems like yesterday that he was here, watching her suffer. *My job, truly, is not easy.* Curiosity and pain overwhelm him as he watches them drag her limp body into the church. The subtle thudding of her heart tells him that she's hanging on. Her end is not yet nigh.

I can't bear to bring her back so soon.

Father Simmons greets Clarisse's parents at the door. Not even Death can contain the low growl that erupts at the sight of that evil man. *His comeuppance will be quite satisfying when I come to collect that bastard. His day can't come soon enough.*

Slipping to the side of the church, he conceals himself, watching from the window and listening.

"What happened?" It's Father Simmons who breaks the silence first.

"We've sinned, Father." Arthur Monroe is woefully drunk. Death can smell it in the air. His nose twitches and, for a moment, he considers taking on his human form so he won't be able to smell the wretched odor so well. A bit of vomit is detected as well. *Gross.*

"She... she said things. Things about a trust account? That... that you've been helping her?" Deborah still manages to find a way to be greedy, even when she, too, is hammered. Clarisse remains slumped on the floor. A strange feeling stirs in Death's gut. *Leave her. Do not intervene.*

It's been ages since he's had to think so hard about restraining himself. Punishment is necessary here. Period. *She's overstepped. She's the fool that didn't listen.* Still, he aches.

His ears train themselves back on the conversation at hand.

"I did all of this to make her last days comfortable." Death freezes. *Last days? She's not on my docket.*

He frantically goes over his "list." Usually, he lets the Reapers have it controlled in dissected parts, but he can see it all at once if he wishes. Filing through, he finds her name. *She's not due. What the—?*

"My Children of Light, your drinking has cost you your child. She must be a sacrificial lamb. Clarisse is a threat to us all, cavorting about with that thing she calls an 'angel.' I pity her, but the Great Light has called her home. I was shown in a dream that her end is coming."

Death's heart lurches. The date on his list gets bumped up. His eyes widen.

"We've been having the same feelings, Father. We took out a life insurance policy...."

Father Simmons quirks an eyebrow. "The Church of Light has been struggling. Perhaps such a policy could be split so as to keep the Church breathing." Everyone nods.

Death is spitting with rage. They're speaking about the girl as though she's cattle. *Why does it bother me now, though?* He senses another presence.

"What did I tell you?" Death freezes, whirling around to find Terrence standing right behind him. He's carrying papers with him. They fall before Death; for a moment, his rage subsides.

When he starts reading, though, his blood begins to boil.

"Father Simmons made himself the beneficiary?"

"To everything she owns. Her trust. Everything will go to the church. He set her up because she knows too much. I read his journals. He's been planning to murder her ever since she figured out that he's a cult leader and not a real priest." Terrence sneers. A moment of silent anger passes between them. Regret tugs at Death's heart. Terrence was once his brother in arms—his right-hand. He could use a sounding board these days. Especially now.

"Do you see why I stepped in?" Terrence glares at Death. Setting his pride aside now is not something he plans to do.

"Yes, and it is still foolish. Her date has been updated. Her time has come." With that, Death turns his attention back to the window. "And if you try to stop this, I will have no choice but to stop you with force."

He thinks that's enough. Terrence, though dull in many ways, is still a sharp student when it comes to opponents. He was wise enough to figure out that Death isn't here for retribution. Rather, he's here for the girl. The strange girl who can make stars. *Just like mine.*

It's the last peaceful thought before he's hit head on.

"You're stupider than I thought, Terrence," Death snarls.

14

SPEAK AND BE CLEANSED

Clarisse

W hen she wakes, she's strapped down to the *chair*. She sees Terrence standing at the doorway of the church. He's covered in... *blood*. The congregation is gathered.

She swallows, knowing the pain that's about to be inflicted on her.

Why did I pass out?

"*You used too much power too fast, Clarisse. Can you try to break free, now?*"

Clarisse struggles against her restraints.

No... what happened to you?

"We are gathered here, today..." Father Simmons begins.

Clarisse blurs Father Simmons' voice out. His face is motionless; he doesn't offer any sort of sympathetic stare. He doesn't seem to recognize that they've spent the better part of the day working together to help her get free. Right now, she's an *example*.

"*Not if I can help it.*"

Terrence starts to move when a starry wolf jumps out and attacks him. The congregation doesn't seem to notice. It occurs to

Clarisse that they might not be able to see anything outside at all right now. The battling wolves might be invisible to them. Or they're too entranced by Father Simmons and his chanting to realize what's happening behind them.

"Death has a cloak over my presence. I can't get you free. Please, try!"

Before he can say anything else, Death has him bowled over and they're fighting once more. The violence paralyzes Clarisse, holding her rigid in her seat. She's been having too much fun in the past few days. The time for her to pay has come. She can't escape.

Realizing that she can't free herself of her restraints, she backs off. It's too late. She's spent. Closing her eyes, she accepts her fate.

She's vaguely aware of Terrence and Death sparring in the entryway. Vaguely aware of the whipping to her back that's been stripped bare, only her bra sparing her the shame of being exposed to everyone. They're "whipping the evil out of her."

Her numbness transforms to anger, her veins tensing up at every lash. Clarisse glares up at Father Simmons; while she's subdued, her eyes are searing hot—a telltale sign that they must be glowing again.

"You know the truth," she hisses.

The congregation gasps; among them, she sees her parents standing. She's filled to the brim with hate. Just looking at them makes her want to vomit. By the way they're staring at her, she knows the feeling is mutual.

If I come home like this, I won't make it.

If she can't get free of her restraints, she knows she has to come up with something to get out of going home. These hours of exorcisms spend her energy.

Terrence, you have to help me.

Terrence is caught up with trying to keep Death at bay. Death drags him down every few seconds. He looks like an antelope in the grasp of an angry lion. Each attempt at yanking free lands him back on the floor.

The torture continues, beating her flesh raw with pain, blood streaming down her body. She can't breathe. Her lungs strain, trying to get in air while hot irons scald her lashed skin. This method hasn't been used in a while. *I'm in deep trouble.*

She braces herself for impact each time, screaming at the top of her lungs. For years, she withheld reactions. For years, she went along with their pain. For years, she let the torture bring her to unconsciousness. But not today. Today, she's got a plan in her head that will only work if she makes this experience far more theatrical.

She writhes, yells, and even as her body goes numb to the pain, she makes it look like she's in agony.

"What are you doing? What's going on in there?" Terrence sounds beat. Beyond beat. She starts to sob; her tears are for him now—not for herself.

"What is wrong with you, child? Can't you see he's using you? Look where you ended up?" Death stands in the entryway of the church. For a moment, he's left Terrence to collect himself. She hopes Terrence is okay. She wants to break free, but she's still too weak.

"Look at yourself. You can't even get up, Clarisse. Your power is killing you. Stop using it and I will set you free. You cannot keep going on using your powers like this." Death's voice looms over her like a raging ice storm.

Watch me, you jerk.

She glares at Death. *How dare you! You say you've seen this before? Do you see what they're doing to—*

Boiling water douses Clarisse and she lets out a bloodcurdling scream. *They've never done that.* Her skin feels like it's melting off. *Anyone who didn't have powers couldn't survive this.*

"Death, I see you." Her voice trembles.

Thanks for giving me my greatest playing card. Clarisse sneers at him, even though her words to him are silent.

"What?"

Clarisse lets out a horrid, gasping scream. Her body falls limp in the wake of that last heave. Using whatever little power she has left, she lets the glow from her skin go dark. Everything in her is screaming at her not to move.

"What are you doing?" Death's eyes are ablaze with fury as much as they are with confusion.

What does it look like, genius? Don't you see this all the time?

Terrence breaks into the church; Clarisse surmises that the spell has been broken because everyone around her gasps at the sight of the two wolves standing in the entryway.

"Clarisse, your demons have been expelled from you. They will leave now." Father Simmons steps away from her with this final assessment. He stumbles away, acting more than eager to distance himself from the two wolves standing in the center of the church.

Terrence shoves Death out of the way, knocking him over. He's thrown from the church and they are, once again, locked in a hidden battle outside.

Clarisse stays completely still. Her eyes are wide open, burning with an urge to blink. Someone releases her from the restraints on her chair. The feeling of those hands tell her it's Father Simmons.

"Clarisse, you may stand. You are cleansed."

Clarisse doesn't stand. Instead, she remains motionless.

I need to hide my heartbeat.

She doesn't know if that's even possible, but now that she's seen Death block out sounds, she knows it must be. Clarisse doesn't know how powerful you have to be to do it, but to block the sound of one human heart can't be *that* hard.

When someone leans down to listen to her chest, they shriek.

"Father Simmons, I don't think she's—"

"Fear not, everyone. She's just stunned. Her heartbeat may be faint from the strain of such an exercise. She's cooling down. Come, my flock. We will pray."

And, like that, they leave her body on the floor. Clarisse restrains herself from getting up as time passes.

She can't hear Terrence or Death anymore. Her powers are spent. If anyone tries to hear her heart it will tell them everything. Her parents are soon the only ones left with Father Simmons.

"Father, will she get up? Or?"

Clarisse strains to hear. They're whispering. She knows that they think she's dead, based on her outstanding performance. But she knows if they find out she fibbed she *will* be dead. Her body can't take any more of this.

"If you had heeded my warning, maybe you wouldn't have ended up this way."

After everything you just witnessed, you have the nerve to say that to me? And it's not like you came and warned me ahead of time. You waited until after I met Terrence who, frankly, seems to give far more damns about me than you do.

"Insolent child, this isn't about caring for you. This is about upholding the balance! Saving you from damnation and keeping things on schedule is my job— less-so the first part. Your parents did the warning I could not."

So, you would rather have me suffer like this?

"If it keeps you from messing things up? From destroying everything all because you can't keep your emotions in check? I'd do this all to you myself if I had to."

Hearing the change in Death's voice makes the hairs on her neck stand up. He approaches her; this time, no one screams and no one tries to step in. She dares to crane her neck a bit—she hopes no one catches it. To her relief, the congregation is facing away from her in silent prayer. What she does catch is Death walking between them. Straight towards her. She wants to get up and run. Scream. Anything. But she can't; he passes through the huddled mass of Father Simons' followers undetected. She returns her head to its original position so as not to arouse suspicion… to look away, really. They still can't see Death as he comes to stand over her, his mouth wide open. his teeth are ruby red.

Blood…? Did you kill him?

"No. He's badly injured. Now, you need to promise me you won't use your powers anymore. Promise me."

It takes everything in Clarisse's body not to let out a groan.

Fine. But on one condition.

"And what is that?"

You let Terrence and I go free. After this, you let me leave with him.

Death's eyes look like they might catch fire.

"I beg your pardon?"

If you don't, I'll keep using my powers. I'll show them to the world and burn brighter than any star you've ever seen—even the ones in your coat.

"And I will win either way, silly girl. I get you all in the end. I'm offering you an out."

And I'm asking you for a small favor in exchange for my cooperation. How hard is that?

Death laughs. The sound is beautiful but, given the position he holds in Clarisse's mind, she wants to shank him for having the audacity to find humor in any of this.

You don't. Look, I don't want to be outed as a freak. I just want a normal life. It's as you say, either way, I'm going to die. You're going to take me. If I keep using my powers and it 'kills' me, like you say, then what do you have to lose?

She almost yelps as she feels hands start to grab at her. Father Simmons and her parents hoist her body up. *Oh goodness, they are going to dump me somewhere.*

Before she can finish trying to sway Death, Terrence comes leaping into the room. This time, she knows he's seen—her mother's scream can't be for anything else. She wonders if Death can be seen now, too.

Everyone comes to a standstill. Death moves to fight him, but Terrence dodges out of the way and starts *talking*.

"Listen up! What you have done has summoned Death himself to collect your daughter. I have fought for her. Tried to keep her safe. Did you not heed my warning? That I was an angel here to protect her? You all have violated the sacred order that the Light has me uphold."

Death scoffs. "You fool! Do you know how hard it is going to be to wipe their memories of this?"

More people scream and Death *hisses*.

Ah, so both of you are visible right now.

She can feel Death glaring at her before he bounces around to face her, confirming the fact.

Clarisse's parents tremble.

"I did what I had to do to protect my flock from the likes of you. Deceivers. Evil. Manipulating." Father Simmons looks pale as he stands before Terrence.

"Would a devil be able to raise someone from the dead? Isn't that strictly a power of the Great Light? To drive away Death himself?" Terrence spits. "Would the Devil know that you've been conspiring to have Clarisse killed? So *Arthur* and *Deborah* could cash in on the life insurance policy you took out on her? So you could split up the assets and walk away millionaires? Sell little trinkets and profess to be a god-incarnate? While I was trying to free her from you all when I first got here—and was so *rudely* interrupted—I took the liberty of going through some of your belongings, Father Simmons. I saw the documents. It doesn't take a genius to understand them—the gravity of them. Let's face it, she's a threat to you. And after all this time, you would take your so-called 'daughter' and sacrifice her for money." Terrence spits. "Is it not the job of an angel to stop such sins?"

Clarisse is on her feet, practically jumping in the air. Her muscles give silent screams of agony. Her skin is seared. Death's stars turn a deep red; he looks like a swirling, cosmic terror. The bumps on Clarisse's skin raise to attention. Her heart burns from the revelation that Father Simmons wanted her dead, too. Tears start to come to her eyes, but she wipes them away. Right now, she needs to keep her focus at all costs.

It shouldn't surprise me that much.

"I'm not taking your deal, Death. Show's over. You can't scare me with threats of dying. Don't you see? I've been dead my whole life. I'm alive now." Her hands are shaking, but she doesn't stop. "Let me make those choices for myself. Let me decide if I want to live on the edge or not. You're a liar. This isn't dangerous at all. That magic was saving my life. They would have killed me. Buried me somewhere and covered up the murder like nothing happened. So, who's really the villain here?"

Her vision becomes a bit slanted; she steadies herself.

"Why did you sit there and let this happen? Prevent Terrence from helping me? Does this look okay to you? And you would have done the same?"

Clarisse gestures to Death, drawing attention to her almost bare chest. "What, you thought this would scare me from doing any more magic? From spending time with Terrence? If anything, you have just accomplished the opposite of what you set out to do. I bled today for a false cause over a false narrative. I'm done with you. You will win in the end; you'll come get me when it's time, no doubt. But I can tell you that you're the shittiest creature I've ever met. You do your job and you don't give a damn about anything else. And all for what? Why does it matter so much that I'm using my magic?"

Death's voice is booming. Clarisse feels something like hail stones hit her shoulders, but she stands her ground. The moon and stars are screaming to her. The universe is on her side tonight.

"Mortals aren't meant to! And he's using you, Clarisse!" Death explodes. "Are you seriously that naïve? You aren't going to even stop and consider the consequences? Why do you think Terrence, who was mortal once, is focusing on you, of all people? Do you think he's helping you out of the kindness of his heart? Do you think he cares?"

Clarisse glares at him. "You know, you talk a lot of shit for someone who's never bothered to intervene on *any* of this. Who admitted he *wanted* this to happen! I've been used my whole life. My. Whole. Life. By a piece-of-scum priest who uses me as insurance for his fake ass cult and my parents who see me as a burden for even existing. Was it my fault that I was born with these powers? Was it my fault that I was born with an innate inability to control them?" Clarisse crosses her arms. "I don't care what Terrence is to you. Friend. Foe. It doesn't matter. To me, he is my friend because he is the first and *only* person who has ever taken up an interest in protecting me. Looking out for me. Doing the things that you *could* have done but chose not to." Clarisse holds up a finger to shush Death before he can speak more. "But you were just 'doing your job.' I know. You can't get involved. Unless it involves people you don't like."

The words seem to sting. Death's eyes almost look like they're glistening with something like… *tears?* "Fine. If you don't see the benevolence of my actions, then I won't bother you anymore this fine evening. Use your powers, for all I care. When I show up early and the ramifications of what you've done catch up to you, don't bother crying then." He turns and leaves the church.

Clarisse focuses her energy on the people standing near her. Her parents and Father Simmons.

"Now, I'm going to leave. I'm not coming back; don't bother trying to find me. If you come to my place of work, I will make it the most horrible day of your lives. And *that* is a promise. I'm going to go home, collect my things, and I'm going to leave."

Father Simmons clenches his fists. "Clarisse, I'm sorry, but I—"

"You made a choice; so did I. You gave me everything I needed today. I'd say thank you, but I think this penance was enough in exchange. I'm tired of paying for something that's not my fault. You're a shit person, you know? I really did think you were a father-figure, but now I know. You're just a freak in a robe. And you guys," Clarisse turns her attention to her parents, "I genuinely hope you rot alone in a nursing home."

She has the upper hand here. She's still not sure how she managed to convince Death to leave her. *"He's not supposed to be seen by mortals. Or speak to them. Unless it's their time, of course."* Clarisse turns to Terrence with a smile. *Thanks to me, I take it he has a lot of clean up to do?* Laughing, she runs her bloodied hands through her hair. She won't be surprised if the Church of Light doesn't remember a single iota of what happened today. Death would be back. He has a mess to clean up now. Because of her.

Serves the jerk right.

It was strange, though. The redness in his stars doused the minute she called him out over his hypocrisy. She can't help but wonder....

Does he actually care?

"No, Clarisse. It's hard for anyone to understand Death, but I worked for him for years. He's not an emotional being. He only intervenes when things corrupt his schedule. That's it. He doesn't care about when you die unless it's not when he has it planned out for you. I can explain more later but, right now, I think you need to finish up business here."

Clarisse turns to face the congregation, a smile perking on her lips. It's the most rebellious thing she can manage to do now. Her body threatens to collapse out from beneath her at any moment.

"As Death told you, you will not remember this. There's really no point in me saying anything to you. I just know that I'm going to be gone. I'm not coming back. I won't pester you any longer."

Terrence harrumphs with approval, flicking his tail. Despite his battered state, he uses any spare energy he has to heal Clarisse. She feels his warmth, confirming she made the right choice. *Death is a jackass.*

They limp out together, Clarisse's body aching despite the lack of visible wounds. Terrence looks worse for wear, having been torn from stem to stern in his fight with Death. Clarisse yearns to help him in return. But right now, they have to leave. Together.

Clarisse places a hand on Terrence's coat of darkness, no longer hidden to the world. Her inky black-shadow friend offers her a tired smile that she matches. Tears of relief start to pour from her eyes; he, too, starts to cry a little.

We won, Terrence.

"That we did, my little star."

15

FLEEING

Clarisse

Clarisse rips through her closet, stuffing her clothes away, grabbing her paperwork, her journals—anything and everything she can. She doesn't know where she'll go, but she hopes her trust fund money will come through for her. As far as the documents said at the bank, the money is hers until she dies. *Then* Father Simmons can have it.

I'll have to change that.

They don't have a car, so they walk. She thinks of asking Terrence to carry her, but he's still looking pretty battered from his fight with Death. Healing him, whether directly or indirectly, is her number one priority right now. Their feet are aching when they reach the motel. The good news is that it's right next to Clarisse's new job at the mall.

She finds they have a vacancy and that the cash from her graduation is enough to buy a few nights to stay. It's a dirty place that's less than savory, but she'll take it. *Anything to get away.*

Terrence agrees to come in separately to avoid having to shape-shift and be explained away as a service dog again.

Room 37B. She takes her keys, hoping he heard her.

Her body screams with relief when she finds that her suitcase has already been unpacked on the bed. She wonders how Terrence managed to get it upstairs without being seen.

"Terrence, are you there?"

"Yes," he moans.

"Are you okay?" She walks in to check him over, unable to hide the terror on her face when she sees him. Death did so much damage to him outside the church foyer while she was being exorcised. She wishes she could heal her friend as he did for her.

"Why didn't you save some healing power for yourself?" She's crying; it's soft, but she doesn't know what else to do. Everything is overwhelming her.

"You're mortal. I'm not. And you're my friend. I don't know if Death has sown any seeds of doubt into your mind, but please know I care about you so much. I would never do anything to put you in harm's way on purpose." He heaves in and out, his breathing ragged.

"You say you can't die, right?"

Terrence manages something like a nod. Clarisse steps into the hotel bathroom for a moment to run a washcloth under hot water. She wrings it out, ignoring the few cuts and scrapes that scream from being twisted about. It stands to reason that Terrence couldn't heal everything. These will have to heal on their own.

"Here, hold still." She sits next to him on the bed, cleaning his wounds. He winces visibly a few times, but he doesn't say anything else while she dabs at his scars and wipes the dried bloodstains from his shadowy fur. It feels more like fur now than it did when they first met. Clarisse is astounded at how she still knows so little about her friend.

"Terrence, what are you made of?" The question sounds way more awkward than she intended and she blushes.

He manages to wheeze out a short laugh. "I'm a shadow, much like you would assume. What *type* of shadowy substance is up for debate. The details of my nature were never explained to me when I passed. Death is never all that elucidating to those he collects, whether they work for him or move on."

Clarisse turns her head to the side, focusing on the scrapes around his mouth. "Work for him? Death mentioned you were a Reaper. How does that come about?"

"I was cursed by the Selyento—the Tree of Life. I'm not sure why, but it's why I'm stuck in this form and I'm not able to look like a human. I can look like my own shadow and nothing more. As penance for my curse, I was allowed to work for him with the ultimate goal of being 'cleansed' in mind. That never happened. I died during the Black Plague. I've been dead for almost seven-hundred years."

Clarisse gasps. "Wait, what? And you've been left in this form this whole time?"

Terrence whimpers a bit when she finishes by gently rubbing at the last scrape. "Yes."

"And he never said *what* you were paying for? Or the Tree of Life?"

Something in Terrence's face shifts. Clarisse can smell the lie he's about to weave, but she doesn't stop him.

"No, he never did. Nor did the Tree. It's ridiculous, really. Death is a huge joke. I hate him," Terrence grumbles. "He's no fun. All logic and facts. 'Everything happens because of forces you don't understand.' I hate that, Clarisse. I want to save you from that as much as I possibly can. I want to be your hero. No one was ever mine when I needed them."

Clarisse picks at her fingers, wondering what part of what he said was a lie. It doesn't matter right now; she tucks that thought away for later.

"Well, maybe someday I can be your hero."

She whispers to the buzz in her veins. It's slowly coming back, though still faint. The moon and stars whisper again. A small light pulses from her hands.

At first, Terrence doesn't notice. He's closed his eyes and is letting the pain consume him in the hopes of getting through it faster. When Clarisse puts her hands on him, he snaps up.

"Hold still," she commands.

He doesn't move; he looks fearful as she begins to work. "Clarisse, that's probably not going to work. I appreciate the effort, but...."

The scars on his body close. For a moment, he doesn't speak. "Do you know how hard it is to master something like that?" His red eyes glow with a fire Clarisse can't place; the question itself is so quiet Clarisse almost misses it. "What?"

"A healing spell. Do you know how hard it is? Especially when the wounds are inflicted by a god?"

Clarisse shrugs. "I guess not knowing how difficult it is to do something probably helps. Just jump in. Ask questions later. You're hurting. It wasn't all that hard."

The bags under her eyes tell a different story, tugging her to sleep. She slumps onto the mattress, not bothering to switch into pajamas. Her powers are fully drained now. *I'm glad you're okay Terrence.*

"I'm glad you're okay, too. Get some rest. You and I both need it more than ever."

16

TIME CRUNCH

Terrence

While she sleeps, Terrence watches. Every sound is a threat to them. He worries about the stars that twinkle outside the window. Death is probably cleaning up the mess at the church.

He can't risk losing this girl to that evil creature that's been on his heels since he defected. Death doesn't understand his goals. He can't. It's beyond his comprehension to understand the ideas Terrence has for what the world *could* be with the help of people like Clarisse.

The night passes slowly. Terrence, as tired as he is, must continue keeping watch. He hopes Clarisse will wake before long. He needs sleep, too. Granted, she's far more fragile than he is. He can't lose vigilance now because of nap-time, of all things.

When cracks of daylight peer through the window, he lets out a sigh of relief. She wakes.

"Clarisse? Are you alright?"

"I'm doing much better, thank you." She says it, but her skin looks gray in the light of the early morning. He wonders for a moment if draining her like this is too much. Maybe there's a grain of truth to what Death had to say about magic having a "cost."

But they're too close to victory to start doubting. He won't let her get that far because he knows the limits. His own curse was because he was inexperienced. Now, much wiser, he knows where the line needs to be drawn. Tangling with Death was stupid, but he won't let a mistake like that happen again. He needs to get this girl out of here and fast.

"Clarisse?"

"Yes?"

"Why don't you get dressed? We have a big day ahead of us; I saw something about complimentary breakfast downstairs, on the way in."

Her stomach growls like an angry bear. They share a laugh. Terrence shifts into his dog-like form and Clarisse shuffles through her briefcase to find something more appropriate to wear. Her clothes stink of carnage from last night. It's a miracle she managed to stay asleep at all with the smell.

He tunes in on her thoughts.

"I don't want to look like a weirdo in my blood-stained clothes, Terrence. I'd take a shower first but we might miss breakfast, so it'll have to wait."

And, yet, you shoot lights from your hands, can hide the sound of your heartbeat, make me look like an angel, and look like a terrifying, halo-wearing goddess when you're mad at people. Who's weird, here?

Clarisse snorts. She's become much more confident in herself since he showed up. He smiles, reveling in the moment. Magic *is* the answer. He's making a difference in this girl's life.

Before long, they'll unlock the secrets to immortality and be helping people all around the world, just like her. He'll restore order —put it back to what it was before everything went wrong.

"Are you okay?" Clarisse looks at him with fear twinkling in her eyes. He guesses that his expression has been blank for quite some time with him just standing there in the hallway plotting like an idiot.

"Yes, Clarisse. Just thinking through everything that's happened in the last few days. I'm sorry to have brought so much pain on you." He stops himself, realizing he's speaking aloud. To their collective relief, no one is standing in the hallway.

"Terrence, we're going to have to be more careful about that."

You're telling me. It's all my fault you got caught. I'm so sorry, Clarisse. I never meant for you to get hurt.

His heart aches just thinking about everything the poor girl went through the other day. How Death can live with himself is beyond him.

If that starry freak can even be classified as alive.

He shakes himself, following beside Clarisse with such closeness that he nearly knocks her over a few times. His eyes scan the room, looking for any sign of the various forms that Death has been known to take. Anything suspicious and he would have her running out of this motel as fast as he could carry her. And he would this time. He would strap her to his back and have her ride. It's insurance for him and her, collectively.

Would you have really made a deal with Death like that the other day? Would you have really agreed to surrender your power in an attempt to save us?

"Yeah, why?"

You do realize it's foolish to make deals with cosmic deities where you literally have no leverage, right?

Clarisse shrugs as they enter the dining room.

"You were hurt. I had nothing to lose beyond what I have—my life. And he's going to win it anyway. Obviously, it wasn't going too hot and he wasn't interested. But hey, if I could help you in any way, I was going to."

Clarisse smiles at him. Just the sight of something so beautiful fills him with wonder. Her smile is everything.

He shakes himself to keep from staring too much, knowing it makes her uncomfortable. He watches her put two plates together— one for the both of them. *Perks of wearing this dumb vest, I guess.*

She sets the plate down for him, looking extremely apologetic that he can't eat at the table with her. But it's no matter. He finds the gesture to be one of the sweetest things that anyone has ever done for him.

Before long, they're both full, finished, and tired again.

Clarisse, do you want to head back up and sleep some before checkout? I need to go stake out some places for us to hide, so you can't use any magic while I'm gone. Anything like that would risk bringing Death right to us.

Terrence hates the idea of leaving her, but he needs a hideout so he can think.

Desperately.

And it's harder when you've got a whole human with you. Being a shadow wolf made hiding a whole lot easier. He hopes that by separating, Death will follow him if he picks up wind of where they've gone.

He knows he can't avoid confrontation forever, but he wants Clarisse to be far stronger when that day comes. Today, she's worn. Her power is surging back faster than he expected, but it's still not enough for her to do anything major.

"I'm so tired. I may just extend our stay for the day. Does that sound okay with you?"

Terrence nods, though he's uncomfortable with the thought of staying in one place for too long. It can't be helped, though.

I'll be back this afternoon. Just stay in the hotel. Sleep. Read something if they have books for you to take a look at. Did you bring any of your own with you?

"A few."

Terrence chuckles at the sight of more than 'a few' books teeming in her suitcase. They outnumber her clothing easily.

Alright, then you should be plenty entertained. Please, be careful.

"How long should I wait before I come looking for you?"

His heart churns.

Clarisse, if I don't come back by nightfall, you run and don't look back, do you understand? I'm trying to keep it to where you can have your job and your dreams like you want, but if I don't show up, you need to get the hell out of here as quickly as you can and never return to this town, do you understand?

Clarisse doesn't like this answer—he can see it in her face.

"I don't want to lose you. You're my best friend."

You won't. I'll be back. That's the worst-case scenario, got it? Even if it's past nightfall, I'll come looking for you. I just don't want you to be a sitting duck, got it?

Clarisse crosses her arms, but by the way she stands, he can tell he's won her over. At least at this point.

"Be careful."

I will.

He waits until they're back into the hallway alone and takes his leave. Time is ticking, and he has to find a place for them to hide and *fast*.

17

AN UNWELCOME GUEST

Clarisse

Clarisse extends their stay with little effort. Not many tourists are blowing through Ashville, despite it being the middle of summer, so there isn't any concern about the room being double-booked.

I wonder why.

Clarisse laughs to herself, turning on the shower. She bites back a screech at the feeling of cold water hitting her raw skin. Where she doesn't have scars, the skin is new. Terrence replaced quite a lot of it after being seared by hot irons and lashed with whips. The new skin still isn't used to feeling such intense things like ice-cold water.

Maybe this is why babies cry....

She accustoms herself to the feeling and stays in the shower for quite some time. Wondering if Terrence is back, she steps out and wraps a towel around her. Looking around, she swears at the realization that her clothes are still on the bed.

Idiot.

She doesn't hear him, so she knows it's safe to step out. When she flings open the door, she screams.

Sitting in the middle of the floor is a wolf made of stars.

"Clarisse!"

She grips the towel as tightly as she can around her body. "Death! What the hell? What—what are you doing here? Can't you knock? You can talk to me in my head, can't you? Why wouldn't you be like 'Hey, caught you, put some freaking *clothes* on before you come out here?'"

His stars are tinged with pink; she wonders if that means he's embarrassed. He uses a quick spell to put her clothes back on her body. "There, better?"

"Not really, no." Clarisse lets the towel fall to the floor. She wishes she had more time to dry off because her clothes are damp now. But it's better than being stark, freaking *naked*.

"What do you want? I thought you said you were done with me."

Death sighs. "I have decided you are still worth the effort."

Clarisse sneers at him. "Oh, how generous of you. I'm so glad you decided I'm *still worth the effort*."

He seems a bit miffed at this; she decides it's probably best to stop pushing the Grim Reaper. It's a bit foolish that she's disrespecting him at all, she realizes.

Am I stupid?

"Yes."

Really?

"You asked."

She puts her hands on her hips and assumes a stance that conveys as much annoyance as she can possibly muster. "Have you ever heard of manners?"

"Yes, though it seems you missed the lesson on how those work."

Clarisse's eyes widen. She would ask him who he thinks he is, but she knows better. That would end in some kind of sarcastic quip about being Death-incarnate. Then she starts laughing.

"What?"

"I'm not telling."

"You can't just laugh and not tell me," he grins. It's an unsettling image since it looks more like a snarl. "I like a good joke."

"Oh, do you? I was just thinking it would be funny if I were to ask what makes you think you're so important that you can tell me about what manners are."

Death laughs. "I'm Death, silly girl… wait, that's why you were laughing, isn't it?" He starts to chuckle. His stars turn gold rather than their usual, twinkling white.

Did I actually make him… happy?

"*No!*"

The stars lose their yellow hue.

"Enough of exchanging thoughts. There's no need to hide our conversation. There's no one else around, anyhow." Clarisse rolls her eyes. There's the no-nonsense Death Terrence described working for. "I've come to talk to you about Terrence. I don't think you fully understand what you're dealing with. *Who* you're dealing with."

Clarisse opens her mouth to argue, but she realizes she doesn't actually have anything to say. She *doesn't* really know who Terrence is after only knowing him a few days when he's put all the focus on her. Not convinced he's out to get her like Death says, but she wonders if it's time she actually listens.

"I see your wheels turning. Good. You do have sense."

Clarisse glares at him. "You really know how to piss someone off, don't you?"

He shrugs. "I'm only being truthful."

"Okay, well, there's this thing called 'tact' and you could really use a lesson on.…" She huffs, crossing her arms. "Never mind. This is hopeless. Fine. Give me the spiel. It's not like I can make you leave, anyway. What is it you want to tell me about Terrence and how awful he is and all this crap you keep yammering on about?"

Death looks surprised at her tone.

"Before you get after me again about manners, I'm gonna pull the teenager card. I'm still a kid. Okay? So, I'm sorry I'm snappy." She can't believe she's actually giving this guy a break. He almost *destroyed* her one and only best friend. Not to mention threatened to kill her. But she needs to stall. This is her only option.

"I appreciate the apology and you are correct. You're rather young and I should give you more leeway. I first want to apologize for my actions. Your point earlier about me being hypocritical was more than fair."

This isn't how Clarisse imagined Death would start a conversation. Shock blooms on her face and, for a moment, his stars flash yellow again.

He laughs. "Yes, I am capable of recognizing the error of my ways. I am very caught up with my job, you know. Do you know how many people die every second?"

Clarisse shakes her head.

"About two. Now, you must understand, while I do have quite an army of Reapers to help me do my job, I'm rather preoccupied with the order and natural balance of things. It's easy for me to overlook the little details, like how people feel and how someone such as yourself might be inclined to do foolish things to try and escape an unarguably abusive past. I do regret not doing something to remove you from your situation, but, you must understand. I can't remove everyone from a situation of abuse. Life must take its course. I only stepped in when you started practicing magic because of *who* you're practicing magic with."

Clarisse blinks. "What do you mean?"

"This is going to be confusing, but I'm going to try and explain it anyway. Ask questions as you see fit. You first need to understand that there are thousands of timelines that encompass a person's potential future. Every choice you make creates another set of thousands of outcomes. How you act determines a plethora of futures that are even more dependent on what you choose to do with the cards you have."

Boy, you did say it was going to be confusing.

Clarisse's mind is dancing in circles trying to keep up. "So, basically, actions have consequences but certain actions produce specific consequences? And there's no way to tell which one I'll end up with until it happens?"

Death grins again; his teeth, somehow, are even more terrifying than Terrence's. She holds back the urge to shudder.

"Precisely. You would make for a sharp pupil. Perhaps once you pass on, I'll have you put in a school for magically-inclined souls. The problem, my dear, is that you're practicing magic within your mortal body. Being near Terrence has affected the range of your capacities. Tell me, how did you go—within a few days, mind you—from making 'little stars' to making full-blown illusions and healing people?"

"How did you know about the healing thing?"

"Magic leaves a trace. It's how I found you." *Damn it.* "Terrence should have known better than to let you heal his wounds. Tell me, how did you feel after practicing that level of magic?"

Clarisse thinks for a moment. It unsettles her that he's starting to make sense. *Is he right? Is there really a cost to using magic?* And why does Terrence have anything to do with why her powers are amplified?

"I see you're starting to connect some pieces. I realize this is a lot to take in; I'm sorry I didn't approach this subject with more care." He pauses, his eyes full to the brim with a thousand other thoughts. "I'm sorry I pinned you like that and didn't rescue you. I mean, they were going to lose their memories anyway; I should have pulled you out of there. It just isn't customary for me to intervene. Can you understand why?"

Clarisse lets out a breath. "I understand. I'm upset, but I understand. It's a stupid custom, but if you tried to intervene for everyone, then this wouldn't be Earth. It would be Paradise; this place isn't meant to be perfect or without suffering. You're not a superhero. You're Death."

"Once again, you show great promise. You're catching on rather quickly." Death takes a few steps closer to her.

She's more comfortable around him now than she's ever been. "Would you like some coffee?"

The question blurts its way out of her mouth before she can stop herself. Even Death looks like he's never been asked that question before.

Who asks the Grim Reaper if he wants a cup of coffee?

"*You, apparently.*"

What is it with you people and seeing inside my head? Ugh. So do you want a cup?

"Yes. Black, please."

Clarisse gags. Coffee with nothing in it?

"It's healthier for you that way, you know."

Well, apparently, according to someone, you win all the time anyway, so I might as well enjoy my cream and sugar.

Death laughs.

"Alright, spill the beans. Tell me everything I want to know." Clarisse hands Death his cup of black coffee and avoids cringing at the sight of him levitating the cup to have his magic toss it back into his gaping maw in a matter of seconds.

"Aren't you the least bit curious about the fact that Terrence was a Reaper? That he worked for me?"

Clarisse grimaces. "I haven't really had much of a chance to ask him. I've been a bit busy, if you haven't noticed. And I just didn't think to worry about it," she shrugs. "I know that seems dumb and you can judge all you want, but I don't really have any friends. He is my only friend."

Death sighs. "You're far too trusting. That could hurt you in the future. But I'll elaborate as much as I can. I'll take you out of here if at the end of this you decide you want to be freed of his grasp; if not, I will let you continue on in your errant ways. Deal?"

Clarisse narrows her eyes as she takes a sip of her creamer-filled coffee. "I was told not to make deals with gods. Ever again."

Death grumbles something in a language unfamiliar. "Fair. But I'm upholding my end of the deal, whether you agree to it or not. I won't hurt you or Terrence today. *Today.*"

Clarisse shivers. She takes another sip of her hot coffee, suddenly wishing she made a lot more cups.

"I suppose I should start with Terrence's origin. Has he told you how and *why* he passed?"

"I know he passed during the Black Plague. He had powers like I do; he said he was cursed when he entered the Afterlife and took up a job with you in order to pay penance for what he did."

Death nods. "Yes, that's part of it. But that's still missing the why."

Clarisse throws her hands up, exasperated. "Then go ahead and say it! Just tell me! I don't want to have to sit here and guess at *everything.*"

"Impatient, are we?" Death winks. "Alright, so I'll tell you everything and let you ask questions at the end. Terrence contracted the disease in the early 1300s. Upon realizing he contracted the disease, he tried to use his powers to heal himself. I came and warned him, much like I am to you, now. I told him trying to cheat his way out of dying was going to get him into trouble. But he didn't listen."

"So magic does lead to immortality, then," Clarisse triumphantly beams. "That's why you're trying to stop me."

"I thought you said you weren't going to guess and let me tell the story?"

"Sorry," Clarisse murmurs.

"Unlike what you think, I don't control when a person dies. You made that apt observation just a few moments ago that choices have myriad consequences; the true one isn't realized until the moment it occurs."

"Oh."

"Yeah, 'oh.' So what I'm trying to tell you, in short, is that by doing magic, he altered his timelines in such a severe way that it violated the standard outcomes. Without making this too confusing, I'll just say that certain consequences *shouldn't* be possible and, when they are, it makes judgement day a real pain for the person who violates the natural order. And *that* is far beyond my scope of control. I do intervene on the part of people like Terrence to try to give them jobs that satisfy a punishment sentence so that they can truly pass on in the Afterlife without ending up damned to Kohlu or stuck wandering in Yehta."

"Wait, what are Kohlu and Yehta?"

"Hell and Purgatory. I'm surprised you've never heard of those terms before."

"Dude, no one has ever heard the words Kohlu and Yehta. Like, what the heck even—you know what, I'm not even gonna ask at this point. So, why is Terrence still damned to look like a wolf? And is he really a god like he says?"

Death laughs. "A god? No. A damned soul with a lot more power than would do him good? Absolutely. *I* am considered a god; how many gods of death have you seen in various mythologies? Plenty. How many *Terrences* have you seen represented?"

Clarisse thinks on this for a bit, coming up empty. She's heard of shadows and shadow gods, but something tells her that Terrence doesn't qualify. "Why would he call himself one, then?"

"He has a particularly elevated sense of self, thanks to his powers. Ego is something he's got more than enough of."

You're one to talk.

"Excuse you?"

Nothing.

Death groans.

"Look, what I'm trying to say is that you'll end up like Terrence if you don't stop. You cut seconds off your life. You're free to practice magic in the Afterlife and the occasional slip up here isn't going to get you damned. But altering things? Changing your outcomes like this? Clarisse, you're risking eternal damnation. You will end up taking time off your life. It could be minutes... days... years... Think of magic like alcohol. In small doses, it does no harm. But when you drink a lot of it? Think of what that does to your body. And now imagine what it would do to your immortal soul."

Clarisse is greatly disturbed, but tries not to show it. "Terrence wouldn't put me in danger like that, Death. How do I know you're not just trying to keep me from becoming immortal?"

Death looks like he wants to slap her... if he had hands to slap her with.

Does he have hands?

Death grins, shifting forms. Now, standing before her, is an olive-skinned man with jet black hair. The only thing that resembles the starry wolf are those beautiful, golden eyes that lack pupils. To put it simply, he's *hot*.

Uhhhh....

"Like what you see?"

Shut up!

"Now that we've settled your endless, childish curiosity, may I continue?"

Clarisse sticks her tongue out at him, not caring how stupid she looks. "Wait, but why do you choose to look like a wolf?"

Death shrugs. "It's comparable to the idea of the church grim, and I like wearing my stars. It's the only form that lets me do so. Though, this is far more appropriate when dealing with humans who aren't... *hostile*. Anyway, getting back to my point: Clarisse, Terrence is duping you. Anyone who calls themselves a false god and claims to want to help you with nothing in exchange... I mean, apply his logic to what you just said about making deals with gods. Aren't you implicitly making one with him? And what's *your* leverage? Your powers? And don't you think he could have helped you without you using them?"

"But Death, I chose to use them."

"Did you? He spoke aloud to you in his shadow form in front of your parents, putting you in a particularly rough position, right? You did what you thought you had to do. While that *is* a choice, it's not really a fair one, is it?"

Clarisse shakes her head. Death wasn't present for *any* of what he just mentioned. The hairs on her neck stand on end.

"Wait, how do you know...? Never mind. I'm so done with you people knowing everything. Look, I admit there are a few flaws in his story. But why did he leave? Why would he want to stay damned?"

Death cocks his head and Clarisse avoids the urge to swoon at how beautiful he is now that he's in this form.

Why am I like this?

"I don't know, but I'm certainly flattered."

Clarisse's cheeks burn. Death sits down on the bed and pats it, motioning for her to sit next to him. She freezes, her legs refusing to move.

"Uh, I think that's a bit close for comfort."

"I don't bite. I'm just trying to make things more comfortable. I really want to make it up to you for how rude I've been in the last few days. Please."

Clarisse takes a hesitant seat next to Death.

"Look, I know you've been through a lot. And I realize I'm probably not going to convince you today but, please," he grabs at her hand and looks her deep in the eyes. It's unsettling to have his eyes burning into her own the way they do now. "Don't you think you should at least *consider* what I have to say? Don't you think it's odd that I, who am 'only interested in collecting souls,' am trying to keep yours from being collected so soon? What's in it for me?"

"What's in it for any of you?" Clarisse buries her face in her hands. "I don't know what to do," her fingers muffle the sound of her despair.

"I know. And I'm not trying to tell you that this is an easy decision or that you're wrong for believing what Terrence has to say. I just want to make sure you're informed going forward. I want you to have a chance to live. The last thing I want to do is come get you and have you become a victim to that idiot's grand *plans*, whatever they may be."

"Yes, but what do you really gain by helping me?"

Death grimaces. "I get to right a wrong. I get to make up for leaving you in a place that would put you in this position in the first place. This is my fault, Clarisse."

The answer doesn't satisfy her. She looks up at him. "No, it's not. Life just isn't fair. It's like you said. It's not your job to intervene."

"I put you at risk, Clarisse. I had no idea you were actually this powerful; it astounds me that you've not died doing what you have in a mortal body at this point. Please, take it easy. I want you to flourish just as much as Terrence says he does."

He looks serious, but Clarisse isn't sure if she can believe him. She doesn't know who or what to believe anymore. Embarrassment swells up inside her. Why hadn't she thought to question these things sooner?

"Why am I so gullible?" She drops her head.

Death moves like he's going to touch her, but stops mid-motion. "You're not gullible. You just haven't been exposed to anything like this. All you've known is what it's like to live in a cage. No one can blame you for taking the first chance you can at escaping."

Clarisse tries to face him again, but she can't. She turns away. "I need more time to think about all this. I appreciate you not coming in and chasing me like a monster this time. Thanks."

Death sighs. "I'll be around again. If you need me in the meantime, look to the stars."

"Wait, what?" Clarisse looks up and finds herself alone. She can't believe that, for a split second, she *misses* his presence. She wants someone to hold onto. She wants this confusion to end. She opens her suitcase, finding her wolf plushy still stuffed inside. She clutches him to her chest and hides her tears in his worn fabric. Before long, she's asleep. But the dull ache in her heart never leaves.

18

TENSION

Clarisse

"Clarisse! Wake up!"

Clarisse rolls over; she groans, her eyelids clinging on to the deep sleep they are reluctant to leave.

"Clarisse!"

Cold water dumps on her head. She bolts up out of bed, shrieking. "Terrence! What the heck?"

"Sorry, uh, I just had to wake you up because *I need to know what Death said when he was here!*"

Clarisse blinks. It takes her a moment to even remember what he's talking about. A fuzzy image of a wolf made of stars and then a handsome man start to surface. Death had been here. In this room. Telling her about Terrence's past.

"Wait, wait! How did you know he was here? I didn't know what to do, I'm sorry Terrence. He showed up and I'm not strong enough—"

Terrence snarls.

"I'm not worried about that, what did he say? Did he hurt you?"

"Tell me how you know he was here." She folds her arms, agitated about the water all over her pajamas.

Terrence grimaces, his nose wrinkling up into a snarl that drops cinder blocks of ice down her spine. She remembers what Death said and is afraid now. Why should she trust this creature? Sure, he's helped her. But at what cost?

She's conscious about keeping her thoughts doused. Something inside her brain clicks; she envisions a sort of vault locking her thoughts away. The buzzing in her veins is reminiscent of every other power she uses; she just hopes that this is enough. The look on Terrence's face tells her that he knows she's keeping things from him. *It must be working.* His red eyes glow a bit, flashing with anger. "Clarisse, no secrets. What did he say?"

"He told me why you died and the cost of using magic," Clarisse picks at her nails that she's started to let grow since Terrence arrived in her life. *Mom never let me have long nails.* She does her best to play it cool in this conversation. An unfamiliar sense of dread starts to weave itself through her gut. She doesn't feel comfortable with this creature anymore.

"Details! I need details!" He's yelling now; Clarisse fears someone next door might hear and come looking. The last thing she needs is more drama in her life.

"That magic is what killed you!" She hisses the response. "If I keep using magic it will not only kill me but *damn* me like it did you!"

Terrence whirls around, facing the wall opposite her. Clarisse swears she sees fire spout from his mouth. "I knew he would try to sway you with that!" His voice is suddenly deep, like gravel that's been doused in volcanic ash. *As if I know what that sounds like...*

Clarisse clutches her wolf plushie to her chest, ignoring how childish she feels. "What do you mean?"

She's not sure where the courage to ask her question comes from, but she's glad for it regardless. Flashing images of all the times Dad screamed at her threaten to send her into a world of panic. Her breath shortens and her lungs feel like they might collapse. *He can't be like Dad. No. Hang on.* It's still not enough to save her from those flashing memories. They consume her while he continues to rant on.

"Clarisse, it's his fault that I'm damned. I'm trying to make it so that you can't end up like this! If we can make you immortal, he can't damn you and you can enter the Afterlife without having to die! That's what I'm after. I want to *give* you a life that never ends and one free of suffering. Tyrladan isn't all it's cracked up to be outside Earth."

Clarisse is terrified at what she's hearing, more ice lacing itself in her veins. Winter itself has consumed her very being. She starts to shake; control over her emotions leaves her. Her heart feels like it's going to explode with rage and fear and sadness all at once. Her ribs feel like they're caving in on her. She can't breathe. A choking noise escapes her throat and she slumps over.

Terrence notices the panic attack and rushes to her side. He pushes himself up against her to keep her warm. The violent shivers raking through her body prompt him to wrap her as tightly as he can in his embrace. She's grateful that he noticed.

"Clarisse, I'm sorry he put doubt in your mind. What have I done to make his words worthy of shaking your faith in me?"

Clarisse's eyes widen. Those words sound familiar, like something Father Simmons would say. Just thinking of that man makes her want to spew vomit all along the walls. Now she can't move. S*he's* a deer in the headlights; the truck is only seconds away. Her vision blots in and out as the anxiety overwhelms her now.

"I'm just telling you what he said," she whispers. "I didn't say I believe those things or think that they were fully truthful."

Terrence hisses.

She yanks back from him. "Stop treating me like I've betrayed you or something. What was I supposed to do? He's *Death*. There's no scenario where I win against him."

Terrence takes a deep breath, finally lowering his voice. "Are you afraid of me?"

"Generally, no. Right now? Yes. You're scaring me."

She cringes, wondering if it's the right response. An urge to put her hands up to guard her face surfaces, but she keeps it at bay.

"Okay, okay. I'm being unfair. I suppose I haven't told you enough, either. That's understandable. I need to fill you in on what it is I'm trying to achieve."

Clarisse notices that he seems to be speaking more so to himself than anyone else. It hurts her. Rips her to the core. Her mind reflects on how calm she'd been around Death. How calm she'd been with Terrence when he first arrived. She yearns for those moments. But, right now, her guard is up. She's on high alert.

"I'll fill you in. But, right now, we need to leave."

Clarisse is shaking, wishing the pent-up tears would flow. She stifles the ocean in her eyes like she has since she was a child. Although, she's more terrified than she's ever been."

"Look to the stars." Death's words echo in her guarded thoughts. She's grateful that they still seem to be safely tucked away, though she worries it might not last as long as she needs.

It's going to be a while before she can call him, but a glimmer of hope glows within her that he can sense her desire to speak. *Being with Terrence is being inside a cage.*

His teeth glisten and wink in the light. "Clarisse! Earth to Clarisse!"

"Sorry, I'm just still really tired," she lies. "I guess I just spaced out."

He huffs. "I found us a place to stay. Get your things together."

"How are we going to get there?"

"I've called us a cab. We're going to keep up the service dog charade and have them drop us off so we can walk the rest of the distance."

Clarisse doesn't argue, too exhausted from all the panic. She's not sure how she has the strength to stand or to put everything back in her suitcase… to follow Terrence out the door, knowing full-well that her mind is turning him into the very monster Death painted him to be.

But what if Death is wrong?

She wonders if she can "call" long-distance to Death. He can beat the crap out of Terrence and she can follow him somewhere.

Why would he help me get out, though? I did this to myself.

They ride in the cab together, silence enveloping the ride. She hates that it's become like this and hopes that she'll have more sense by the next day. It feels like the ride takes only seconds before they arrive at a set of abandoned stores near the woods.

"You sure this is where you want to be dropped off?" The cab driver has a hint of caution in his tone, as if he knows this is a rough area.

No, my service dog is a fake god from the Afterlife and he's holding me hostage. Please help.

She looks at Terrence and nods. "Yep. This is it. I'm doing some exploring; I thought this would be a good place to start."

Terrence seems pleased with the response.

At least he's reasonable now. I can't risk upsetting him again.

The way he acted in the hotel room indicates that he's unstable when it comes to the subject of his death. She mentally beats herself up for not thinking to ask about that sooner.

Am I going to die? Am I going to look like him someday? Be stuck reaping souls for hundreds of years before I have a chance at being freed from Hell or Purgatory.

She keeps her eyes on the ground, following after Terrence. It seems like years drag by now. Her feet ache from all the walking. She's so drained that she feels she might keel over.

Before long, Terrence comes to a stop. "Are you alright?"

He's calm. The edgy personality vanishes as if it never existed.

"Yeah," she gasps, "this is just a really long walk. Are we almost there?"

"We're already here!" Terrence bounces around just like he did while eating cereal. Clarisse can't help but smile.

Maybe I was making more of a monster out of him than he actually is?

Still, she's not about to trust him. She can't. Not when Death had made so many fair points about being careful.

"Where are we?"

They stand in an empty field at the edge of the wooded terrain they've been trudging through. She wonders if Terrence made the path for them when he left or if it's been here, created by the animals and hikers who decided to pass through.

"Silly, this is where we're going to live!"

"In the middle of a field?" Clarisse stutters, gripping her shoulders as a shiver works through her.

"No, no. We're going to *create* a place to stay. We're going to build a house together!"

Clarisse is at a loss for words.

Has he finally gone insane. Did Death's visit make him snap? Or did I just miss this type of behavior the whole time?

She tries to hide her doubt, but her face betrays her.

"Come on, out with it. What don't you like about this place?"

"It's not that I don't like it here. I just... How are we going to do that? Like, build a place to live? I know I have a trust fund but I'm not sure if I'm going to retain legal ownership—at least total ownership—of the funds... there was a lot of confusing legal jargon at the bank. I... how are we going to get materials? I don't start work till Monday and if I do I have to be on alert for...."

"We're using magic," Terrence interrupts. It's the first time that he seems annoyed with her, so Clarisse keeps her mouth shut.

Every red alarm bell imaginable goes off in her head.

"Magic?"

"Yes. Building structures is rudimentary when more than one being does it. I've already placed spells around the perimeter to hide the trace of magic from Death, so you needn't worry about that. He won't keep getting in the way!"

Terrence laughs aloud and Clarisse stays silent.

Does he not care that I literally might die if I use magic?

His eyes bore into hers; even though her thoughts are hidden from him, the glint in his eyes is enough to tell her that he's on to her.

"I can tell Death has shaken you. Listen, what happened to me is deeper than just 'using magic.' You haven't even attempted magic that makes you immortal or saves your life, have you? Because that's more in line with what I got in trouble for."

"What do you mean?" Clarisse picks at her fingers.

"I mean that I contracted the plague. I attempted spells to ward off its effects. That is 'interrupting the natural balance' like he said. That's what he told you magic does, right?"

Clarisse hates how her face betrays everything she has to say. She's done so well at hiding herself all these years. And now? Now she was doomed to have everyone know what she's up to. Everyone can read her. Everyone can tell when she's lying, what she's feeling. She's tired of it, making a mental commitment to herself to start working harder at hiding again. Her excitement at meeting Terrence led her to destroy her whole life in a matter of hours. Now that days have gone by, everything needs to be different.

Same shit. Different cage. She hangs her head.

"Don't worry, Clarisse! I'll make sure that none of this magic is the type to kill you until we *do* figure out how to make you immortal."

She doesn't argue. Instead, she puts on a smile and goes along with his plan. "Alright. I want you to know I do believe you. I don't doubt your intentions when it comes to helping me. I really just couldn't keep Death from entering the motel. I didn't know what to do and I didn't want to alert you in any way and get you hurt again."

This seems to appease Terrence. He relaxes himself even more. "I'm sorry I yelled at you and frightened you like that. I'd never hurt you."

Father Simmons said the same, yet, he did all the time. What makes you any different?

She's getting good at hiding her thoughts. She hopes that using that magic is more like a small glass of wine than a shot of whiskey. Death's analogy is still fresh in her head and she's not about to ignore his warning. "Alright, fine. I do want to take it easy though. You say this is an easy spell?"

"Easier than you can imagine with my help."

"Okay. Let's get to work then! So uh... how do we start?"

Terrence laughs. "It's quite simple. I'll show you."

19

THE WONDERS OF MAGIC

Clarisse

The magic is not "quite simple" at all. Clarisse strains, her skin pouring with sweat as she attempts to raise the foundation of the house. The first hour was focused on drawing a blueprint in the dirt. Terrence had quite a lot of elaborate ideas from the jump. She's too tired to fight him.

She doesn't want to include fancy banisters and wallpaper and so forth because she has to *imagine* all those things. He says he's helping, but she wonders if his idea of "help" is simply amplifying her powers, as Death alluded to in their conversation. She wishes she had asked more questions.

But right now, she has to focus. She's never seen how the foundation of a house and how it works, so Terrence tells her that she has to *feel* it. To understand the strength of the house.

Of course, that all sounds like a ridiculous load of bull crap to her. The house plans themselves are shoddy. She's not sure that any parts of the structure will hold, magic or not; she doesn't plan on literally dying to hold it up.

"Come on, Clarisse. You almost have it!"

She doesn't 'almost have it,' because she's almost ready to pass out. Just as she's on her last leg, something begins to tug at her soul —something ancient. The moon and stars start to whisper and hum again; their words may be foreign, but she swears she knows what they're calling her to do.

"Let me try something." Murmuring this last request, she closes her eyes. In her mind, she throws away Terrence's blueprints. Instead, she looks at the outline of what he has in mind. He's not drawn it all that well; granted, dirt isn't the best medium for constructing house plans.

She imagines what the house might look like when it's finished. Dark gray siding—her emotions are dulled and that's the color she associates with staying hidden. Black shutters. An old wooden door. Something out of a horror movie; she's terrified and she might as well embrace how she feels. But it has to look happy enough to trick her dear *friend*.

She strains harder, aware that the world around her is dimming. The load seems less heavy. The structure of the house, in her head, is done. She doesn't know how she knows this with her eyes closed, but she takes a guess based on the weight that's now missing from her veins.

"Alright, now onto the interior." She hears Terrence take a deep breath, but she chooses to ignore him.

She tugs at the magic in the atmosphere, aware that she's dragging on the forcefield to hide them from Death. Its presence is all the more tangible to her the further she goes into imagining the house. Death will know where they are soon if she's using as much power as she thinks. *Then again, it's only blueprints... right?* The feeling of sickness in her arms and legs threatens to wrench her eyes open, but she returns her focus. To preserve herself, she grabs from the forcefield even more. *I need Death here, anyway. He has answers.* Terrence makes no sounds; she takes that as a sign that he's not noticing where she's drawing the extra power from. For now, she can keep designing their abode.

Clarisse builds the house from the outside in. The porch comes first. Steps pop up in her head, made of dark, mahogany wood and two rocking chairs. Her imagined dream homes always had rocking chairs. This one, no matter how nightmarish, still needs them. The door opens; a peephole lets her into a living room. It's an open-floor concept, so it seems to jump right into the kitchen. There is no wall dividing the two; the dining room is visible from the living room. A large flat-screen TV spreads out along the wall; the walls are a pale white. The floors are made of freshly laid, rich, reddish-brown hardwood. She's not sure what trees they came from, but she hopes she isn't cutting down anything expensive or endangered.

She moves into the next room, where a back door leads to a larger foyer; spiral stairs stretch up to a second floor, whose hallway is marked by long, stretching rails that would keep someone from tumbling over at the sight of such a drop. Bedrooms fall into place along with bathrooms, rugs, plants. Everything seems alive in her head. Downstairs, the foyer leading to the upstairs stretches to a pair of double doors that contain a small ballroom.

I love dancing.

"Uhm, Clarisse?"

She opens her eyes.

"Terrence, I'm trying to imagine the house here, would you give me a second—what... what the ..."

Standing in front of them is the house she created. As it turns out, the weight she felt in her veins wasn't from the strain of imagining something so complex. She was *actually* putting the house together. The stars chitter with excitement. Clarisse wonders if they've alerted Death. *Look to the stars....*

"This isn't what we drew!" Terrence cries, jerking her back to cruel reality.

Clarisse whirls on him only to find Terrence laughing like a madman.

"This is even better!" He bounds to the door, wiggling the handle to no avail with his teeth. It's locked. "You're telling me you made this house and you didn't even bother to make the key?" The fire in Terrence's eyes is a cause for minor alarm, but Clarisse keeps her cool.

Opening her palm, she finds a glittering pair of keys waiting for her. This is *her* house. Not his. She doesn't say that aloud, simply tossing him one of the copies and letting him run inside.

Since when do you even need keys? She doesn't hush this thought.

"It has to be a proper house, Clarisse! A proper house needs keys!"

Clarisse rolls her eyes. "You're insane."

"And you're not?"

Clarisse shrugs. "Fair point."

She follows after him, curious to see if her creation looks exactly as it did in her head. To her surprise, it's *exactly* how she "imagined" it.

Terrence presses down on the floorboards. Not a squeak or squelch is heard from beneath them. He looks up at her, tears brimming in his glowing red eyes. "I can't believe… you did it! And it seems that you did follow my blueprint more than I thought. I apologize."

"I just didn't understand what you were asking in a few places, so I had to improvise, but I tried to keep it true to its nature."

The stars and moon are memories she keeps to herself. If they really are Death's secret informants, she can't betray them. To be robbed of their presence and locked inside would defeat the purpose of her new *home*. Though, she does wonder if that's how Death has known where she is this whole time. *And why wouldn't Terrence know?* When she steps inside, every thought and worry she has is stifled.

It's the most intricate house she's ever seen. Every piece of decoration has a proper place. Houseplants sit on bookshelves begging to be filled with various titles. Pale walls are glowing with warm light fixtures that spiral and twirl with lively delight. The smell of freedom paints the air. Much remains to be done, but everything about this place screams *Clarisse*.

Her fingers brush along various empty shelves and the mantlepiece of the fireplace is decidedly quiet. So, a few things are missing here and there but the house is *sound*.

Terrence calls out from a different room. He's already moved on to the next great adventure. Clarisse smells the strange white flowers on the coffee table in the center of the living room.

Terrence shouts out again.

"You made a ballroom?"

Clarisse laughs.

"Yeah, that's why I said I love dancing!" Clarisse leaves the living room at lightning speed so she, too, can behold her long-awaited masterpiece.

They open the ornate glass doors together. The floor is impeccable—it practically shines under the light. It's a pale tan with intricate, geometric patterns that resemble flowers. Chandeliers drip with fiery light that cascades to every corner, already twinkling and swaying to music that's never been played. Clarisse's cheeks are tinged pink with embarrassment and delight. Her soul is on display in this room. Judging by Terrence's face, he's aware that he's looking at the manifestation of some secret part of her that even she hasn't known until now. She claps her hands, filling the room with the first audible sound aside from their own breathing.

"I don't know what possessed you to do this but remind me to never question your decorating ideas ever again," Terrence laughs. "Shall we explore the rest of the house?"

As reluctant as she is to leave this wonderful room, she feigns excitement.

"Sure!"

They don't spare a single room. They look at everything. Beds, shelves, windows, bathrooms, and closets are all looked over with a fine-toothed comb. Clarisse makes sure she hasn't missed anything.

"I just want to say how lucky I am to have found you first. Death would have stomped this potential out a long time ago if he'd known the scope of what you could do."

If that doesn't sound like manipulation in the making, she's not sure what does. It puts a stop to her eagerness. It's a reminder that this house is a cage, not a place to be safe and cozy.

The sound of soft, pattering drops on the roof makes them stop.

"Of course. We can't even explore the garden now. It's raining," Clarisse frowns, crossing her arms.

"Garden?"

"Oh, yeah. I wanted flowers in the back. A little sitting area for us to picnic, read... stuff like that? I hope that's okay."

Terrence smiles.

"You created this. It's whatever you want it to be."

That's what you say.

Clarisse thanks the rumbling thunder outside for breaking the awkward silence between them. It's the strength she needs to speak.

"Well, I'm glad that you were here to help me with everything," Clarisse lies. After making the house stand on its own, she knows that Terrence *is* some kind of amplifier. She wishes she had her journal to write down what she needs to tell Death the next time she sees him. There's no way he missed this. The stars have to be screaming to him by now. *I hope they are.* For now, she resumes her position as a professional liar and actress.

She takes a seat on the bed. "So… what now?"

"Well, today is Saturday. Late Saturday. You don't start work for two days, so, why don't we take the night off? I know you're exhausted. Do you want to order food?"

Clarisse stares at him. "We don't have an official address."

Terrence produces some paperwork from thin air. A deed to the house is firmly placed in her grasp; along with it, a small map with their location proves her doubts to be wrong.

Her jaw could probably scrape the floor. "How did you?"

"I removed the illusion that nothing is here. There should be a small driveway outside right about… now."

Clarisse looks out the window; true to his word, a curling driveway reaches up to the front of the house. Out at the end of it, a small road stretches from through the woods from where that wide path was.

"Will it show up on GPS, though? That's how most drivers get places, you know."

"Absolutely!"

Clarisse smiles. "Pizza?"

"I must confess, I've never had it."

Clarisse gasps. "How have you never had pizza?"

"I don't need mortal food. But after that lovely cereal stuff, I'd love to try a pizza. We didn't get a whole lot of 'fun' food during the plague, as you can imagine."

"Say no more!" Clarisse runs downstairs with her cellphone. She's glad the bill is entirely in her name, or else Father Simmons might have cancelled her plan by now. But this is hers. The house is hers. Her life is hers.

Sort of.

She ignores the brimming feeling of betrayal, and fear washes over her as the dark, shadow wolf follows her downstairs. He isn't letting her out of his sight at all today. *Will I ever get to be alone again?*

She dials the first pizza place that pops up on the map and places an order. While they wait, her mind wonders what life might have been like had she never met Terrence. Even considering such a thing terrifies her. Death only realized his mistakes *because* of Terrence. She would be stuck in that house trying to figure life out. She would still be waiting on the job on Monday and be feigning complete innocence. Facing the consequences of quitting her father's firm so early. She rubs her arms as she thinks of the lashes that would have come.

This was for the best.

She lets the fears swirling in her head subside knowing she can't question her choices now. There's too much at stake.

"They'll be here in forty minutes," she says. Now is the time to simulate as much normalcy as possible. She's not about to let her deck of cards show. For the record, she's not sure what sort of hand she's holding anyway. *Time to play and find out.*

20

SECRETS

Clarisse

W hen she opens her eyes, she's confused. The sunlight streaming through the window tells her that it's well into the morning. Her stomach churns, a little queasy. Last night's pizza isn't agreeing with her.

Terrence took his own room so she could have some privacy. And she's grateful. At one time, she might have asked him to stay with her since he was, at one point, a source of comfort and this is an entirely new place. Grim images of his monstrous response at the hotel have her on edge–she wants nothing more than to be left alone. Right now, she doesn't trust anyone. Not even herself.

I wonder what he's up to.

Her mind is groggy along with her legs and muscles. She doesn't want to start her day, but she hears the pattering of impatient footsteps outside her door. *He's pacing.* Terrence let her sleep, but she's irritated that he would just wait outside like that.

But he can't know I feel that way.

She wears a smile on her face when she opens the door, hiding the pain her mind and body endure.

A manic, terrifying grin is what he's wearing when she opens the door. "Good morning, sleepyhead! I thought you would never wake!"

"Sorry, I just needed the extra rest, I guess." She feigns innocence, stretching her arms high to the sky and ignoring the crackling sounds that erupt from her spine on the way up. It's always sounded like bubble wrap when she pops herself around, but it's bad this morning. Terrence cringes a bit.

"What are you going to do today?"

Clarisse pauses, knowing she has one more free day before her job begins. "I guess we probably need groceries? I can go get those."

Terrence laughs. "Ah, no. I'll be doing that. I can't have you leaving the house without me present. And you're resting today, or else I'd take you with me. The forcefield should be strong enough to keep Death at bay."

Not after I did my magic… but you don't get to know that. Her soul pales at the thought of seeing the starry wolf alone again, but she can't let Terrence know what she's done.

"Can I trust you to stay put while I'm gone?"

Clarisse pouts, hiding how terrified she is that he's slowly taking control of almost every element of her life at this point. And he's not even hiding it anymore. "Yeah, I'll stay put. So, what am I allowed to do then, today?" Irritation laces her voice, despite her best efforts.

Terrence seems like he might be sympathetic, but he ignores her frustration entirely by jumping up to put his paws on her shoulder and place his devious grin right in her face. "You're allowed to explore your lovely new home, do no magic of note, and enjoy yourself! Read a book! You packed some, right? I suppose we'll need more, but you've got plenty to keep yourself occupied while I go stake things out. Get us supplies. Right?"

It's more of a command than a request, so Clarisse nods. She's not strong enough to tell him off. *I glimpsed power just long enough to let it slip through my fingers. I've exchanged one cage for another.* Her heart sinks; it seems like it's doomed to drown.

"Perfect! I'll leave you here, then. I'll be back before long, so don't worry too much. If there's any trouble, I'm sure you can sort things out. I'll have to think of a way for you to call me. As a matter of fact," he stops, "I'm going to get a cellphone of my own while I'm out. That way you can just pop me a text for when I go out in the future."

Great. Now he'll be texting me. Fantastic. Wait... how will he? She blinks, looking down at this strange, shadow creature.

"How in the Hell are you going to blend in? You're a dog... wolf... thing?"

"Illusions, darling! I can project a fake human to go with me and make it look like I'm guiding them." He laughs at his own plan; Clarisse allows herself to chuckle at the thought, too. Still, it doesn't stop the buzzing of a million more questions and the overwhelming sense of dread that yearns to eat her alive.

"That sounds like a good idea." She wonders how she manages to keep going like this. To keep that smile of hers pinned up like a banner, fooling everyone around her into thinking that she's some kind of mindless puppet that doesn't question the things that come her way.

But I haven't really questioned things till now, have I? I deserve what's coming to me.

Terrence is already leaving; Clarisse is glad, though she's missed half of what he's been saying on the way out the door.

"Under no circumstances are you to do magic without me present. Do you understand?"

"Yeah," she calls. "I'm taking it easy anyway. I want to relax."

Terrence smiles, his eyes softening. The danger she sensed the other day isn't there anymore. She wonders again if, maybe, Death is wrong. Or maybe Death is trying to drive a wedge between them to take advantage of her situation and convince her that there really *isn't* hope for her. That she has to live like this.

But her gut says otherwise. Her very core speaks to her, screaming for her to listen. When the door shuts, a certain gloom she's not felt in ages shrouds about her chest and mind. It's that darkness that comes to get her when she's at her weakest. She hates when it comes around, knowing all too well that it lasts for more than just a few moments. She gets into these fogs and doesn't come out for days, months… a whole year at one point.

What do I do?

Her eyes brim with tears as she runs her hands along the halls. She returns to her room, opening up her suitcase and putting clothes in the armoire resting in the corner. A bookshelf grabs her eye; she has yet to finish even one book since starting on her journey. Granted, it's not been a long one, anyway. She picks one out that might be satisfying and sets it on the bed.

One by one, she sorts through all her books and thinks of different ways she can organize them. She's never been able to put her literary choices on display; she can't wait to start adding more. Spacing all her titles out, for now, she makes her shelves appear more "full." Everything is going swimmingly when she gets to the third shelf from the top.

The shelf creaks at the touch, clicking from the walls as the shelf swings open.

"A secret room?" Clarisse gasps.

I didn't imagine this…. Terrence brushed over this shelf at least four times yesterday—all the shelves really. She wonders if this is what he'd been looking for. But it hadn't opened for him.

She remembers an important thought.

This is my house.

The keys only appeared to her. The house has certain pieces and parts that may open only to her; she controls who gets to come in and who doesn't. *I haven't lost all my power.* She won't be able to use this when her dear *friend* is home, but it's somewhere that she can hide for now. *Can Terrence go through these walls like he can others?*

She chews on this thought for a moment. *Probably not.* She giggles, passing through the small, secret hallway. On the other side is a small room. A desk is placed up against the wall with shelves all along the corners.

It's a tiny reading nook.

It's just big enough for her to walk around in and think. Something she's rarely been allowed to do is suddenly fostered by the size and style of a room no bigger than a closet.

What astonishes her more, there are books *lining* the shelves. She'll have to read them in here. Terrence will be suspicious of how she got them; honestly, she wonders how she got them, too. The titles are unfamiliar. She certainly couldn't have imagined these herself.

"Do you like the collection?"

Clarisse freezes. "Death." She turns, finding the starry wolf splayed on the floor, a title hovering before his face; he's paging through at a rapid pace and she wonders how in the world anyone can read that fast and remember anything.

He chuckles; the sound is warm and thaws the ever-annoying ice in her veins.

"One learns to read quickly when they're as old as I am. This one's nothing of note, really. Just some minor spells." It snaps shut and he stands. She wonders if it's the size of the room or if he's actually that much taller of a dire wolf than Terrence. He towers over her. Were the ceilings not a few inches taller, he'd be scraping them as he approaches.

"What are you doing here?"

"I sensed you were unwell. Are you alright?"

Clarisse shrugs. "No. I mean, I made this house. How do you think I feel? I'm... exhausted."

Death sighs, slouching to the floor to sprawl back out in front of her. He seems much more relaxed now that they aren't arguing so much as talking. It's different to see him in this light. Clarisse joins him on the floor, enjoying the feeling of the plush carpet between her fingers as she sprawls out.

"Why did you do it?"

"What?"

"Make this place? When you know that magic wears you out? Right after I warned you?"

Clarisse frowns. "I think Terrence is gonna snap or something. Like, I don't know what to believe. I don't know why I want to believe you so much when he's only ever helped me. I have no proof to say that he's going to hurt me but, after you left, he went kind of ballistic that we met without him knowing. He said he could 'sense' that you'd been there and started acting all weird. I made this place because he said he would help. But he never did."

"He just amplified you, I take it?"

Clarisse buries her head in her hands. She doesn't like that he knows and doesn't like that she's telling him everything with reckless abandon.

Why should I trust him either?

"Clarisse, you can't hide your thoughts from me as you have been from Terrence. I'm a bit more skilled at this. And you're right not to trust me. But, seriously, my job is to keep things in balance and on schedule. You're being moved from that track of acceptable outcomes. I don't want to see an innocent girl damned because some reckless fool who used to work for me thinks he can use her to his whims."

Clarisse blushes, peeking out from her hands to give Death an irritated stare. She doesn't appreciate it when he goes rifling through her thoughts any more than when Terrence does.

Just when I'd gotten comfortable in the confines of my own head again.

Clarisse realizes in a moment just how crazy this all sounds. She wonders if this is still some strange dream. Tears pull at her eyes. She doesn't know who to believe, where to go, or even why she's putting up with all this.

"I still don't know what to do, Death," she sighs. "I mean, you seem like you're being genuine, but it was literally only what, two days ago that you were trying to keep me pinned to the ground when everyone thought I was dead? You left me with those people. I know you say you're sorry, but I have to undo thirteen years of abuse… really more… and just trust you? Like that's what you're asking of me? If you're here to convince me to leave, believe me, I'd love to. But where would I go? Where would you take me? How do I know you're not here just to collect my soul and damn me anyway?"

Death looks flustered at this. "I'm sorry you still feel this way. Look, I only came in to check on you because this took a lot of magic. You're wiped and Terrence is a fool to leave you alone like this. You could get hurt. I'm here to make sure you don't."

"What, are you my guardian angel now? Terrence tried that role and it didn't work too well for him." Clarisse crosses her arms, trying to ignore how rude she sounds.

"Clarisse, I've never once pretended to be something like that. I'm not here to sugarcoat things or protect you from every monster. Nor am I promising you a utopia like your 'friend' who seems to care so much about your well-being. I am here because he was under my supervision once; he took leave and began to try to find someone like you to start putting to work whatever stupid plans he has envisioned in his mind. I'm here to try to save you from that." Death's face, though covered by the skull, seems full of fire. His stars turn red. It dawns on her that she probably preferred Death in human form since he can't wear the mask. But the stars are enough to be a tell-tale sign for her. He's not happy with her resistance.

But what are those plans?

The blank look on Death's face isn't helping. *If he doesn't know, then who does? And why chase Terrence down? And why are only some outcomes for my life acceptable as opposed to others?*

Death groans.

"Look, I understand that you're frustrated with me to no end. But you've acknowledged it multiple times. This is *hard* for me to understand. My life has fallen apart before my eyes in practically no time at all. *Days.* That's all the time it takes, apparently, for someone's life to come to a shattering halt. Can you stop to appreciate that for a moment? I don't know what to do. Am I stupid for trusting Terrence so soon? You say no, but I think I am. And I have to come to grips with that. And part of me, as childish as it is, wants to believe him anyway."

Death sighs. "You're not wrong."

"Well, then, can you give me a little bit of room? I'm honestly terrified of both of you right now and I don't know where to turn. You're the literal *Grim Reaper* and I'm supposed to believe that you're trying to help me *live*? That's not even close to being within the purview of your job description. And why should I be reassured by your statements? You're literally doing this just because it inconveniences you." Clarisse falls down, burying her head on the carpet. It's a lush escape that she wishes she could fall into. Disappearing sounds all the more appealing.

"Clarisse, I'm not sure how to convince you that I'm here because I care. You were so coherent the other day. You understood why I didn't step in; I thought you were maturing and would see the error of your ways. It appears I was mistaken."

Clarisse snaps up, giving Death a stare that appears to startle him, his eyes widening at the sight of her sudden change of demeanor.

"Really? Are you seriously going to talk to me like that? I'm not some petulant child for you to boss around. If anyone has lost their sense of maturity, it's *you*. You were so understanding the other day and I was starting to like you. I was hoping you would come to talk to me so we could figure out what is happening. Maybe Terrence is right. You really are in this for yourself. I'll be fine and the exhaustion I feel is growing pains."

Or maybe I'm deceiving myself.

She knows Death hears this thought, but her mind is eating her apart and she can't control every thought. *I shouldn't have to.* She's not in the right state of mind to be hearing any of this.

"I think it's best if I come back later. Things are too fresh for you to understand, let alone be comfortable enough to make a decision."

Yeah, just leave me alone again. That's what everyone does when I ask questions.

A spark of something horrid passes through Death's eyes. Pain? Regret? There's no time for her to ask him about it.

Clarisse stands, resisting tears while her chest heaves. She runs her fingers through her hair, prepared to rip apart every strand. "I think it's best if you leave. I don't want to talk to you about this anymore."

Death scoffs, though something else still hides in his voice. "Suit yourself. I was already going. Don't expect me to be so kind the next time we meet."

Clarisse laughs, mocking him. "Kind? Since when have you been kind to me?"

She hides the flinching pain in her chest at saying something so awful, thinking back to that moment in the motel.

The flash in Death's eyes appears akin to that same pain she feels. "I see we're just going to have to be at odds. I hope, for your sake, you see the error of your ways or wake up."

He's out the door, leaving her in the emptiness of a room that doesn't feel so full of magic anymore. The second he disappears is the second she wants him to come back. Her hand reaches for the spot where he stood seconds ago. Tears start to fall. She wants the old Terrence back. She wants Death to come back and for them to talk like they did at the hotel. *I was starting to believe I could have something good in my life.* She sighs, wanting her hopes and dreams back.

Curling up on the floor in the fetal position, she lets herself cry before stepping outside, dousing Death's trace along the way out. She can feel his magic and his aura even after he's gone; if she can, she knows Terrence will be able to. It's another power that just manifests to her. A self-defense mechanism. Terrence doesn't need to know that Death was here in a secret room, of all places. She's not about to get flack for that. Not now. Not ever. She doesn't want to see that same monster she did in the motel.

The bookshelf clicks shut. A piece of her dies, but she doesn't care.

Maybe dying wouldn't be such a bad option after all.

21

DANCING

Clarisse

It's been hours and Terrence hasn't returned. Clarisse wonders if she's broken into someone else's house and has been insane this whole time. Pacing back and forth in the kitchen, she waits for a sign that she's not alone.

Every sound disappoints her. They're all empty of Terrence's presence. *It's lonely here. I've never been alone so long.* Hell, at this point, she'd appreciate seeing Death's obnoxious face.

Her heart lurches. She still feels like crap for talking to him with so much hate. For treating him like he doesn't care and doesn't understand.

I really am a stupid kid.

The world seems much darker now. She misses having interaction with someone. It's only been a few days of having someone in her life that's a *friend*. Not a disciplinarian or a false smile using her for fake show-and-tell. *I hope....*

She's torn. She doesn't believe either of the strange wolves in her lives. *But at least Terrence was there when I needed him the most.*

"I wish you'd come home so I can spend time with you. I wish things hadn't gone sour. I want to help you and I need help." She doesn't know why she's whispering these things aloud but can't help herself.

I mean, I'm already insane, why not go a little farther toward the edge of the cliff? What's the worst that could happen? I fall?

She shakes herself, unsure of where these dark thoughts are coming from. Ceasing to exist shouldn't be a comfortable thought.

I've never let the demons get to me. Not like this.

The loneliness creeps up on her more than ever as time passes ever so slowly.

Her feet find their way down the stairs, leading her to the ballroom. She manages a smile. *Dancing might brighten my mood.*

The doors open without her touching them. She doesn't need to. *What does it matter if magic kills me?*

The lights illuminate above her head; she flicks her hands and adds more to the ceiling. Brightness to alight the darkness of her mind. She walks around, looking for music.

Are there speakers in this room? What do they plug into?

In the corner is a jukebox.

A jukebox, of all things? That's what I picked?

The library is full of songs she's never heard and songs she's yearned to hear again for years. Music was a forbidden enjoyment in her house. She took to enjoying the jingles in grocery stores or from the occasional commercial she would pass in windows of different stores. Caroling at Christmas was a magical thing; she always loved listening.

Now?

I can listen to what I want.

Her chest feels like it's going to explode when she realizes who's most likely responsible for the different choices music. The same person is responsible for the books. Shivering, she determines to shake the guilt from her shoulders.

Music pours from the walls, threatening to suffocate her with beautiful melodies that carry her far from her troubles. She doesn't know how to dance properly, but that doesn't stop her. *I don't care if I look like an awkward chicken. This feels good.*

Memories from her life flash before her eyes. She holds out her hands and plays them out before her like a projector would. Though the room is far from dark, she sees the moving figures. They illuminate the room like her stars. Moments flash by her and she dances between them, passing through the holographic apparitions, letting tears fly. *I've lost my mind.* She sucks in a breath as she sees the starry wolf in the library again. The smiles he cast at her in the hotel room. *But who cares if I'm insane?*

The lights burn different colors as her mood shifts. *Hey, they even look like Death's stars.* She wishes she hadn't scared him off, knowing he may enjoy the show. *I wouldn't be alone.* He might be someone to spend time with.

Why am I thinking of him so much? Why not Terrence?

The sun outside is gone. The windows to the ballroom are pitch black, sending shivers up Clarisse's spine as the room grows cold. The contrast of the lighted room and the inky nothingness makes her full of unease; her stomach starts to churn and she can hear each and every thud of her heartbeat. *Ignore it. Just ignore it.* If she stops to stand still, the pain will catch up with her. The guilt. The loss. Everything. Sadness is the enemy and she's determined to fight it off.

She's never had space or been allowed to approach her feelings. Now that she's allowed, they've become too large to confront all at once. The looming figure of all her worries lurks in the corners of her mind. *Ignore it. I'll keep ignoring it.* A clump of ice rakes down her spine, pulling her to a halt. *Something's wrong.* When she stops dancing for a moment to catch her breath, her mind focuses on a *presence.* "I'm not alone anymore," she whispers. That's when she spots it. A scream emerges from her throat, screeching and guttural.

From the window, a pair of eyes become visible. They're bright, milky-white, and look something like her own stars, blinking.

That's when more eyes become visible. Lots of eyes. Too many to count. They peer at her from every corner, burning into her soul. She stumbles about in the hopes that they might disappear. Her skin burns as she pinches it with reckless abandon; if it weren't for the way those horrible eyes stared, she might be more careful not to draw blood. It drips down her arms as the pupils spin wildly in whatever direction she goes.

A low growl echoes from outside the ballroom. "What the?" Her body freezes, dizzy and faint from running about in an attempt to escape.

The windows shatter; the monster steps inside.

The creature looks like an arachnid centaur. From the torso up, Clarisse looks at a "man" with a whole lot of eyes on his bald head. His skin is pale; she doesn't think any creature this ugly would *dare* step out in the middle of the day. From the torso down, a massive spider clicks along the ballroom floor.

It opens its mouth, blocked by pincers, trying to say something. Words Clarisse doesn't recognize pour from its mouth. They are reminiscent of words Death and Terrence have used. She's not sure what the language is but, to her, it doesn't matter. Right now, she can't hear anything over the sound of her own screaming.

She runs for it, trying to escape the ballroom. The crackling feeling erupting from its direction makes her realize her folly too late. This creature possesses magic of its own. The doors slam shut and, from the look on its face, it doesn't seem too pleased with her response.

Clarisse turns on her heel, looking desperately for anything that might serve as a weapon against this horrible monster that's going to have her cornered if she doesn't move soon.

To her dismay, there's nothing. The lights that were buzzing all around disappear at once. If she can't find anything, she's going to have to conserve her power. She can't afford to be exhausted if she's running from this… *thing.*

It scuttles toward her, its movements choppy and uncertain—like it doesn't know if it should stare her down first or just charge her before ripping her to shreds. Clarisse's skin pales to the color of paper. She's not looking, but she feels that way at the very least.

Someone? Anyone? Please?

She hopes that Death is secretly still nearby; maybe he can save her.

But it's not his job to intervene. Why wouldn't he have told me it's my time though?

Clarisse shakes her head, stuffing that angry thought away for later. If she lives through this and sees him again, she's going to give him the cursing out of a lifetime. She doesn't care how long he's existed. Her rage is going to be the worst he's experienced.

She shuffles to the doors of the ballroom, pushing at them from behind so as not to look frantic. This creature won't get the satisfaction of knowing that she was terrified in her last moments, if this is how she goes.

"What do you want?" Clarisse mentally slaps herself. *As if this thing is going to*—

"You. Your power. I want to consume it," the creature hisses. Its voice is baritone, like someone smashing on the lowest keys on the piano.

It sends shivers up her spine.

"You want to what now?" Clarisse steps back, her voice quavering. Her eyes stay locked with it, though. Cowering isn't an option anymore. Staying strong is her best bet.

"Don't run, foolish mortal. I have you now." Its pale eyes glow, not looking pleased with Clarisse's attempt to resist. She runs along the corners of the ballroom, wondering how long she can keep running and if, perhaps, she can even wear it out.

A blast of power surges past her, smacking into a wall and destroying the paint and wood. It splinters everywhere, shattering Clarisse's hopes that she could at least win in a game of stamina with this strange thing.

It gets closer and Clarisse can't help but let her teeth chatter. Those pincers are the most menacing things she's ever seen. Her eyes spin wildly about in the hopes that she'll catch a glimpse of someone capable of stepping in. Death. Terrence. *Anybody but this thing.* Her breath is more and more frantic. *Is anyone here to help me?*

Still, there's no one.

Clarisse stops running, puffing her chest out and letting her body glow. Her energy is wearing thin and sprinting about isn't going to stop it. *I'm going to have to face this thing.* She has no idea how to fight, but this creature doesn't have to know that. It's best to keep up the illusion for as long as she possibly can. Terrence *has* to be coming back.

Her thoughts return to Death's point that he's likely only an amplifier.

Of course I'd think about that now of all times. Her mind spins. *I wonder if there's a magical term for an amplifier in that weird language they speak....* She resists the urge to smack herself. *Really Clarisse? That's what you think of right now? Focus!*

It dawns on her that the spider centaur has been watching her with something like amusement on its face the whole time she's been battling her inner monologue. *So much for posing as a threat.*

"You're a strange little creature," the spider-centaur-whatever thing hisses. "Perhaps I should keep you as a pet after I take your power."

"Oh please." Clarisse gags, sticking her fingers into her mouth. She doesn't know where this sense of bravery and snark is coming from, but she isn't about to abandon it now. It's like a fuel she didn't know she needed to keep going.

She's never felt this much danger in her veins before. Dealing with her father on many a drunken night and even her mother during certain angry spouts never felt this horrifying. Not even exorcisms chilled her to the bone like this is. This creature is something otherworldly that's *literally* broken into her house. *Her* house. The one she just made.

Anger takes hold of her being. The dull light on her skin turns red. The creature noticeably shifts.

"I didn't think the little creature was capable of being enraged... curious...."

"Who are you, and what do you want?" Clarisse asks the question with more command over her tone this time.

"I am from Tyrladan, little one. Kohlu."

Kohlu.... Didn't Death say Kohlu was like... Hell?

She doesn't allow herself to think about that for too long. There's too much on the line—too much at stake. Clarisse balls up her fists, holding them out at her sides as though she might start swinging. It would be a pointless endeavor, but she wants that same energy flowing through if she's going to put up a fight.

"That doesn't answer my whole question. Who are you?"

"An… acquaintance… of Terrence's. We don't quite see *eyes* to eye," it laughs.

Clarisse groans. "Are you serious? You think *that's* funny?"

She rolls her eyes, wishing that she was anywhere else in the world but trapped in a room with this freak. It feels very childish in some ways, but she knows not to fall for that false sense of security. This thing is dangerous.

Does it really know Terrence?

So far, it hasn't read her thoughts—at least it hasn't given her reason to think so. But she's careful not to think too hard beyond the task at hand.

Kick this thing's ass.

"Who are you?" Her question echoes through the silence. The creature pauses, considering her for a moment as though she might be a hamburger about to be eaten for lunch.

"My name is Ralun."

"Ralun?"

To her surprise, it's enough to get him talking.

"Yes, I was sent by Terrence long ago to help him collect souls. A creation of his. He abandoned me long ago. He's weak. He lost sight of his true purpose. I've taken it upon myself to start trying to do the same things he was."

"Wait, what?" This bit sounds interesting. "What kinds of plans?"

Ralun laughs; Clarisse feels herself burn with fury.

What I wouldn't give to punch the daylights out of this guy… but I need more information first.

"Nothing a mortal like you could ever hope to understand," Ralun smiles, his pincers opening wide for her to see the awful rows of teeth sitting behind them. They're stained black.

"Gosh, do you need a toothbrush? That's super nasty," Clarisse quips, stifling her laughter.

Who are you, Clarisse?

All this recent self-discovery is making her dizzy. She's never been able to understand herself or her emotions. Jokes were forbidden. Laughter was rare. And now, here she is, mocking a spider-centaur monster like it's no big deal. Like she's carried that humor with her the whole time and it's finally able to get out and give a big welcome to the world.

And now I'm going to die.

She needs to ask Ralun more questions. If he worked for Terrence once, maybe he can provide more information about who he was. What his plans are. Why he abandoned them. Before she can distract Ralun any more to start getting answers, he lunges.

Her body, without warning, releases a sea of angry stars. They burst from her hands, whirling balls of angry fire. They're hot. *Searing.*

The first one lands on Ralun's skin, leaving more than a mark. The flesh where the light lands turns black, like the burning embers in a campfire. He deflects it quickly, but the damage is done.

He lets out a roaring scream. "You imbecile!"

The cry is pathetic and Clarisse would laugh if it were a scene from a movie or a book. It's a classic, cartoonish villain response from the lame *clean* comics she was allowed to read on occasion. But she can't afford to lose focus right now.

He whirls on her, his legs scuttling much faster. She's surprised at how fast he moves.

She dodges just as he slides on the ballroom floor, crashing into an adjacent wall.

Heart thudding in her chest, she turns around to assess his landing point. She charges up the light in her hands, two balls of white-hot fire arising from her skin the second she summons it. This is straining her. She feels the weight of using all this power thudding in her veins.

"Come on, Clarisse," she mumbles to herself. "Knock this guy out. You can do it." She sounds most unsure of herself.

Ralun hears her ridiculous mantra and laughs. "You really think you stand a chance against me? You're a mortal—I am not. You cannot wipe me out of existence. Very few gods possess that power.

So, what are you left with? You can die. Your soul can be stolen. You're weak. You might as well give up now and beg for mercy and forgiveness for the insolence you've displayed thus far."

Ralun's words reach from all around the ballroom. Sweat trickles down her forehead. She can't admit defeat to this freak, but he makes a lot of sense.

What kind of chance do I stand?

The fact that he can't hear her thoughts, though, tells her that he's at least weaker than Terrence and far weaker than Death.

This sparks a little hope in her, though she knows she's never taken either Terrence or Death in a fight head-on. It's not really much of a comparison to make. Still, she holds onto that little spark of hope, gripping it tight as she runs around this ballroom, watching her dream house shattered from the inside. In her *favorite* room, no less. Channeling the rage at witnessing all this will do something to keep her fires ignited; maybe, it might even make them more dangerous.

Ralun sends another spark of energy whirling toward her. That's what it looks like, anyway. Clarisse doesn't have any other way to describe what comes arcing her way. This time, it hits home. Her body sears with blistering heat and she lets out a scream. He approaches. She's moving against an immovable barrier that feels like the twine of an electric fence. Every move is punished with another jolt. She smells her flesh burning but makes the choice not to look. Not now.

If I survive this, I can cry later.

Were it not for her experience with pain, she might have buckled. For once, she's grateful for all the torture she's had to endure. It's made her *strong*.

"You think this hurts me?" She mocks him. *Might as well*. She's moving as hard as she can against her invisible restraints as he gets closer, but nothing gives.

"You think it's wise to bait me in a moment when you're weak? When I have you cornered?"

Clarisse spits in his direction, not willing to give him the satisfaction of begging or crying or, worse yet, *apologizing.* She's tired of that.

Her eyes glance around in the hopes that Terrence or Death will come to her rescue. That *someone* will step in.

Ralun towers over her, gripping her neck in a chokehold. "You keep looking around like someone will save you, but you're beat, you pathetic child."

Stars of a different kind start to strain in her eyes. The voices of the moon and stars that usually call to her are distorted. Her own lights are flickering, threatening to give out.

"What do you want?" She strains, voice cracked from the stress of his grasp.

"Your power." He hisses, his eyes wide with hunger.

"Really? It doesn't seem to be doing me any good." She feigns nonchalance. "It's not enough to beat you, it seems." Clarisse shrugs. "So why bother with it?"

Ralun laughs. "You just don't know how to use it. It'll be better served in the hands of someone worthy of it."

So, if it's something you want that bad… maybe I can beat you…. Stifling a grin, she focuses on keeping him talking. "And just what will you use this power for?"

If he's idiotic enough to answer, I'll know if I have a chance or not.

"Overthrowing Terrence, of course. And continuing his original plans."

Bingo. She keeps playing his game.

"What plans?"

"Wouldn't you like to know?" Ralun sneers. "I don't know why I'm talking with my meal. It's rude to play with your dinner."

Clarisse pales. *Dinner?*

Her knuckles turn white as she grips her hands and pushes harder than ever to break whatever spell it is he has on her. This time, she has luck.

Whatever it is holding her snaps. His grip on her neck is broken and she stumbles free, taking the opportunity to leap far away from him so he doesn't get a second chance.

"Get back here!" He shoots another arc of energy at her. She stands, holding out her hand to stop it.

Something connects.

A wave of light leaves her hand—those same balls of starry fire she's been creating—and it blocks whatever it is that he's shooting. She looks at her fingers, staring in silent awe.

The next arc he fires hits, knocking her flat on her butt. Her jaw is bloodied, hair matted with sweat and grime. She has no idea how long this has been going on, but she's had enough.

Holding out her hands, she summons her building rage.

"Stop!"

The command rings out and, to her surprise, Ralun stops moving. He, like she was earlier, is suspended—unable to move. She can see he's struggling against her but it's to no avail. *I have him trapped.* Disbelief threatens to break her focus. *No Clarisse. Keep pushing.* She channels her energy toward him. A gasp escapes her lungs from the strain. *He's right. I don't know how to use this power. But you bet I'm going to figure it out.*

She imagines him going away, like she imagined building the house. At first, nothing happens. Then the screaming starts. Smoke and vapor begin to erupt from his body; the harder she focuses on ridding herself of the pest, the faster she sees results. Finally, his form evaporates. She blinks repeatedly, in awe that he's really gone. Left standing in the wake of a nightmare that, for a moment, she doesn't believe even existed, Clarisse pinches herself in hopes that she'll awaken in that nice bedroom of hers upstairs.

The longer she stands still, the more aware she becomes of how much pain she's in. Charred skin screams under her touch. She looks down, lurching at the sight of the wounds littering her body. Her limbs cry for relief as she slumps to the floor, her stars dancing in front of her face and fizzling into nothing.

The hairs on her neck stand up; she realizes it's stupid to believe he might be gone for good.

Where'd he go? Did I really get rid of him? Is this a trick?

Her eyes dart around the room full of ruins, her chest heaving. *Can I heal myself like Terrence did?* A lot of these magical moments are happening on accident. She can't keep rolling the dice and landing on happy outcomes every time. It's not realistic. It's unfathomable. *And if Death is right… costly.*

All around her, the voices of the moon and stars call to her. They warn her that she's not alone again. Clenching her fists, she stands, ready to fight again.

"Clarisse?"

"Terrence." Before he can reach her, she slumps to the ground, one last scream of agony shattering the still of the night to pieces.

~

Death

From the window, the Reaper watches Terrence arrive. He regrets leaving the mortal alone. Death, for the first time in his existence, feels something like *guilt* writhing in his gut. He watches Terrence's mouth open in a scream as the girl slumps to the ground. The terror in his ex-Reaper's face is evident. He can't hear that awful scream, but he knows the sound all too well.

Ralun had been here before he knew, making him come to her rescue too late. He used his own magic to ensure Clarisse's "spell" was completed—if you could even call it that. Ralun wouldn't return tonight. Death sealed him off in Kohlu, making sure he wouldn't escape for quite some time, if at all. Clarisse did a number on him, wounding him badly. Death doubts that she knows just how much damage she actually did. But for now, he's just happy to see her under the care of someone who won't physically harm her.

At least for now.

He shivers, dimming his stars as Terrence takes a cautionary peek out the window. Death won't be seen. Regret washes over him for snapping at Clarisse earlier.

She's just lost. Confused. Angry. And I didn't give her much reason to trust me today. I was just making headway and then had to just….

Death sighs. In moments like this, he wishes his Creators imbued him with more emotional understanding. The toll would have been heavy at first, especially given the nature of his job. But it would make it easier when he came to get people who were grieving— easier to understand them at least. *But all the harder to pull them away from their loved ones. Their hopes. Their dreams.* He lowers his head.

In times like these, rare as they might be, he regrets the job he's given. Death longs to break in and steal Clarisse from Terrence's grasp. Now, she'll wake up and see Terrence as the hero. Terrence will get the glory. Terrence will be the one she clings to. Death's job of convincing her that Terrence isn't in this *game* of his for her sake will be nearly impossible unless something else shatters her. And he doesn't want to see her broken.

Maybe it'd be best to just let the magic eat at her slowly.

But this feels like betrayal. She'll be damned just like Terrence. He doesn't want her to have to work for him to earn the years off a sentence she shouldn't have to serve.

He curses the mechanisms of Tyrladan. The way magic is viewed is unfair. Mortals should be able to wield it at least in some capacity without such stiff consequences.

Right now, though, he forces himself to watch. There's nothing he can do. He'll have to wait. Reaching, he grasps for a thought of Clarisse's, hoping he can hear what they're saying—what they're doing. How she feels. It's a foreign thing for him to try to empathize with another being, but, for Clarisse, he's open to trying.

His attempts fail, leaving him wanting. She's still unconscious from the looks of things. Just as he's ready to turn away, he's hit with something awful. Something dark.

His stars darken as he tries to understand what he's just seen. Whatever it is… it's not good.

22

ACHES

Clarisse

Clarisse's bones are beyond sore when she opens her eyes. She's in bed—her eyes, though bleary, settle on the bookshelf she decorated. Her heart yearns for the titles beyond the secret doorway. It's a strange thing to focus on, but it brings her something like comfort knowing the books are waiting. Her mind isn't right. It's all twisted and crummy.

As awareness returns, she feels the eyes of someone watching.

"How are you feeling?" Terrence stands over her.

"I… I hurt." Her ribs ache just by moving enough to speak. She moans. Fat tears manage their way down her cheeks. She can't hide them. Her emotions are raw. Stars erupt from her hands. They're not meant for battle this time. Instead of their usual bright, cheery colors, they're a solemn blue. Sadness incarnate. Pain. Suffering. An echo of everything she's experiencing in her very core.

Terrence crawls next to her, resting under her arm so she can hold him like a makeshift teddy bear. Everything hurts, so she figures being on her side can't be any worse than lying on her back.

And she wants to hold someone—something. Anything will do; she doesn't fight when Terrence offers himself as tribute.

For the time being, any doubts she has about him are resolved. He's the one there for her. She doesn't pester him with questions about where he was when everything happened. By the look on his face, he feels bad enough.

He didn't know.

"Of course, I didn't."

She realizes that her mind's guard is let down. *Is the secret of the bookshelf hidden by Death's magic or my own?* Even jogging her memory with it is dangerous; when Terrence doesn't seem to notice or bring it up, she assumes that her hunch must be correct. It is a secret only she and Death carry. Some sort of magic is keeping it from Terrence even when her mind isn't guarded. It's a relief to know. She's glad to avoid a fight or any tension. *Just let me feel comfort. All I've felt is pain.*

"Thank you," she whispers into his fur. Its void-like substance becomes familiar; she doesn't mind that his body heat stings against her injuries.

"For what? I left you," he huffs. There's a tremor in his voice that sounds as though he's been crying. "I left you alone and that awful thing came in here and could've *killed* you. Or worse…." His red eyes are drenched in sadness. There's no mistaking the twinkle in his eye for anything other than the presence of tears.

"I take it I missed my first day of work?"

Terrence hangs his head. "I'm afraid so, darling. You've been asleep for a week now. I couldn't wake you. I called him and told him you'd been in an accident. He's happy to take you on once you've recovered."

A twinge of hope starts in Clarisse's heart. "So, I'm not out of luck entirely?"

Terrence gives her a sad smile. "No, but you're going to take a while to recover. I realize my mistake now. I need to train you to defend yourself before I ever leave again." He tucks himself tighter under the covers.

She can't see his face, but she knows it's probably warped by sadness and tears. She tries not to think about it too much. Worry for him eats at her.

"You shouldn't worry about me. You could have died, Clarisse. Far before your time."

Clarisse lifts the covers to look Terrence in the eye. "Terrence, I'm okay," she whispers. "He's gone. I managed. I don't know how and, yeah, I got hurt. But that's part of life, right? We can't avoid getting hurt."

"By spider gods from the Afterlife? Yes, Clarisse, that's normal. That's a normal way to get hurt."

Clarisse sputters to life with laughter. It racks her ribcage with pain, but she doesn't stop. The feeling is enough to make the ache worth it.

"You know what I mean."

His head lowers against the mattress, ears slightly flat against his head. He does, in moments like this, look very much like a normal "dog" or "wolf."

"I do know what you mean," he starts, "but I told you I would work with you to set you free. To release you from the pain you experienced. I don't want to bring you *more* pain. That's the last thing I'd ever want to do."

The words echoing in her mind from previous conversations with Death become dull. He can't possibly be plotting against her. Death is blowing things out of proportion or has things all wrong. However, something Ralun said comes to mind.

"Ralun talked about your 'goal' or 'master plan' when we fought? I assume he's just crazy but did you really work with him once upon a time?"

Terrence looks a bit surprised, but if that emotion was present, it disappears within seconds. "I figured he'd bring that up. I did, in fact, work with him. He worked for me, rather. When I first broke away from Death, I had... aspirations. I realize now that many of them were foolish; some of my ex-followers have yet to see that. When I realized that I had the powers of a Selbena, I got a bit... power-hungry. I didn't allow myself to see my own limitations.

Much like you, I was 'high' on freedom—freedom from working for Death."

The wheels in Clarisse's head turn at full speed. Suddenly, the disconnect between Death and Terrence makes more sense.

"I've matured now; I'm sorry to say it but he likely won't be the first that you run into."

Clarisse freezes, her muscles tensing. "What?" She winces, trying to pull herself up into a full sitting position, immediately regretting it but following through.

"I had more followers. They'll show up, too. Ralun was not the most radical among my legions. I'm going to have to train you to defend yourself, Clarisse. I'm sorry. I'll be here next time, of course... but if I'm ever going to go out and get supplies for us, I have to know that in the short spells when you're alone, that you're able to keep things at bay without coming so close to... dying...." He chokes the word out like he can't believe it either.

"Terrence..." Clarisse tries to find something to say, but comes up empty. Instead, she slides back beneath the covers and lets her body lay flat.

She feels childish as she clutches to the old hope that the covers will shield her from whatever *other* dark creatures are out there. She hadn't thought to ask Terrence about other beings like him. Nor had she thought to ask if they might want to *consume* her or murder her because of her abilities.

Morbid curiosity overwhelms her. "Terrence? What happens when another being consumes you for your power? And don't you dare make a joke about cannibalism."

Terrence snickers, a mischievous gleam in his eye. "What would make you think of me as being so callous?"

He sneers at her, sitting up. His massive frame blots out the light from the window. Clarisse shudders that, despite his shadowy form, no light passes through him. She wonders why that never bothered her before. Shivers spark and pop along her spine.

He is darkness incarnate.

"Basically, when they consume your energy, your soul is removed from the powers it possesses. You might be reincarnated as something else; you might just pass on altogether. Usually, it's the latter, but by becoming unattached from a part of yourself, things can get… tricky…."

Clarisse's eyes widen. "Wait, what?"

"You become severed. Part of you lives on inside the creature that consumed you—the part of you that possessed power is absorbed by them. Part of your conscience has to decide if it wants to go with that part of you or be reincarnated… it's complicated."

The way he says it makes it worse; Clarisse can't fathom something so awful.

Severed?

"Can you get your power back once it becomes severed from you?"

Terrence pauses. The look on his face tells Clarisse that it's best she proceed with caution.

"I would think it would be impossible to do so. It depends on how powerful you are, how long you've been severed, what kind of being consumed the power and so forth. I've never heard someone ask that question. Consumption is rather rare since it is considered to be so barbaric. I take it Ralun threatened you with this?"

Clarisse nods.

"Well, if it helps, creatures have to be incredibly powerful to sever someone. He likely would have failed and just slaughtered you. He might have gotten pieces of your power but at that point, it's not the same as consumption."

"Ah, good. I would've just died then. That makes me feel *so* much better."

Terrence's ears flatten with embarrassment and Clarisse realizes it's probably best to let that one drop. She knows he feels bad as it is. "I'm kidding, Terrence. But thanks for clearing that up. I was worried when he mentioned it. Is there any way you can guard yourself against consumption?"

A light seems to sparkle in Terrence's eyes. "There are plenty of spells you can learn." He hops from the bed. "Right now, though, I would get comfortable with one of the books on your shelf or spend some more time sleeping. You're going to need a lot of rest."

"I'm hopeless," she groans. She reaches for a book, but she can't summon the courage to magic it her way. And standing terrifies her. Terrence notices her struggling and grabs the copy for her.

Terrence pauses in the doorway after making sure she's comfortable. "You're not hopeless. I hope you realize you managed to fight off a very dangerous creature from the Afterlife single-handedly. That's more than amazing. You deserve to see yourself as a righteous badass." With that, he disappears.

A smile quirks on Clarisse's face as she buries herself in her book.

I am badass.

23

SOMETHING LIKE NORMAL?

Clarisse

A week passes and Clarisse can sit without everything burning. She spoke with Mr. Harris and explained things away as a horrible ladder accident. He wasn't happy, but he was far from angry. Just disappointed, at least in how he sounded, that he couldn't have his seamstress as early as he wanted. But her job was secure— all she had to do was show up when she was ready with her paperwork.

She's fumbling with the pages right now, wishing she felt strong enough to go. Terrence steps into her room, pausing to look at the stack of finished books on her table and chuckles. "Bored, are we?"

Clarisse rolls her eyes at him. "Now, you know that's a dumb question."

Terrence sticks his tongue out at her. Since the incident, they've been enjoying each other's company with far less tension. The fiasco at the motel seems like eons ago. By not using magic for a week, Clarisse feels recharged—new. It makes her suspicious that Death is probably right. It probably isn't healthy. But Terrence hasn't been pushing her and no new creatures have come through the door. He's been steady at her side since that night, making sure she's never truly alone, except to go to the bathroom or shower.

"I know, I know." His interruption breaks her from her thoughts.

She smiles at him, holding her papers with a thin string of hope attached to them. "Do you think we can go to the mall today? I really want to start working."

Terrence's face scrunches up. "Work? Gross. I think you should stay here with me." He puts on the most dramatic face a shadow wolf can muster and starts fake sobbing. "What about the home? Who will read all the books on your shelves again? Who will keep me company when I have to sit there like a dog and be *quiet* all day, pretending I don't exist."

Clarisse cackles. It's all ludicrous. She realizes, though, that this likely means that he's okay with her going back out. Her heart starts thudding faster. "Does this mean you'll go with me?"

He gives her a look of *"Duh, stupid."* She doesn't have to read his mind to know it's what he's thinking.

"Would you like to run into another creature of the darkness alone?"

Clarisse shakes her head rapidly, pausing a moment to grab at her neck when the pain catches up to her. The twinges remind her that she still has to take it easy.

"No," she grumbles.

"What? Are you offended to have me with you in public?" He adds on a fake sniffle to return to his dramatic approach.

"Oh, brother. Of course not!"

He breaks into laughter, giving Clarisse a mischievous smirk. "I suppose we can go see Mr. Harris. Is all your paperwork in order?"

"Yes!" Clarisse is on her feet before Terrence has time to say anything else. She's running to the bathroom, a pair of fresh clothes in hand.

"How long have you been holding your outfit for?"

"Don't worry about it!" She shuts the door with an excited slam. Slamming doors was strictly prohibited. Here? It's *her* house. *Her* rules.

She giggles, throwing on her outfit, making sure to brush her hair and make herself look presentable.

"Maybe I can buy some makeup after work? Or on break?"

There's silence.

"So I can look more presentable for work?"

"Do you not own any?"

Clarisse pauses. "Well, no."

"How did I not notice this?"

Clarisse opens the bathroom door, a pair of khakis and a button-up shirt her chosen attire. She's grateful that Terrence grabbed clothes while he was away, even if that meant more time fighting Ralun alone. Mary Janes and old dresses weren't going to work and she didn't have the time or strength to sew something new.

"Because you never asked?"

"Point taken." Terrence looks her up and down. "Not bad. You clean up nice," he teases. For a second, the comment stings. She's never been given compliments that didn't come with taunts attached. When they don't come, the ache relaxes a bit. Still, she knows she's not pretty. She's awkward. Underweight. Gangly. Short. Her acne is clearing up but, still, she's not anything to look at. So not being called ugly is a first. Light brown eyes and dull brown hair never has any bounce to it just don't speak to her. *Or do me any favors.*

"Why do you have such little confidence in yourself? I think your eyes and hair are beautiful."

Clarisse shrugs, walking towards the door.

Terrence rushes forward, stopping her at the entryway. "I need an answer."

"Well, I'm not the prettiest thing in the world. I know that. I just wish I'd been born with better... attributes, I guess. I'm very plain."

Terrence frowns a bit, cocking his head to the side. "First of all, you're not ugly. Nor are you plain. Clarisse, you're *eighteen*. Not everyone is born to look like a supermodel. And beauty is very subjective. You're beautiful in your own right. You have survived hell and made it look easy compared to anyone around you. You've taken all these changes in your life in stride and I've only known you for half a month. That's nothing in the scheme of things. And already, you're starting to 'fill out' since you can eat properly and I'm sure you'll feel and *look* better—not just aesthetically—now that you're able to take care of yourself. My goodness, child. Give yourself a break. I think really think you look wonderful. And you look better and better every day now that you're free to take care of yourself, regardless of your figure or hair color. All of that is pointless. It's the way you wear your soul that counts; you wear it with stunning grace."

Clarisse is redder than Rudolph's nose and she buries her face in her hands. "Th-thanks," she stammers.

Terrence laughs. "Not a bit shy, are we?"

"Nope, not at all," she lets out a nervous string of clipped laughter, moving past him into the hallway. He looks a bit confused, but she trusts that he can figure it out. It's not like she's going to just *believe* him that she looks good. Why would she?

"You will. In time."

Crap. I forgot.

She chooses not to seal her mind off, even though she is well enough to resume that task. Having him in her thoughts is comforting. She only seals off the ones that have anything to do with Death; even then, those feel like sins.

"Hey, Terrence?"

"Yes?"

"How are we going to get to work?"

Terrence grins. "Not to worry!"

They step outside the house and, in the driveway, is a car. Clarisse screams. "When did you get that and how?"

"I have connections. Now quick, get in."

Clarisse stares at him like she's been shot. "I... I don't know how... I've never...."

"Oh, don't worry about that. It's simple!"

Of course, it was not simple. It was a miracle that either of them managed to step out of the car alive when they pulled into the mall parking lot.

"Driving lessons," Terrence slurs. "Remind me... to get you...

driving lessons." He's panting like a real dog, shifting into that form, his tongue becoming more pink and *normal* as he heaves from the terror that they encountered. Clarisse is waiting for blue lights to pop up at any minute. An insane asylum is just a car crash away.

I won't be able to control anything if I get myself into that kind of trouble.

"You'll get the hang of it. Now, you have a job to get to."

Clarisse nods. "Wait, don't I look kind of normal for someone who fell off a ladder?"

"Snap! I didn't think of that!"

Terrence mutters something for a bit before giving her a hard stare. She finds herself with a brace along her back.

"Can't have broken arms if you're going to sew, now can you?"

Clarisse rolls her eyes. "Fair."

A few people stare while she talks to Terrence aloud. She makes note that she needs to keep their conversations in their head as the mall doors swing open.

Last year's top forty songs greet her as she makes her way to the second floor. Mr. Harris' eyes brighten at the sight of his new employee. She doesn't even have to say anything, just hand him the paperwork and, to her surprise, he hugs her.

"I was so worried about you, kid! Here I thought I'd just lost my best future employee before she could even start!"

Clarisse laughs nervously. "Yeah, it was scary. I felt so bad; I'm really sorry I had to call off like that. Luckily I didn't break my arm. Just sprained my back really bad. I think I'm good to do some sewing now. Just gotta keep this brace on."

Mr. Harris sets her paperwork down and claps his hands together. "Not to worry at all! I'm just glad you're not hurt! You don't strike me as the type to just up and leave your job, anyhow."

"Not unless it's a job under your father…."

Shut up, Terrence.

Clarisse smiles, choosing to let silence serve as her answer. Mr. Harris isn't wrong. She hated every moment not being able to start at a job that meant so much to her. "So, when do we get started?"

Mr. Harris laughs. "Eager, are we?"

"Absolutely!" Clarisse spends the next few hours reading manuals, filling out more paperwork, and taking in everything she can.

On her break, she buys some makeup. At the end of her shift, she enjoys a small dinner from the food court before leaving. After they get home, Terrence beams at her as she takes off her shoes and collapses on the living room couch.

"That went wonderfully," he chirps. "I can't believe how well you did! Well, I can… but whatever. That was great!"

Clarisse laughs, sweaty from wearing her back brace all day; she's more than relieved when she peels it off. Her body still aches, so she doesn't feel so bad for faking a specific injury when, in fact, her back and *more* were hurt from the exchange with Ralun.

"You're honest to a fault, you know that?"

Clarisse rolls her eyes. "We literally lied about everything we did when we were talking to my parents."

"Fair. Fair. But overall, you really don't like being deceptive, do you?"

Clarisse shakes her head. She reaches into her bag—a new one she purchased at the mall along with her makeup—and pulls out a newspaper. She doesn't typically care for her town's shenanigans, but today, she figures she'll give it a read.

Nothing seems extraordinarily out of place. The usual thefts are reported; a few community initiatives that mean nothing have already begun to fade from the cheap ink. What catches her eye, though, is the "missing" section of the paper. A few runaways, children, and pets have been listed. But at the top of the page is the worst possible thing she can imagine.

It's a photo of her.

"Terrence?"

"Yes?"

"I think Death's spell to erase my parents' memories worked a little too well." She hands him the paper, her heart threatening to explode.

"What do we do?"

Terrence frowns, his face furrowing where his eyebrows might've been were he not woven of darkness itself. "Well… this could be problematic."

Before he can say anything further, things get worse. They turn just in time to see a strange, large, fanged serpent weaving through the door.

Another monster has found its way inside the house.

~

Terrence

Before Terrence can react, the black, smoking snake swipes at Clarisse. The fangs make their way through her flesh, leaving angry red marks in their wake. She screams. He pounces between them, refusing to let Clarisse get hurt a second time.

This creature has no name that Terrence knows of, but he recognizes him as one of Ralun's followers. News of his defeat must be spreading like wildfire in Tyrladan. No mortal has ever survived an encounter with Ralun, much less defeated him.

He bares his teeth at the snake, emitting a low growl that fills the air with spitting heat. The room's temperature rises to a boil. Clarisse isn't moving. As far as Terrence can tell, it's going to be up to him to save her.

Which is only fair.

He brushes her aside, pushing her onto the floor in front of the couch so it can act as a protective barrier. Snarling at the awful serpent that's weaving in and out, he awaits an opportunity to strike. The serpent hesitates.

Terrence smiles, wildfire brimming in his red eyes, spilling out from the edges. His body is aflame, the shadow of his fur akin to charcoal in a furnace. He's ready to end this.

"Don't you dare touch Clarisse again."

"S-she killed Ralun."

Terrence laughs out loud, sensing Clarisse's confusion on the air.

He worries about her and the bite. It can't be good, with only so long to help her treat it. His powers are limited. He's better at outright destruction than healing or creation. It's why he's been more of an accelerant for her than an outright help.

The truth is, if he'd tried to build the house with her, they might have a tinderbox instead.

But now? Now was the time for his exact skill set.

The room is engulfed with flames. They skate along the furniture and walls, leaving them unscathed. The flames stay hungry. They only have one thing they can cling to—their intended target. The snake screams.

Terrence defeats the creature in little more than a blink.

"Pity," he scoffs at the ashes where the snake once lay.

He rushes to Clarisse on the floor, her skin pale and sweat beading along her skin. Her body tremors from the venom traveling in her veins.

"Clarisse," he says frantically, "look up at me."

He tries to avoid sounding as panicked as he is. She needs reassurance, not fear.

He helps her up onto the couch. "Clarisse, I need you to use a healing spell. Like you did with me. I need you to focus; I know you're tired and I know that you've been hurt like all hell, but I need you to live. You can't give up on me."

To his surprise, he's crying. He's never cried before—not like this. This little woman is his only friend. He regrets much of what she will have to do to help fulfill his plans, but he never intended to have her hurt like this. She was supposed to be the key, supposed to help him find utopia—to build it with him. To be by his side as his friend.

"Clarisse, please."

She's shaking, but he breathes a bit when he sees a light start to glow in her fingertips. Her hand cradles her arm where the fangs did their damage. The entry points become sealed; within seconds, the healing is done. At least partly…

Her head lolls to the side of the sofa. For an hour, he listens to her pulse. In time, it's strong and regular. A breath escapes his lips and relief overwhelms him.

He carries her up to his room once he's sure that disturbing her won't make things worse. Setting her on the bed, he sits by her side with no intention of leaving. A thought dawns on him and he summons the newspaper from downstairs. Admittedly, he's taxed. Using magic in the mortal world at such magnitude isn't easy— especially when emotions are involved.

The newspaper planted in front of him, he reads. He's appalled at how well Death's magic does at erasing people's memories. Clarisse's parents truly know nothing about their daughter's escape, according to the reports. Father Simmons has a statement added into the report alongside her parents' statement, describing her as an adoptive daughter. To them, nothing happened. There was no exorcism. Not in their minds.

While the physical scars are gone from Clarisse's skin, Terrence knows they're deeper than that. He fumes at the thought that they can just *forget*.

How dare he give them that much of a pass. They wanted to murder her.

His eyes soften at the sight of her chest rising and falling. He's glad to see the pallor to her skin has disappeared, replaced with its normal, healthy glow. The magic she used was too much too soon, but if she didn't heal herself, Death would have been imminent— literally and figuratively.

He closes his eyes, thinking of ways to combat this new threat, alongside the monsters that appear every time Clarisse walks through the door.

"If they see her at the tailor's or Mr. Harris realizes she's missing," he grumbles, "I have another fiasco to handle aside from the one we're already facing."

Clarisse mumbles something in her sleep and his eyes widen.

Can she hear me right now?

She grunts, rolling over, tousling her hair in the process.

I suppose not. He chuckles.

She's a ray of sunshine in his dark world—he can't imagine a life without her. Truly.

Now he just has to work out a plan to hide her. To keep her safe.

But how can I do that?

For now, the most he can do is confine himself to the spot next to her on the floor and plot. His plans are best thought out without interruption. He'll take advantage of the quiet.

Don't worry Clarisse. I'll keep you safe. I'll figure out this mess. We'll change the world together, still. You'll see.

24

BREAKING

Clarisse

Clarisse wakes up, her hair a sweaty, matted mess. She's had nightmares back-to-back. Now that she's blinking and aware, they recede to a distant past. She's never quite that good at remembering dreams. Snippets might come back to her, but they're all nonsensical and never worth remembering anyhow.

She pulls the covers off, making a beeline for the bathroom. Vomit threatens to rise up; her skin is sticky with sweat. Barely keeping herself from puking, she takes a moment to collect herself. She needs a shower and bad. She doesn't see Terrence; her heart rate quickens at the thought of being alone in the bathroom. He can't follow her in there anyway and she doesn't want to risk being seen naked by some *other* monster if they keep showing up.

The memory of the snake… *thing*… is fresh in her mind, though most of it is a blur after she was bitten. The venom worked fast, leaving her a curled-up ball of pain and delusion on the floor. She can't remember anything in terms of how she felt or what she thought, other than that she was ready to meet her end.

She briefly recalls Terrence ordering her to heal herself. Before she takes a shower, she steps back out into the bedroom. She needs to make sure he's there before she does anything to make herself more vulnerable than she already is. Any power she had was zapped in making sure the venom was removed from her system.

"Terrence?" She walks into the hallway, grimacing as she notices the bloodstains on her shirt. She must have clutched her arm there while she was on the floor. While the marks on her arm are gone, the remnants of the violence are not.

I wonder how you get blood out of shirts.

Her feet find their way down the stairs; Terrence is curled up on the couch in the living room.

His ears perk up when he sees her. "Clarisse, are you alright?"

"Yeah, I was just worried. I wanted to know where you'd gone." Terrence sighs. "I'm alright. You should be more worried about yourself, I would think," he chides gently. "You need to get back up and into the bed."

"Terrence, I need to take a shower. I'm covered in blood and sweat." She covers her mouth. "I want to hurl. I need to get into some pajamas. I'm not ignoring my needs, I'm just… making sure you're okay." She lowers her head, not sure why he's upset with her for getting up to go see him, but the worry in his face is evident. "Are you sure you're alright?"

He cocks his head to the side. "Sometimes, I think you're too insightful for your own good. No. I'm not alright. I'm a bit drained. It's hard to do rough magic under so much duress. Plus, if I hadn't erased that creature as fast as I had, that venom… it… it would've *killed* you."

Clarisse's jaw tightens. "Killed me?"

"Yes. Any creature from Tyrladan is probably going to kill you if it strikes you, slices you, or bites you in any fashion that involves poison. It's a miracle you… you survived," his voice cracks. "I thought I'd lost you."

Silence envelops them both. In moments like these, Clarisse is reminded why she trusted Terrence. Whether or not his motives are sound in Death's eyes, they're at least genuine.

Or so I believe….

She's relieved when he doesn't respond. It means she's still strong enough to keep him from intruding on her thoughts. She worries that even using that much magic, though, will damage her body. Even now, the tendrils of the land beyond life brush against her--tempting her to give in. Her soul feels... *loose.* Like her body is a pair of clothes she's ready to take off and put through the wash for the last time.

The thought makes her grow pale.

Am I dying?

"I hope you'll forgive me, but I'm going to carry you back upstairs. I can't imagine how you're handling the trauma of everything you've been through right now."

Clarisse nods as Terrence leans down so she can sit atop his massive shoulders. He carries her up the stairs with little effort, setting her down once they've reached her bathroom.

"I'll go back downstairs while you shower. I've got extra protections around the place so there should be no more intrusions. And if there are," his eyes glint, "I'll be there with consequences for them in no time. So just relax and enjoy your shower. I'll set your pajamas out for you."

Clarisse stares at him for a moment.

"Are you sure you don't want to talk? I'm okay, Terrence."

No, I'm not.

Clarisse hates lying, but she doesn't need her only friend worrying for her. Not right now. She needs to do that for herself first, once she's alone.

"I... I know you are. Just wash up. I'll be alright. I have some things I need to think about in terms of how I can protect you moving forward."

Clarisse lets it go from there, softly closing the door behind her. Satisfied that the door is latched and that there are no other monsters lurking behind the curtains, she takes off her clothes and steps into the shower.

The cold feeling of being split in "two" lingers. She wonders if she might close her eyes for the last time if she keeps leaning up against the shower wall like she is. Every time she shuts her eyes, she worries they won't open again—that each breath might actually be her last. Once she's satisfied that Terrence is downstairs, she lets herself sob.

She keeps it quiet—she's mastered that much, but her body racks from the pain. Everything hurts, like she might give out.

Her head pulses as she takes extra care to lather every part of her with soap. It smells of lavender and honey. She focuses on the scent as a way to dissociate from the pain. It's not as successful as she needs it to be; she crumples to the ground and holds herself in a ball on the shower floor.

Am I dying?

To answer her question, her chest heaves. She feels that she might lose a lung if she keeps coughing this hard. Stifling a scream, she sees it—blood. It leaves her mouth and coats the floor of the shower. Her body convulses. She prays Terrence can't hear her. All at once, the flashing images of Death's warnings spiral to the forefront of her mind.

How much of my future have I sacrificed? What have I done?

She can't breathe. Her lip trembles. The panic in her body overwhelms her. She can't help or fight it now, so she gives in. Terrence still hasn't heard; the bathroom door isn't being smashed in and no one is coming to her rescue.

I can't keep going like this.

She wobbles, grabbing the railing in the shower as she stands, turning the water off and grabbing the towel waiting for her on the rack just outside the shower.

I've lost a lot.

Her lip still trembles. She carefully wraps the towel around her body and steps into the bedroom, grabbing the pajamas Terrence set out for her.

I need to see Death. Now.

She knows it's a fool's errand to try and get him to come here now. It would take too much strength. She doesn't know how to summon Death aside from actually dying. And that's everything she's trying to avoid right now. Performing spells is basically suicide and she's not about to risk everything for a conversation that she already knows the ending to.

She runs her hands through her matted, wet hair. For some reason, it sets her off. Manic desires to make herself pretty overwhelm her. Frustrated as she keeps hitting knots, she goes back into the bathroom and grabs a hairbrush. When she starts pulling, she stifles another scream as hair begins to fall out of her scalp if she pulls too hard. Her hands are shaking as she goes even more gently against the tyranny of those knots that seem to be conspiring against her—to make her bald. Her breathing is erratic and her pupils have become so dilated that she can't see the irises anymore. *I need to stop. Hair can wait.*

She wants to talk to someone. Anyone. But for some reason, a little feeling in her gut says Terrence isn't the person to be talking to.

He's worried enough as it is; I think he's actually lying. I think there's more to this.

She's not sure what to do. A thought strikes her.

Would there be books on summoning Death in my library?

Clarisse realizes she's sinking to the ground, a hairbrush still going through the strands of her ever-thinning hair while she walks about. She wonders if she can grow it back, pieces of her soul cracking in two at the sight of every strand that leaves.

I need to stop brushing. A sob breaks through her. *I don't want to die yet.*

She tries to compose herself when she hears Terrence's footsteps.

"Clarisse, are you alright?" When he enters the room, the air heats up. He smells danger; she can see it in his eyes. "What's going on?"

She puts the brush behind her back; in the process of pulling it behind her, she rips a chunk of hair from her head. This time, she can't help it. She screams.

Before she can do anything, Terrence is with her. He pulls her so she can sit on the mattress and does his best to soothe her. She can't hide the bloody towel now. His eyes land on it before she can swipe it beneath the bed or anywhere that he might not see.

"Clarisse?" She coughs.

"Terrence… I'm dying…."

Terrence freezes. "You're not dying. You're not dying. That's impossible; we've been so careful!" The way his voice cracks betrays him. Oddly, it only irritates Clarisse.

Clarisse rolls her eyes. She can't hide her frustration with him right now. Or with any of the things she's having to deal with. This is too much for her to handle. He should *know*.

"We have not. I had to fight off a damned spider monster and heal myself from the fatal venom of some freak snake—both of them crawled straight out of literal *Hell*, I might add! I don't even know what I'm doing, either, so when I actually use the magic, I'm having to use it at the extreme and it's not controlled. Terrence, I don't even know *how* to fight. I let my fear drive a natural instinct that's probably really volatile. Did you ever stop to think of that?"

Her chest is rising and falling so fast she fears she might shatter her ribs—she's like a porcelain doll right now. "Death was right. I am taking years off of my life by doing all this. Is there any way to undo the damage? Is there any way to stop this? Because now, as you say, they're all going to start showing up. More monsters from Hell. More responsibilities. More 'small' reasons to use magic. That all adds up! I'm only eighteen, Terrence!" She's crying so hard she can't see. Wincing, she expects him to get angry for mentioning Death and flinches when he gets near her face. Only when her own tears clear does she see his.

"I'm so sorry, Clarisse," he whispers. "I really never meant for you to get hurt. I know you've heard a lot of things about me. And many of them *were* true. I do have plans. I wanted you in them. But you were never supposed to get hurt. You were never supposed to succumb to the same fate I did."

"Am I damned?" She can't stop the question before it comes tumbling out. She looks at Terrence and considers his form. Does she want to be *just* like him? Working against a punishment that robs her of her humanity for all eternity for trying to save herself? "How is any of this fair? Why do we have to pay for being different? Not even Death seemed happy with those rules; if he's not happy with them, why not change them?"

Terrence hangs his head low. He doesn't say anything; Clarisse can tell from the look on his face that he's just as defeated as she is. Her heartstrings are tugged by his obvious show of remorse.

"Terrence, look at me," she demands.

The sudden shift in her tone grabs his attention.

"I want you to understand something: you're my best friend. I don't want you to beat yourself up for whatever happens. I just wish you'd told me your plans sooner so I could've made more educated choices. And not painted Death as just an enemy to dismiss. You never dismiss an enemy, Terrence. Never. And just because I talked to him, doesn't mean I don't trust you." Clarisse takes a breath. "And I'm only going to say this once. When you got mad, it made me more inclined *not* to trust you than trust you as I always did. I was honestly terrified of you when we left that motel. I thought you were going to hurt me."

Terrence looks taken aback at this. "Why would I ever hurt you?"

"Terrence, you gave off some super-scary vibes when you found out I talked to him. I know now you were just angry at Death, but I... I didn't know what to do for you or how to make you stop being angry with me. I need answers, Terrence. What you've been up to... Why? I want you to explain things."

Terrence sighs. "I can tell you about those things tomorrow. Right now, you need to go to bed."

Hurt feelings fill her body. She knows he's dodging; after opening up to him like this, it breaks her in half to have him just walk away from the conversation. "Terrence, we need to talk."

The temperature in the room spikes again.

"Clarisse, I'm not in the mood."

Once again, she's left in a cloud of sadness and confusion when he leaves the room.

Does he hate me for telling him? Will he ever tell me the truth?

Her heart catches in her throat and her eyes water again. She can't sleep now. She's just learned she's dying and he just... up and *leaves* her.

"What are you up to? Why won't you tell me the truth?" Her eyes fall on the bookshelf in her room. Judging by the way he stormed off, Terrence isn't coming back any time soon. It's time to get some answers. And she's betting that the library behind her wall might have some.

25

THE BEGINNING AND THE END

Clarisse

Confident that the bookshelf is shut behind her, she rummages through the titles lining her walls. It hurts to move, but determination alone fuels her. While some are pleasure reads, others are more informative. Books on the consequences of using magic, the lore of Tyrladan, and so much more wait at her fingertips. She gives herself a mental smack in the face for not reading some of these sooner. There's an arsenal at her disposal that she hasn't used.

The ballroom is still in shattered pieces because Terrence either can't be bothered to fix it or is unable to and Clarisse is now on the brink of taking her last breath.

Alone.

Her mouth goes sour as the image of Terrence leaving her keeps coming back. He's blowing hot and cold too much for her to understand. She starts by opening one of the books about dying; she doesn't see anything about Death specifically in terms of his physical form, but she knows that he likely wouldn't make such a clue *that* obvious.

Hours pass while she wishes she had a window to see the sunrise and sunset. The plush, gray carpet grabs at her body, making it hard to stay awake as she turns the pages.

In this book is the process of dying, different ways that people die, and limited information about the soul. Her eyes fall on an intriguing chapter: *The Origins of Life and Death.*

In the beginning, there were Two—Tryta and Siralto. Together, they wove the fabric of the known universes into the land known today as Tyrladan. Within it, they filled its infinite branches with worlds anew. They created the Balance. They created everything that lives and breathes.

Tryta and Siralto loved each other from the beginning, working together to create a system treating all fairly and without favoritism. Every creature was given a purpose, defined and true.

Clarisse yawns. "This is a horrible way to catalog such an important thing. Who wrote this?"

She flips the book over but can't find an author's name. Shrugging, she continues.

They were the model for everyone to follow. Their minds knew no bounds. One day, Siralto transgressed against Tryta by creating Earth. A world where people could reproduce. The Earth's resources were finite; the inhabitants would eventually outlive their means. An experiment, she called it. But Tryta, our Lord and Savior, saw the evil of such a plan.

Seeking to right the system, by murdering his wayward wife, he created the mechanism that would save this world in Tyrladan from becoming overfilled with Life—Death.

Clarisse snaps the book shut. Her eyes are wide and her veins are filled with fury. She searches again for an author name, ready to throttle whoever it was who wrote about Siralto that way. Something in her tells her that a lot is missing from this recounting of the "beginning," as the author called it. She wonders why this even bothers her in the first place. All her life she'd known religion to be a giant scam, thanks to Father Simmons. All she knew about were stories of the Great Light. Clarisse wonders if Siralto inspired those stories. Or even Tryta.

Were they even there? Was Earth just an experiment by Siralto? And how is creating something on her own a transgression against Tryta? What kind of controlling, manipulative, asshole....

She hears footsteps from beyond the door. They echo from the empty hallway outside her room. Clarisse quickly tosses the book aside, sliding the bookshelf open and clicking it shut behind her. She sits back down on the bed, trying to make sure she looks like she's been there for a while when Terrence enters the room. The twinkling of sunshine through the window tells her that it's going to be time to go to work soon. She groans.

"Tough getting sleep?" Terrence's voice is cold; Clarisse is a bit shocked at how he's acting, having learned that she's going to die. Of course, she remembers that once upon a time he was a Reaper.

Has it made him less sensitive? Why does he keep flipping back and forth like this?

Her mind can't process it all. "Yeah. Didn't get much, honestly. I'll get ready for work."

She leaves him standing there, being short to him in return. Somehow, she feels like maybe he's not so sorry after all. What plans was she a part of? He never really cleared that up.

If he'll explain at all. He likes being tight-lipped when it comes to talking about eventualities.

"I'm ready to go."

The ride to work is silent, but she is getting better at driving. Much more focused on the road, she ignores Terrence altogether. Out of the corner of her eye, it looks like he's bothered by her silence. This is *his* fault, too. She shouldn't have played along, and she won't walk into this trap either.

"Alright, let's go." He follows her in.

"What do we do if someone recognizes me?"

"I'm not sure."

No one is there to catch her talking to Terrence this time, but some passersby catch her face when he drops that last bomb on her.

What do you mean?

"I don't know what to do. This is all beyond my capacity to understand or handle."

His eyes are blank of any emotion. Her heart feels like it's been shredded to pieces. Her mind starts to understand what she's seeing. Is he... mourning now? Acting like she's already not there, to make the end easier?

A million different thoughts spin through her head while she works. She skips lunch, her stomach in too much pain to bear anything in it.

As a result, Mr. Harris lets her off early. "You're making good strides, kid. I'm really proud of you!"

The twinkle in his eye gets Clarisse to smile, but it doesn't reach her eyes with her high level of pain. Her veins look like spiderwebs; she knows she'll have to start covering them in makeup to prevent suspicion. *I wish I could just go to a doctor.*

So far, no one has noticed her as the girl in the newspaper.

"Thanks," she smiles. "I hope I can keep making you proud as long as I can."

It's a strange thing to say, she realizes, but Mr. Harris doesn't catch the darker meaning behind it. Of course, he doesn't. How could anyone possibly figure out that she's dying? That her time is almost worn out?

"I think you will!" He stays this cheery while he locks the door behind them, whistling some tune she doesn't recognize. She doesn't bother to pester him with the name. Why should she?

I'm not gonna be alive long to enjoy it, anyway. And my ballroom is... destroyed.

Her throat chokes up and brings her feet to a halt. After a few deep breaths, she catches up. She can't afford to let anyone see her break, let alone her boss. She wants to be remembered as strong —stoic.

They part ways; Clarisse is still bothered when Terrence doesn't want to address *anything*. He won't answer her questions and remains a brick wall of nothingness on the way home. She, frankly, wants to throttle him for putting her in this situation in the first place and then leaving her to wonder.

"Are you ever going to talk?"

She finally presses the issue when they've got the car in park and are in the driveway. By some miracle, she has yet to be noticed or stopped by police for driving without a license.

"What do you mean?"

He blinks at her, trying to give off the appearance of innocence. That, of course, doesn't work.

"Are you serious? You talked about me being a part of your 'plans.' There's a whole admission you gave that you realized there were risks involved in what we're doing and you're not going to address them? At all?"

Terrence's eyes flicker and, for a moment, Clarisse swears she can see sparks in them—actual little flames.

"Terrence, I thought you said my explanation for being afraid of you was sound the other day."

He only nods.

"Don't give me a reason to be afraid of you now," she stammers. Her skin is clammy and she's sweating. Something about this whole situation doesn't seem right. He looks like a ghost... an eerie shadow.

"Please, I'm not trying to make you angry or not be appreciative of everything, but... I don't think I have a whole lot of time left. And I want to know if there's a way to reverse that or if I need to 'settle my affairs' and enjoy what time I do have left."

She thinks the request sounds reasonable but, to her dismay, Terrence chooses not to answer. They stand there for some time, without resolution.

She huffs, crossing her arms. He's getting harder to read and predict every day. Part of it, she realizes, is her fault. She's not letting him hear her thoughts anymore; while he can't hear them, he has to know that she's hiding things from him. He's not stupid.

But after how he acted in the motel….

She shudders at the thought. Realizing they've been sitting in the driveway, just simmering in silence, she tries a new approach.

"Terrence? I think we need to attempt to be more communicative. Why don't we go inside and play a game?"

His ears perk up, giving her hope that there may be a chance at reviving their friendship. She doesn't want to lose him, no matter how reckless he's been with her life and limb on behalf of some plan he won't yet reveal.

"What kind of game?"

"You pick." She figures being amiable is the best approach. Flexibility is the best way to get to him. How else can she hope to salvage anything with him?

"I think we should play checkers."

Clarisse nods. "Alright. Let's go inside and play."

She needs him to be cooperative. Sound. She needs answers now more than ever if she's going to save herself. The depression at the thought of dying weighs upon her every molecule. It's not at all like reality is portrayed in modern media—as much as she's seen of it, anyway. Instead of sobbing and crying and being dramatic like they portray it, it's a dull ache in her chest that never seems to leave. It's exhaustion creeping at her veins and eating her alive. It's a sense of loneliness even when she has someone with her. It's tearing her apart. And she needs it to go away.

Something inside her tells her that it won't. Not for a very long time.

26

GAMES

Clarisse

Clarisse's eyes glaze over as Terrence procures a checkerboard from thin air. Once, such an act might have captured her imagination; now, magic is nothing to her. A nuisance more than anything.

"Hey, Terrence?" She sets their pieces on the board. She chooses red, wanting some color in her life… even if it is so stark and violent.

"Yes?"

"How much effort would it take me to repair the ballroom? Like, if I recharged enough and we can figure out how to 'fix' me, is that something we can do?"

He nods and she waits a while hoping he will continue. Nothing comes. *Why does he keep this veil of secrecy? Have I said something to permanently damage our relationship? I haven't done anything wrong… I just want answers. I'm the one dying here; it makes no sense for him to stop talking like this.*

A cannonball of terror settles in her gut.

Was it the confession about being afraid of him? Or my constant pestering about how to reverse the effects that magic has taken on me?

Her head spins as she places her last piece. Terrence has been done for a few minutes, silently watching her. She wishes she could read his thoughts and understand him more.

He makes the first move. "The person with black pieces goes first, traditionally. At least for the first round. 'Coal starts fire' is the term used for that rule."

Clarisse finds that confusing, but nods and smiles to pretend like she understands.

"So now that you've gone, I can move?"

"Straightaway!"

She's only seen other people play, but she picks up with ease. It's minimalistic. It doesn't require you to think if you don't want to. *Sometimes I wish I didn't have to think at all...* He beats her every time, but she's enjoying herself. Occasionally, she catches herself drifting off to sleep. To remedy this, she thinks of something to say.

"So, Terrence? What inspired you to help me?"

Terrence blinks, his focus on his next play suspended.

"I... I just saw you and thought you were a lot like me," he shrugs. It's still odd to see a wolf attempt such human gestures. As a consequence of the fact that he *was* human, Clarisse realizes. It must be so strange to be trapped in a body completely different from your mortal shell. She tucks away the fear that she'll be the same when she reaches the other side. It's something for her to worry about later. *Later.*

"What about me reminded you of yourself?" She walks herself into a three-jump trap he's set, though it doesn't bother her at all. He grins as he takes her pieces as trophies. She's an easy opponent, but it puts him at ease. And it makes *him* easier to pry for answers. Those are the pieces she's interested in collecting.

"Just... you grew up in a very sheltered life? Where things were very backward... I grew up in the Dark Ages, Clarisse. Everything was like that, then. Children were to be seen and not heard if seen at all. When I realized I had magical abilities...." He moves a piece to the far end of her side of the board. "King me."

She obliges.

"In any case, why does that matter?"

Clarisse laughs. "Can't I at least be curious?" She moves into another trap, giving him the last of her checkers. They restart the game. She knows she's already doomed to failure, but that's okay. She's getting somewhere with the game that matters.

If I can't get him to give his plans to me directly, maybe I can reverse-engineer them by understanding the person behind them.

It's a crazy sentiment—an attempt at understanding why an ex-Reaper has gone militant against Death himself sounds like she's lost all of her brain cells.

Granted, she's dying.

Who cares when you have nothing to lose? When you've already signed away your soul?

The board set up again, they play.

"Why did you decide to leave Death's keeping? Why did you stop being a Reaper?" This question borders on the edge of danger. It might shut him up, but she makes it sound as light and casual as possible.

"You know, I'm glad you asked."

She lets out a mental sigh of relief.

"I left because of the same backward rules that got me damned and have drained you. I know Death supposedly doesn't 'agree' with them, but if he doesn't agree with them, why uphold them?" He double jumps, taking more of her pieces. "I don't think that the way that Tyrladan works is particularly efficient. First of all, why have people die at all? Why put them through this horrible system where so many tragedies occur—so many evil things—and then have them pass on to be judged by a damned tree? And for what? What do we accomplish?"

Clarisse can't hide her confusion. "Wait, you're literally judged by a *tree*? I thought that was a metaphor or something."

"Yeah, it's called the Selyento. I've mentioned it before." He moves another piece. "No one knows why that was the chosen mechanism. I still don't understand it all that well. It's information for the higher-ups only. I was second-in-command among the Reapers and I still wasn't qualified enough."

Clarisse's jaw drops. "You were second-in-command?"

Terrence laughs. "Did I not tell you this?"

She shakes her head. "Terrence, no offense, but you've told me almost *nothing* about yourself. I'd love to know more about my best friend. You don't have to share more with me than you're comfortable with, but like, really? How can you just drop that bomb on me when we've known each other for *weeks* now!" She plays it up, appealing to his ego.

A worry nags at her that his "hot-and-cold" personality will show through, but this appears to please him. If anything, she's realized that her friend is a narcissist. He doesn't like admitting to faults—only to areas where he finds himself to be strong. She's been picking him apart and it's the only thing that seems to help her make sense of him. It makes her blood boil that he's justifying his actions of using her with some grand scheme that "only he understands." He hasn't said that directly but she's not stupid. She can figure that much out for herself just in watching him.

"I suppose I can tell you more." *How generous of you.* Clarisse smiles, though, urging him on. "So, yes, I was Death's right-hand man. I'm particularly gifted in collecting souls of the damned. I don't know if you've been able to tell—and I'm sure you have—that I'm able to raise my core temperature and often feel 'hot' to the touch. As a consequence, I'm able to go in and out of Kohlu unscathed."

Clarisse raises an eyebrow. "You can literally drag people into Hell?"

"Precisely. That's not an easy trait to find. When it is found, Reapers of that sort are coveted since the others don't particularly like to get burned. Kohlu's fires are enough to damage even those who are immortal. Perhaps not *kill*, but the sensation isn't fun. Death can go in there, but he's busy doing logistics, collecting high-value souls, and collaborating with Fal and Aynda to ensure that the bigger picture is still being followed; hence, my frustration with him for not standing up to the mechanisms by which Tyrladan currently operates."

Clarisse pretends to understand who Fal and Aynda might be, and just nods her head. She wonders if Tryta and Siralto are to blame like the story or if it's just a myth. "How were the mechanisms for Tyrladan... *made?* Or why did they come to be the way they are? If that makes sense?" She doesn't want Terrence to know that she has a whole library of Tyrladanian lore at her disposal. It could be dangerous for him to have possession of something of the sort. Dangerous for her and dangerous for him. She knows it's best to keep her mouth shut for the time being. For now, it's about playing the long game.

He beats her again at their current game. "Shall I go easier on you?"

She chuckles. "No. I don't want a sympathy game."

"Fair enough," he winks, resetting the board. He's been doing it with magic, losing patience in watching her setting up the checkers every time. At least, that's what she thinks. He has a short fuse, it seems. He gets sloppy when it comes to details, which is the opposite of what Death does. She can see where the rift between them likely arose. Terrence is all emotion; he doesn't give enough credit to his logical side. Even his methods of playing checkers are getting more and more reckless. Before long, Clarisse will be beating him. He's gotten predictable without noticing it.

"And as for how... I hear rumors of how Tyrladan was created. This Tryta and Siralto thing... I think it's a load of hogwash. I think things just came to *be*. If there truly were divine beings that created the world, don't you think they would have made it better? And to operate on this idea that one of them turned on their spouse and killed them for thinking differently... for trying to be independent... I hate that."

Clarisse coughs. "Wait, what?"

"Yeah, there's this story about Tryta and Siralto. Everyone blames Siralto for all the suffering and pain that people experience on Earth since she created it without Tryta's permission. He killed her, and ever since, Death has existed and people here can pass on. I don't buy it and, if I did, I'd be pretty angry about Siralto's part. I mean, who blames a victim of murder for how they died? That's ridiculous if you ask me. If Tryta is real, I'd love to give him a piece of my mind."

Clarisse takes careful note of the temperature rising. Something tells her that he isn't as dismissive of the story as he says—he would have to know that *someone* or *something* put this whole Tyrladan thing together. Life after Death? A place to go that operates on weird strictures and such? She's buying the story, whether he does or not. And if he's taking the story so personally, she doesn't understand how he can lie to himself and say he doesn't believe.

Better to act like such a tragedy didn't occur, I guess. I'd love to give Tryta a piece of my mind, too. What a jerk.

"In any case, after years of serving him, I got a bit reckless and decided I wanted to take over the passing. I wanted to recreate or revamp those mechanisms that make it so people have to die. I wanted to restore Earth to what the mysterious Siralto intended before the world was stuck in this machine where magical beings are punished for violating the natural order. I figure if there are stories of such an existence, that there is a kernel of truth in every fairytale, right? And so, I set out to try and figure that out. I did magic when I was alive and, ultimately, it did kill me." He sighs. "I thought that I'd begun to understand what magics were safe and what weren't, which is the only reason why I let you practice any. I thought if you built up a resistance—almost like weightlifting—that you would eventually be strong enough to do greater things without consequence."

Clearly that didn't turn out.

Clarisse smiles with soft understanding. It's incredibly selfish, what he's saying. He let her be at risk of the very same thing he fell victim to. But it's still not adding up. *Why?* There's no satisfying answer after their conversation. It makes her blood boil, though she does her best to keep her composure. "Do you think it can be gotten around? That there's still hope for me?"

Terrence fixes her with a stare that looks something like sympathy. Sometimes, she wonders if he remembers that she's a real person with real feelings and not a test subject. "I think so. If we just let you rest and you let me do more research, I'll be able to figure this thing out. Trust me, I did the soul-collecting thing for centuries. I think I know what I'm doing."

And there's the ego.

"I hope you're right." She finishes the game, taking all of his remaining pieces from the board in an easy move. He looks shocked.

"I think that's enough playing for tonight, Terrence. I'm tired and I want to be ready for work tomorrow."

27

THE TRUTH WILL BE REVEALED

Clarisse

With the door firmly shut behind her, she throws a fist at the wall. It's juvenile—pointless. All it does is leave her with bloody knuckles and a hole in the wall. She doesn't know where else to drive her rage. Downstairs, her "best friend" is hiding secrets from her that could help her live.

"Did he seriously think that I wouldn't be upset? That his plans wouldn't come at such a huge cost?"

She whispers the questions, but they keep rolling in her head with violent force. He was seriously going to try to create a *utopia* where no one dies? And where does she fit into that picture? He's holding back from her—not telling the whole truth. She fears for her life now more than ever; the irony is that she yearns to meet with Death to ask him questions.

The memory of their last meeting is a painful lance in her hopes of finding answers. How can she expect him to help her now? She threw off his advice as little more than trivial.

Some childish part of her clings to the fantasy of happy endings. But she doesn't want to end up like Terrence: deluded. Attached to things that are impossible and immeasurably reckless. He put her life in danger. Took advantage of her situation. Led her with promises she didn't think twice about.

I should've known better.

She doesn't cry. It exhausts her to do that anymore. He's not worth the energy. Walking into the bathroom, wrapping her arm in a washcloth, paying careful attention to the scraped skin on her knuckles, she cleans it off. She isn't surprised in the slightest that the pain wears off immediately.

Why should anything make sense anymore?

She looks at herself in the mirror, looking worse than ever. Her face is drained of all life—like some warped painting. Her movements feel out of sync with her body. She's not sure if she understands fully how she feels. It's surreal.

When she steps out of the bathroom, she avoids her bed.

Why sleep when every hour may be my last?

She steps into the secret room, picking up the book from the previous night. To avoid irritation, she skips any other parts that have to do with Tryta and Siralto. *Of course... they just keep pinning the 'demon' title to her. Why? Why does she have to be the martyr? The example?* Clarisse has had enough of that her whole life. She wishes she had been stronger.

But right now, time is of the essence. Every moment spent worrying is a moment wasted. She needs to focus.

Finally, she falls on a chapter that looks promising.

The Reapers:

Creatures whose designated purpose is to collect the souls of mortals who are ready to pass. See the instruction manual for Reapers for more information. Provided by Death.

Death:

Head of the Reapers. Can only be summoned by a passing soul or via an intense connection in the stars....

She reads no further.

The stars?

She stares at her hands. Using magic is perilous; letting Terrence lead her astray sounds equally perilous. The twittering presence and whispers of the universe outside tempt her, though. If she could understand them, would they do it for her? Shaking her head, she knows that's not the way. She would have to use her own.

Is this something I really want to do?

Her stomach churns. She lowers herself onto the carpet, the world swaying. Her vision fails her and she wonders if it will ever return. Apathy fills her. She doesn't listen to see if Terrence stands outside. She slides open the door and steps out into her bedroom. To her fortune, he's not there. Clarisse takes the book with her, carefully studying other chapters.

She's not sure what time it is when she goes to sleep. It's late, that's for sure. Clarisse wishes she'd gone to bed sooner, but she needs answers. She can't bring herself to regret not sleeping more or taking better care of herself. It's not like Terrence cares anymore, either. Or at least he doesn't seem to.

Morning comes too early in the wake of dreams she starts to remember for the first time. Death was a common theme, though most of her interactions with him were garbled. She can't remember what she said or why she said it. There were strange creatures and a weird tree. She wonders if it's anything like the tree that will get to determine if she's damned for eternity or not. Part of her wishes this was all a giant joke—that this wasn't happening to her and that she stands a chance.

She puts on an old dress that she stitched together. It's graying, just like she is. It's been in her wardrobe for forever, but she's proud of it all the same.

She almost makes it out the door without Terrence. Not bothering to talk to him, Clarise settles in with Terrence next to her. An uncomfortable rift is felt between them. She sees remorse in his face, but he's not making any efforts to fix it. He sits in silence, bathing in it like some kind of *freak*.

Clarisse wonders if her thoughts are getting more jumbled

because she's dying. Or if maybe she's just getting more moments of clarity because she doesn't have enough strength to give a crap anymore.

Maybe I've seen too much.

She casts Terrence an angry, sleep-deprived glare as they make their way into the mall. The ball is in her court now; he needs to share more or start playing as far as she's concerned. In her mind, he's killed her. It's his fault that she was led astray. *Not that I was any better off before.*

When she makes it into work, she plasters that fake smile on her face so Mr. Harris won't be suspicious. "Good morning, sir."

Mr. Harris tries to smile, but instead, he places a newspaper in front of her.

Her photo is circled. Their eyes meet and Clarisse feels her heart try to explode in her chest.

She shakes her head. *There's no point in lying now.* "I'm not in any trouble, Mr. Harris. I ran from home. They beat me there. They treated me like crap and so I up and left. That priest that brought me here leads a cult where they burn me if I step out of line. They strapped me to a chair and did horrible things to me, and I finally had enough. I'm an adult and found a safer place to stay while I work for you."

It all comes tumbling out while a few tears fall. She's never told *anyone* other than Terrence the truth. Mr. Harris looks more than shocked, his eyes wide.

He places a gentle hand on her shoulder. "Clarisse, why didn't you say something? You need to take legal action against these people!"

She shakes her head. "What's the use? The burn marks are gone. I treated them and I heal pretty fast, so there's no evidence. What am I going to say? How can I prove what happened?"

Mr. Harris crosses his arms. "Oh no, we're not standing for that. I'm taking you down to the police station and we're filing a report. Today. Shop's closed; you'll get paid anyway. I'm not having my favorite employee get hurt because she thinks she won't be taken seriously. I'll blast those idiots to smithereens myself if I catch them stepping foot in here and I'll be damned if I don't have the legal protections to do so."

She brings herself to look him in the eye. It's hard to do that with other people. She wonders how long she's gone without actually looking someone in the face. Probably her whole life.

"You believe me?"

"Clarisse, no offense, but I had an inkling that something was different about you for more than just your skills. When you first came here, you looked like a ghost. Underfed. And for someone who just turned eighteen? And knows nothing about the world and had to have a priest help her figure out how to get her life started?"

Clarisse blushes. She didn't realize how obvious it looked to outsiders that something was wrong.

"And you're telling me that priest guy *burned* you?"

"Over the years, yeah…." It occurs to Clarisse that she probably doesn't have any scars left to show him, but she pulls up her dress sleeve anyway. To her surprise, there *are* scars left. Some have returned, her magic wearing off. And there are old ones, but they're there. *My magic can wear off?*

Everything is confusing. She almost forgets that Terrence is with her. He looks positively enraged at the sight of her scars. She wonders if he's angry at her for showing Mr. Harris or if he's angry on her behalf like he used to be.

At this point, she doesn't care.

"Clarisse, these… these look *awful!*" He stops short of grabbing her arm to look at her scars, instead placing his hands over his mouth.

"Yeah, I know…." She hangs her head, wishing she could disappear. Everything got way too awkward way too fast. She feels like a little kid being called to the principal's office, though in her case, the principal was Father Simmons and it usually ended in some ritual to "cast out demons."

Her eyes fall on Terrence.

Too bad those efforts were for nothing.

She swallows a lump in her throat. Clarisse doesn't know why she thinks of Terrence as a freaking *demon* when she's seen creatures like Ralun and that awful snake. But the thought is there. It stabs at her heart and does its damage. She feels winded and has to sit down.

She's crying. "I'm sorry, Mr. Harris. I'm sure you didn't want to hire a screw-up like me."

Mr. Harris pulls her into a hug. "That's absolute bullshit, Clarisse. I didn't hire a screw-up. Your parents and that priest are screw-ups. Simmons? Was that his name?" Mr. Harris gets up and picks up the phone.

"What are you doing?"

"I'm calling the police."

"What?"

"I'm calling the police. You need to speak to someone. You're a missing person, too. They're going to want to know and you deserve to speak first."

She would fight on any other occasion, but she's too tired. Her vision fades in and out. She feels herself slumping against the chair and then her vision goes black for a few moments. When she opens her eyes, she's greeted by quite a few police officers. Mr. Harris stays by her side while she tells them *everything*. From the beginning. Her lips tremble as images of the past come tumbling from corners of her mind long forgotten.

Every scar's story surfaces and is brought to life. Sometimes, she's heaving with sobs and in other moments, she goes numb and speaks her secrets aloud like a hollow shell. All of her fears and thoughts from the last eighteen years burst free. How she was scared she was going to be murdered. How they hurt her every chance they could get. How they gave her scars. The police drive her home with no questions, even though she admits to the fact that she's been driving without a license. Clarisse notices, only at the end, that most of the police officers are either angry or upset—or both. Tears are all she sees as she's escorted from the mall; the ride home is a blur, too. When they ask about where she lives, she lies and says the house is being rented to her by someone who heard her story and lives out of town.

They buy it. She shows them her journals. They're waiting for her on a desk in her room—placed by Terrence, no doubt. All she has to do is point to them and the police gather them all up, asking questions as they read. Pages upon pages detailing her parents' abuse are submitted to evidence. They ask about the ballroom and she says it was damaged in a storm.

Everything is slow and fast at the same time for what seems like hours.

"Do you mind coming down to the station tomorrow to give these statements in a formal capacity?" Officer Burns is looking at her, his graying mustache the most defining feature on his otherwise plain face. He looks more than concerned for her. For a moment, he reminds her of a father-figure. Someone that would've cared and looked out for her while she grew up.

She looks over at Terrence.

But that's a lie. No one cares. No one's going to look out for me.

Still, she grips at Terrence's fur as she nods.

"You rest up, kid."

Mr. Harris followed them there; he takes a look around the house. "I'll go with you tomorrow at lunch if you want. When you give your statement."

Clarisse swears his eyes are watering when he makes the offer. She nods.

"And I'll come to pick you up. No more driving without a license. We'll get that squared away, too." He turns around to leave.

"Hey, Mr. Harris?"

"Yeah?"

"Thank you."

He pauses for a moment. "You're more than welcome. It's a shame you even feel the need to thank me in the first place. How have you survived this long?"

Clarisse shrugs. "I can't say I have."

Mr. Harris moves as if he's going to say something, but Clarisse can see it in his face. He doesn't know what to say. How can he? How can anybody? *She* doesn't even know what to say.

"Well, just prepare for your day tomorrow. You have a long one ahead of you."

Clarisse nods, her inner spark gone. She isn't sure how the day happened. It all ran together so fast… she's completely beyond herself. When the door finally shuts, she starts crying. To her surprise, Terrence's "I care" façade is back.

"Clarisse, I'm so sorry," he starts, "how are you——"

"Don't." She holds up a hand. "You haven't cared all day. For the past few days. And for the record, you won't tell me anything. Seems to me I'm only worth caring for when it benefits you."

She can tell by the look on Terrence's face that this stings worse than if she had just slapped him. But she knows it's probably just a ruse, just like everything else in her pathetic life.

She turns on her heel. "I need sleep. My day just rushed past me and I have to go down to the precinct tomorrow and talk about eighteen years of abuse and hell. Again. Since, you know, I've been taken advantage of since the moment I started breathing. And since this magic shit? Even more." She casts an angry glance at Terrence. "Who knew that my parents were right, too? This magic really is the worst thing that could have happened to me."

"Clarisse," Terrence starts.

She flips him the bird. "I hate myself. Don't talk to me. I'm a freak and I *deserve* to die for what I am. I get it now—why mortals can't have it. We can't handle it and we're gullible freaks that walk ourselves into traps like the one I'm in right now."

She runs to her room, slams the door, sliding down to the floor and cries so hard that her body shakes. She wonders once more if the pain will ever stop.

28

MAKING AMENDS

Terrence

Terrence stands in the living room, shocked at everything that transpired. He's proud of Clarisse for finally saying something —happy that Mr. Harris took enough initiative to get her to speak out about her ordeals. The magic parts will get inflated by the media as part of Father Simmons' cult, no doubt, so she's not in any danger of being exposed.

He thought everything was going well. They had a lovely conversation the other day. Granted, she did look *angry* after it. He had chalked it up to her being tired.

Tears prick at his eyes, realizing that her silence has been a cold shoulder. He wishes he said something. He wishes that he had tried. She feels *used*. He's realized it too late. He wants to go up there and hold her and tell her that he truly is sorry. That he does care; he's just… bad at it. He lets his emotions go way too far and they get the better of him.

I would never hurt her, though. I would never try to use her for my own benefit, solely. I genuinely wanted to share this with her.

He hangs his head.

Guilt eats at him. He knows he can't leave her up there like this. She doesn't sound good. He can hear her wailing and wonders how long it's been since she's given herself proper space to cry... not in silence like she usually does. Terrence doesn't disturb her on those nights, but they're not a secret to him. The smell of sadness taints the air—her other emotions are strong, too. Fear. Anger. Confusion.

I need to talk to her. Now. I need to... explain.

He's never felt the need to be responsible for someone else. Why should he have? He was a Reaper first and a rebellious spirit of darkness next. And now he took on this little human as his only friend and kept secrets from her to the point that it's destroyed her.

Way to go, Terrence.

He walks upstairs.

What if I go get her a gift? Maybe some flowers?

He smiles, though it's a sour feeling against his teeth. Thoughts of trying to repair things keep surfacing.

Yes. And then we talk. Go over everything I've needed to say to her—and should have—from the beginning.

She's still crying, so before a gift he will comfort her. He owes her that much, right?

His knocking hardly makes a noise when he gets to the door; he wonders if she even hears it.

"What?"

The question is strangled by tears and sorrow, lancing Terrence straight through the heart.

What is wrong with me? How could I have been so blind?

He chokes. "I... I'm so, so sorry, Clarisse. I know I've been a real ass lately. I haven't been forthcoming with you. I... I don't know what to say or do to make anything right with you. You're my best friend. Please let me come in and talk things out with you. I don't want to lose you."

When the door swings open, he's met by a very red, tear-stained face that's something like his friend's. He's never seen her display her pain so openly before. It crushes him even further.

"May I come in?"

She narrows her gaze, but he stands strong. He can't give in to pressure, leaving her alone. Her pain-induced rage has left her books scattered in torn heaps all around the floor; her bed's been disheveled, some of the sheets and blankets ripped through. She looks like a caged animal. He doesn't blame her. After all, he's been there. Far too many times to count, really.

"You may." She covers a cough with her hand.

For the first time, he really takes a look at her. Her skin is graying; her eyes have dulled. How anyone is missing this is something he'll never be able to answer. He wonders if this is what brought Mr. Harris to be suspicious this morning. If this is what they were talking about when the police mentioned how bad she looked.

The scars on her arms are returning and his mouth drops. He didn't get a good look at them earlier. Years of spiraling pain worked their way up her arms and, undoubtedly, to her back where they whipped her during the exorcisms.

He gulps.

I… I'm a horrible person.

He looks at her, unable to hide his tears. *Scratch the other plan.* He's staying right here, by her side, enveloping her in his warmth. He curls around her while she slumps to the ground, gripping his fur like a child might grip their favorite blanket.

"Terrence," she whispers. "I… I don't want to die. I wanted to have a chance. Why don't you tell me the truth? Why don't you tell me if there's a way to save me? Why don't we ask for help?" She looks at him, her eyes pleading. "You need to call him."

His heart lurches. *Death? Now?*

He twinges from the pain of the fights they had earlier, his skin still sore. Terrence is not ready for another. But looking at Clarisse… he knows he can't let her stay like this. He knows he can't let her succumb to the same fate he did. "I… I suppose you're right."

For the first time in his life, he's willing to set aside his ego for someone else. It crushes him as he realizes it. He loves her. How much is hard to say. But this little human has become his everything in a matter of weeks. He would do anything to make sure she was alright. It takes everything in him not to punish himself with as much harshness as he can muster for letting her suffer like this. For not explaining.

Granted, he's not even sure how to explain. How to help her. How to justify having put her in his plans the way he did, without a second thought for how it might affect her.

She knows that much, but the damned thing... the potential consequences... that's beyond him to explain, anyhow.

He needs to get her answers. Skipping out on answers isn't an option—no more excuses. No more running. He isn't sure how everything will play out since he's a literal fugitive from Tyrladanian law. But he can hold his own. Clarisse? She doesn't stand a chance if he doesn't say something.

"Clarisse, I'm going to summon Death for you."

Her eyes widen, the epitome of a deer in the headlights. Time seems to slow itself around her every way that she moves. "You... you are?"

"Yes. Not today, but I am. I need to get some things in order, but I will. Don't stress yourself out. I want to have someone here to mediate and give us both answers... answers on how I can help you and how you can help yourself. If at all." He hangs his head, knowing full well that it might be too late.

Not if I can help it.

"Would you like to ask me questions in the meantime?"

Clarisse chews on this and he sees the wheels in her head turning at sixty miles per hour. He suppresses the urge to chuckle. Everything about this girl is wonderful. The worst part is that she doesn't know it and might not get the chance to ever realize her worth.

"Yeah... do you really not believe in Tryta and Siralto?"

He pauses. "Why do you ask that?"

She sits on her bed, looking at him with a strange glint in her eye. Something like... *excitement? Curiosity?* He's not sure, but he's there to listen. He's there to answer. He's there because she needs him and he will be there as much as he can be. In whatever capacity he can manage.

"Well, earlier, when you were talking about them? You didn't sound too happy about the story. Like... if you thought it was all fake... then why does it hurt you? Your feelings? And then, if you don't believe in them, how do you think the whole of Tyrladan came to be? And what's it like there?"

She's gushing over with so many questions that he can't help but laugh. It's deep—hearty. Full, like it was when he first met her. He wonders how everyone that meets her isn't instantly taken with just her personality. It's wonderful and warm, like a hug. He curses at himself again for missing that so much. For letting his hot-and-cold emotions get in the way. His bad days are no excuse for treating her like an afterthought.

"I... I can't say why. It just angers me that the world I live in... we live in... caused two supposed Creator-tier Selben to resort to falling apart via murder. On Tryta's part, anyway. I suppose in some ways I believe *someone* has to be responsible for Tyrladan. It's alive. Breathing. Much like everything else. It's all more than I'm capable of understanding. But... why have Death? Why not make Earth an expanding space just like the other worlds? Why not cater the number of humans to the size of the planet? Were they both insane? But a simple one-off project did not require someone being doused out like that. Erasing someone is not something you should just *do*."

Clarisse winces. "What about the snake you erased?"

"That thing? It was going to hurt you and is of no consequence now. That creature should've known better than to hurt what is *mine*. Given that you are *my* friend, he should've known that the risks were high. Being erased was the natural consequence for such erroneous behavior on his part."

Her face twists up with fear and regret.

He hops up next to her in the bed. "Clarisse, I would do anything to protect you. I really would never hurt you. I'm sorry I've frightened you and left you in the dark. I've been more than selfish in all of this. I should've heeded Death just as you wanted to. I shouldn't have led you astray. Just because he's my enemy doesn't mean he's right. I just got so... *blinded*... I wanted to create a world as the one Siralto intended. With you. Your powers are to create. I was hoping that, by working with you, I could help you harness that; so we could create the pieces to the puzzle that were missing. You're a light-bearer of sorts… like she was. And I just… I wanted so much for you to be able to harness that power and become the woman you were meant to be."

He stops. "I realize now you were already that woman. I just can't stand the thought of watching you grow old and watching your flame die. I hope to all that is holy in Tyrladan that I haven't stamped out your light even sooner."

Her eyes glisten with tears. Has he made her sad again? Terrence pouts, his ears flattening. He hates that and wishes he could cloud his emotions, or at least express them, like a human.

This temporary state of disgruntlement is disrupted when she throws her arms around him. She's shaking from crying so hard.

"It's not your fault. No one is at fault. This all just sucks. You're still my best friend. And I know it's hard for you to get along with Death. Will you get in trouble if you call him?" She pulls back a bit, staring him deep in the eyes to the point where it's a bit uncomfortable.

He laughs nervously. "I'm kind of a fugitive. You saw how he treated me. It's not like I've been the most active target they're after, but I'm pretty high on the list. My dormant state has saved me. Now that I've been active and helping you, I'm sure I might be one of Tyrladan's most-wanted."

Clarisse's eyes widen, her jaw slackens. "What will happen to you if you call Death? Will you be punished?"

Terrence does his best to shrug in his shadowy body. "Maybe. I don't know. I've never known anyone to do anything quite like I have."

"Will you be erased?" She blurts it so suddenly that it's like she's slapped him in the face.

Terrence never did stop to think of the consequences of getting caught. He never planned on it. "I hope not. That may be my fate since I've corrupted yours."

Clarisse pouts. "No, no, no! You will not call Death!"

He lurches. "I'm sorry, what?"

"We can figure this shit out together," she states with such firmness that it convinces Terrence that it's best to just keep his mouth shut. "Look, I'm gonna die someday. When I do, I want you to get the hell out of here and run. I don't want you to linger. I don't want you to get caught and end up wiped from existence because of me. Literally just... *gone.* I don't want your energy absorbed and kept inside some other demon while the essence of you is reincarnated somewhere else. However, all that works. I don't care. I want you to be *you*, Terrence. I want you to be safe."

Terrence groans, his shoulders slumping in defeat. "What do you propose that we do, then?"

Clarisse smiles. "We take it day by day. Look, if I stop using magic, maybe I'll get better. I just won't use any. Nothing. Zip."

"No more hiding your thoughts from me, then?"

... How did you know?

"Do you think that I wouldn't notice an active mind like yours going silent? I was growing rather lonely when you decided to seal off your thoughts."

Clarisse blushes. "Sorry."

"You don't have to apologize." Terrence laughs. "Listen, Clarisse, if you're not going to let me find Death for you, will you at least let me go out tomorrow afternoon to contact some associates of mine? I want to see if there's something I can do to reverse this process. I'm not promising that I won't ever summon Death though."

Clarisse glares at him. "If you so much as think about breaking that promise, I will haunt your erased ass for eternity. Don't think I won't—I will find a way."

It comes rushing out with so much force and fear at the same time that, for a second, Terrence stiffens up. It sounds like a legitimate threat.

"I'll work with what I have then," he smiles sheepishly.

He tucks up close to her as she gets ready to sleep. Now that her thoughts are no longer hidden, he hears something particularly interesting.

"What do you mean you've had a secret library this whole time? And that Death has been here?"

She giggles.

"How dare you, you little—" But he's laughing. And he can't help it. They laugh for quite a while before she mellows down into a restful sleep. He supposes he can wait until morning to go check out this amazing little library of hers with books provided by *Death himself*.

He shakes his head. "I wonder if we've been sitting on an answer this whole time."

He plans on seeing a few runaways or rogue Selben that might help him tomorrow. It'll be a quick trip into the darker corners of Tyrladan and then he'll be right back. And this time, he's putting protections on the house and making her stay in the library. He won't come back to find her face-to-face with another ex-follower of his.

"I can't afford to lose you, Clarisse."

She's asleep, but he hopes she can hear him in the depths of her dreams somewhere. Her hand twitches, clutching his fur a bit tighter. He takes that to mean that she does and settles off into a light doze himself. Before he knows it, the day has come. And Clarisse has one Kohlu of a task ahead of her.

29

MAKING A STATEMENT

Clarisse

Mr. Harris arrives an hour before they have to open the store. Clarisse is awake, making breakfast, and offers him some pancakes which he gladly accepts. It's strange eating breakfast with a guest in the house. They laugh together; Mr. Harris is sharing stories of strange customers and the awkward requests for various outfits they've asked him to put together over the years.

Clarisse hangs on his every word. She feels a lot better today. The weight of fear is gone. Terrence is acting normal. She isn't being forced to use her powers or even tricked into using them voluntarily. He's going to get help and he *isn't* going to go get Death.

He knows about the secret room. She's going to finally get to say something about the horrible things her parents and Father Simmons did to her over the years. It's enough to make her want to dance… and maybe puke at the same time. She wonders if she can put a radio in the kitchen for the dancing bit. Maybe the mall carries them. Dancing might erase the icy apprehension settling in her bones.

"Of course the mall has radios, you dork! They have makeup. Phones. Why not radios? What, have you lived under a rock your whole life?"

Luckily, Mr. Harris is making a joke right when Terrence drops such a funny insult, so her laughter doesn't seem the slightest bit amiss.

Would you quit that?

"What? I'm only telling the truth!"

He bares his teeth in a grin.

Mr. Harris stops to laugh. "I didn't know your dog could do that!"

Clarisse chuckles, rolling her eyes in Terrence's direction. "Yes, he's quite the character. He knows quite a few tricks like that. Haven't taught him a single one of them either. He came this way."

Mr. Harris nods approvingly. "Well, Clarisse, breakfast was lovely and I'm glad to have shared it with you! We should do this more often." He smiles. "I imagine it gets rather lonely out this way. And I'd be more than happy to be your weird, fun uncle of sorts since your own family is a load of… garbage."

He stops himself from swearing—Clarisse can see the beginnings of a much fouler word on his lips and she claps a hand to her face to keep from laughing. The offer is touching.

"I'd be glad to have you around, Mr. Harris."

Her grin is infectious, making the whole room feel a bit brighter. "Well, kid? Are you ready to go learn some more? Hope my jokes didn't get you up in *stitches*," Mr. Harris teases.

Clarisse groans. "Well, you've got the dad and uncle jokes down, that's for sure."

It's relieving to have someone else drive her into work. She was glad when the police didn't offer her any citations when she admitted to what she'd been doing. Granted, given the circumstances, she doubted they would have done much besides a soft reprimand. Officer Burns seemed angrier at her parents. She wonders what will happen to them now that the world is about to know of their hate. Their evil. The way they treat people.

The hours drag by. The anticipation of going down to talk to the police eats at her. Her forehead is beading with sweat when it comes time for lunch. Mr. Harris motions for her. She follows willingly to the hardest job of her life. *Speaking up.*

"I'm right here with you, Clarisse. You grab onto me as hard as you have to if it helps you get through this. I'll rip anyone's head off that dares to try to call you a liar or belittle you for what you've been through. You got it?"

She lightly tugs on Terrence's fur, letting him know she got the message.

The police station is a dull, brick building that could use some repair. It's not a large town and thus, it probably isn't heavily-funded. There isn't much crime in Ashville to begin with, so she's not surprised to see only a few cars sitting outside the station and even fewer people inside when they open the doors. Her thoughts are blank as she tries to calm herself.

She's greeted by a receptionist—a middle-aged woman named Mia, who brightens at the sight of Clarisse.

"You must be Ms. Monroe." She smiles warmly. "I apologize if things are in a bit of a disarray. We've been reorganizing the office and shifting people around. It's normally much more presentable."

Clarisse smiles. It's weak, but genuine. "No worries. Where am I supposed to go?"

Mia stands up, gesturing for Clarisse to follow. "We've got a little desk set up for you. You can speak with Officer Burns there. He doesn't want you to be in an interrogation room or make you feel uncomfortable so we're trying to keep this as low-key as possible. Would you like a cup of water? Coffee?"

Despite how parched her throat is, Clarisse declines both. She's not big on accepting hospitality from strangers. And something about *being* in a police station makes her feel like she's in trouble. Her parents always used to threaten her that the authorities would come pick her up someday if her magic were ever discovered. Being among the very monsters they painted for her when she was a kid is… frightening.

"Is that Ms. Monroe I see?" Office Burns smiles through his bushy mustache and she can't help but giggle a little at how out of place he looks with his arms stretched wide for a hug. She gladly accepts. It's nice to be given genuine affection for once. Without strings. "Now, based on what we saw the other day, would you like to press charges against your parents or Father Simmons? Or both? And you'll need a protective order."

There's a gleam in Officer Burns' eyes that she just can't place, but Clarisse is too startled by the questions to process what's going on.

"Wait, press charges? You mean—like have them arrested? Tried? And what's a protective order?"

Officer Burns nods a bit. "Sort of. A protective order is simply something that prevents them from making contact with you based on a fear of your life. It prevents them from buying firearms since they're being given a protective order based on grounds for domestic abuse. It is, unfortunately, just a piece of paper, but it sends them a signal that the law is looking out for you and that if they give you so much as a phone call, you have the right to tell us and have them booked on a violation of said order," Office Burns explains. "Given the extent of your scarring, I'd also like to investigate the church and Father Simmons. The protective order would be added protection if you chose to press charges, especially while we perform investigations."

Clarisse swallows. "You mean like, a sting operation and stuff?"

Officer Burns laughs. "No, no. We would just use the evidence you give us and use it to get warrants to search. You're probably thinking more like the television shows you watch."

Clarisse cocks her head to the side and then hangs her head in shame. "I didn't actually get to watch much TV growing up. I saw a few cartoons here and there but nothing more. Sorry. I've read books though."

Her smile is bashful and makes everyone around her stiffen with shame. Shame that they let someone in their community be a shadow of pain for so long. Someone had fallen through the cracks of society. Someone deprived of justice. Now the evidence is cold. Now they're building a case with matchsticks instead of logs. The foundation will crumble without more to go on.

"That's alright, Clarisse."

Behind her, she hears Mr. Harris clear his throat. "I'll be outside."

She turns around and almost catches a glimpse of something like tears on her boss's face. She wonders why everyone is so sad. She's alive. She's okay. She's just... wounded. Scarred. But she can survive even more than what she's been through.

She's defied odds for more reasons than they'll ever realize.

"Alright, Clarisse. I'm going to have you fill out a statement. Write down everything that's happened to you that you can remember. Everything. I don't want a single detail left out. We can use that to give to the Commonwealth's Attorney to see if they'll allow you to get a protective order. It lasts for up to two years in Virginia. The attorney can give you more information once you've filled this out. I think there's more than a credible reason to believe that there will be violence against you if you're left alone with these people again. I'm going to make sure that never happens."

Clarisse just dips her head, taking a pen when it's handed to her. It seems like hours. She leaves out no detail. The idea of being able to have the cops as a barrier between her and her parents and Father Simmons sounds like a much-needed relief. It's still not protection all the time, but it's a subtle threat to them that if they even *dare* to come after her again that, if she lives to tell about it, they'll be behind bars.

My father will just hate this for his reputation, won't he?

The thought makes her giddy; still, she's terrified and embarrassed at the same time. It's a weird moment for her. She doesn't have to embellish anything. Everything she writes, she writes to the near letter of the truth that she remembers. Her hands shake the whole time, her handwriting a nervous scrawl that betrays her every emotion. Part of her wonders if her parents or Father Simmons will come bursting in at any moment—if someone might show up to take her away and put her in a circus for being a literal *freak*—just like her parents always said. Anything she's unsure of, she makes sure to leave out or write only the details she knows for certain.

When she hands it in, Officer Burns takes quite a while reading it. A few times, his face goes beet red. "They think you're possessed?"

She nods. She left out the part about shooting lights from her hands… conveniently. Right now, she cares only that they sound as crazy as they are. Clarisse knows if they protest on the grounds that their daughter is some kind of demon-witch, it will only make them look crazier.

Officer Burns, still reading, grunts here and there.

Mr. Harris steps in, letting Clarisse know she's off for the rest of the day. She hates being given so much sympathy and charity, but she can tell she's not going to be able to turn it away. Officer Burns agrees to drive Clarisse home since the process is taking longer than Clarisse and Mr. Harris anticipated.

Clarisse yearns to be back in front of a sewing machine and learning new techniques, but this is the time to use her voice. To say something. To be able to free herself from the bondage of secrecy that's held her captive for so long.

When Officer Burns sets her finished report on his desk, she swears she sees tears in his eyes.

"Miss Monroe, that will be all that we need from you, for now. Would you be comfortable witnessing against these individuals in court if the time comes? They won't be able to hurt you, I promise."

Clarisse nods, filled with relief in knowing someone is looking out for her.

"I'll give you a ride to your house. We'll get you set up for driver's ed and all that. The county will take care of it. We just want you to get back on your feet. Mr. Harris is a good man. If you're working for him, you'll do well. I'm just astonished… and amazed that you've survived all this." Officer Burns claps a hand to Clarisse's shoulder as he stands. He helps her pull her chair back so she can get to her feet. She's weary, forgetting for a moment that Terrence is still with her. He stands immediately to help her keep her balance. The world seems to be collapsing around her.

I feel worse now. Why?

"Reliving trauma is hard. You were very brave today."

Clarisse grips Terrence a little tighter, continuing her strange promenade out the door and into the police car waiting outside.

The ride home is silent. When they get to the door, Officer Burns leaves her with a lingering goodbye and a promise to check in on her later. A note from Mr. Harris is on the door. She's got the next few days off.

She grumbles, placing the paper on the kitchen table. If she weren't so faint, she'd pace about the room. For now, she settles onto the couch in the living room and lets the ceiling dance in and out of her vision. Everything is a strange blur; she can't make out sharp edges on anything anymore. It's all going away.

"Clarisse?" Terrence is at her side. "Are you alright?"

Clarisse reaches a hand out to him, tears pouring down her face. "They're going to find me here."

Terrence freezes. "What... what do you mean?"

Clarisse turns her head to Terrence. A single blood tear rolls down her cheek. It leaves a dark red stain in its wake. Her body is shaking; the truth rocks her to her soul.

"I'm dying."

30

DEATH

Clarisse

Clarisse is vaguely aware of Terrence shouting. He's pushing her. Nudging her. Doing anything he can to wake her up. Her spirit is floating in and out of her body, leaving her comatose on the couch. Her physical body twitches into something like a smile. If all she got to do before she left was oust her parents and Father Simmons, then that was all she needed.

Right now, she isn't scared of damnation or the consequences of using magic. She isn't scared of the unknown place called Tyrladan that Terrence and Death speak of. Right now, she just wishes Terrence would stop crying.

She tries to reach out to him, but her arm isn't working. The strength she needs in her body to give him the comfort he's desperately clawing for just isn't there. He's nudging her and screaming her name.

Stop crying, friend. He'll find you here if you don't go. I'm okay. I'll see you again.

She doesn't know how she knows to call him from her mind, but she knows he can hear her because his face contorts into a deeper, sadder echo of the fear it held before. He knows she's right and that he's losing her. She doesn't have to be in his shoes to know. His face says it all.

From that morning, she should've known that these moments would be her last. She wishes she spent more time hugging Terrence and spent her last day with him. But those idiots that she called parents needed to pay; Father Simmons needed to pay. There couldn't be other girls like her.

She lets out a shaky breath; from her hands, the little lights float up to the ceiling. In a blink, she disappears from the world of the living.

Outside, the moon and the stars stop screaming. She closes her eyes as she hears the last of their voices trail away.

Clarisse dies.

~

Terrence

T errence can't stop sobbing. He can't stop from letting his body shake. There's a small window of time to escape before Death arrives. He knows that Clarisse's soul won't be taken by some low-level Reaper. She's going with the Grim Reaper, himself. He wishes, for a moment, that he was still enlisted with Death so he could go with her. Escort her.

But he's damned. And at risk. He wants to stay with her.

It's selfish to leave.

As silly as it seems, he stops and lets out a baleful howl. He hopes the world around him hears it. Maybe someone will come to her. Her body is cold as he shivers. The lights that were twinkling about her in her last moments are gone.

All that is left is her shell.

Will anyone be there to mourn her? Will anyone know? Will anyone else love her and cherish her memory as I do?

He doesn't have time to ponder these things. *I won't be able to attend her funeral.* He holds back a scream.

Why didn't she show more signs? What could I have done differently? What could I have done to save her?

His mind is a hurricane of regret and sorrow when he leaves the room.

~

Mr. Harris

M r. Harris comes to the door the next day. His phone calls have been unanswered and, out of concern, he shows up to check on Clarisse. He's grown fond of her in the last few weeks. Now that he knows her story, he considers himself responsible for her—she doesn't have anyone else, really.

The door isn't locked and, when no one answers, he lets himself in. The first thing that hits him is the smell. He brings a sleeve to his face to protect him from the wretched stench. Then his eyes fly open in realization.

Something draws him to the couch in the living room and, there, he finds her. Quiet. Pale. Rigor mortis has already set in and, strangely enough, it looks like her body has started decomposing much faster than it should have within one night.

She looks weak. Small. Fragile. All the scars from years of abuse are visible on her skin now; any walls she'd put up to hide them or heal them are gone. They trace little maps of sorrow up and down her arms and legs and, despite the grossness of the smell, Mr. Harris starts sobbing. He can't help but suck up the air.

Shaking her body, a part of him wishes that it isn't as bad as it looks. *Maybe she's sleeping.* The cold of her skin knocks the wind out of him—the hope that she might start moving again dissipates. He knows he shouldn't disrupt her or move the body; yet it takes everything in him to keep from hoisting her up and holding her… something he knows her parents probably never did.

He's frantic now; he's stopped shaking her. It's no use. *She's gone.*

"You had so much to live for," he whispers, lips trembling.

He searches about for any signs of something she would have

used to end her life. There are no razors, pill bottles... nothing. No Terrence, either. He calls out to him, but he doesn't come. She passed naturally as far as he can tell, though he's not willing to rule anything out. His hands tremble as he reaches into his pocket to dial those awful three numbers.

His eyes keep flitting back and forth to the body. Did he miss something? Was there something he could have done?

While he waits, he settles into quiet sobs. *Was she dying this whole time? And how come I didn't notice?* The questions repeat over and over again; his hand clutches hers. He can't let go. Not yet.

When Officer Burns arrives, they share a not-so-silent moment of mourning. The police are just as shocked to find that she passed on so soon. The house is turned over for evidence that someone might have broken in. Was it her parents? Father Simmons? And still, no one can find Terrence.

The sun is gone all day; Mr. Harris is certain that Clarisse's soul took it with her.

~

A day later they learn she died of a heart attack. The coroner seems convinced that the exorcisms performed on her body had caused her heart to become too weak even at such a young age.

She has no history of medical care and has never had vaccines. Mr. Harris and Officer Burns grow angrier at each new revelation. This child has had nothing.

"She was a strong woman," Mr. Harris says quietly as he sits with Officer Burns at the station. Things have been silent. No one dares to bother the chief and his guest. Calls come and go, but they're mostly petty crimes that can be handled. This... this is something that requires more input.

Mr. Harris has nothing to offer on Father Simmons except for his description of what he looked like and how he acted on the day Clarisse came in and got hired. He offers to pay for the funeral, but Officer Burns waives his hand, saying he's taken care of it. Mr.

Harris knows there's no point in arguing. He's buying the flowers though; if there's double, so be it.

"We need to let the community know. We need to let them know that this evil exists," he says.

Officer Burns nods. "The Commonwealth's Attorney has photos of the body. The evidence from the scarring on her skin paired with her statement don't bode well. We've got a warrant for their arrest—Father Simmons and her parents."

At this, Mr. Harris chokes up. He's too clouded by sorrow to say anything else.

"How did we miss her?" Officer Burns whispers it, almost scared of the words he speaks.

Mr. Harris looks up, startled by the question. "What do you mean?"

Officer Burns lowers his eyes, undoubtedly hiding tears. "How did we, as a community, miss this girl? How did we fail her for so long? How is it that no one that saw her said anything? Did anyone know? Did anyone suspect anything? And why not file a report or ask for an investigation?"

Mr. Harris shrugs. "People are blind. What do you expect? Nobody wants to be anybody's hero these days. The system is jacked and kids get forgotten."

It's the truth; neither of them speak anymore of it. Officer Burns has other cases to deal with and Mr. Harris has suits to tailor. The funeral happens a few days later. The whole town arrives, asking the same questions.

Everyone at the funeral seems to be asking the same questions. How was she missed? Why did no one do anything? Mr. Harris hears it all. Some admit to thinking things were strange about Clarisse—Mr. Harris can't help but feel frustrated that no one bothered to ask questions. *But I'm just as guilty.* A pang of regret swallows him up. He hangs his head, refusing to look at anyone, let alone Clarisse's body.

When they close the casket, not a dry eye remains. When the last stone is upon the mount that keeps her body captive from whence it came, they all leave.

31

CLARISSE MONROE

AUGUST 3, 2000 - JULY 10, 2018

"May you always look up and see."

32

MEMENTO MORI

Clarisse

It's been days and her soul lingers. Clarisse wanders through her home, growing frustrated by the minute. She can't speak to anyone; she watched as Terrence got up and left. It's a wonder he didn't notice her. *Didn't he reap souls like mine once upon a time? Did he lose that power?*

Her heart breaks for Mr. Harris as she watches him walk in. It breaks her once again to hear Terrence's name being called. He never comes.

It's like he never existed.

Her soul wanders to the ballroom. It hovers there, waiting. When the icy presence of another breaks through the doors, she breathes a sigh of relief.

"I was wondering when you'd make it."

She turns; her mouth drops. Death's golden eyes are bursting with tears. He rushes to her and a million different emotions hit her at once. Collapsing under their weight, he swings up underneath her to catch her, letting her come apart in his embrace. His cold soul is a wash of relief to her... a breath of fresh air. Being alone has been sheer agony.

"I... you weren't on my list. I... I'm so sorry."

"How did you figure it out?"

Death frowns. "The stars told me."

"They talk to you, too?"

"I'm made of them, am I not?"

Clarisse giggles, pulling away from him to take in his image once more. "I missed you."

Death's stars burn a bright pink. He doesn't try to hide them this time, though. They start to burn with myriad colors. "I'm so sorry I left you... I should have been more caring. More understanding. Terrence was always better at that part. I'm so stupid and I'm so sorry. What you've been through..." Death shudders; he's letting more tears fall now. "I never should have left you."

"You were doing your job," Clarisse smiles. Pain is still with her, but it's quieter now. Manageable. It hurts her to see Death ache. *Don't blame yourself.*

"Oh, but I will. I should have let the rules slide and gotten you out of there. You're special, after all. Magic should have been enough of an excuse for me to step in."

Clarisse shakes her head. "No, Death. You will not blame yourself. But can you do me a favor?"

Her heart burns, hoping to every star and being in the Afterlife that he'll grant her this one last wish.

"Anything. Name it."

"Don't erase Terrence. Don't punish him if you catch him. Don't respond to pain with more pain. I realize what he did was stupid, but he knew that, too. Please?"

Death pauses, his eyes still glimmering. "As you wish. Though, of all the favors you ask for, you ask me to spare him? Not yourself?"

Clarisse dares herself to whisper. "You can't control what's going to happen to me. But you can control what you do to him." Her voice trembles. "Will you stay with me? I know I'm asking a lot, but I don't want to be alone when I face judgment."

"I would never let you face that alone, Clarisse. Ever. And if I can find a way to free you of any punishment you might face, I will. I'm your friend just as much as Terrence is. A shitty one, but a friend, anyway."

Something tugs at her soul; they're inextricably bound. She's not sure why or how, but she knows Death has to be feeling it, too. Her hands burn with her little lights. Her stars scream across the ballroom, setting it aglow.

She takes a breath. "Let's go, then."

THE END

The Tales of the Selyento
continues with:

Beyond the Stars

THE CURRENT MANSALO CODEX

Grammar Rules

No conjugation for verbs—context alone determines how a verb is used.

' attached to a phrase indicates an understood you. (Either in command or regular conversation).

Qualities of possession (their, your, etc.) should be conjoined with the objects they possess.

∼

A

Ahklena: To redo/to relive. (Magical) The process of reliving your life after you have died (or during).

Ahleh: Return

Ahlura: Magic

Aleh Awlo: South West

Alti: Mountain

Altiya: Heaven/Elysium
Adan: Live/life (command, action, being, etc.)
Arke: Happy

B

Barulatye: Book
BarulatyeSelben: Book of the Gods
Ben: Soul
Bendala: Binding of souls
Bur: East

C

Chella: Open/to open

D

Dya: Dream
DyaChella: To revisit a dream, either yours or someone else's (context dependent)

F

Fleckerleke: Harsh swear word—interpret it as you will
Fal: Fate
Falme: Fate string

K

Kohlu: Tartarus
Kreyuhl: The Passing Point/Place (The garden of the Selyento)

L

Lafura: Soul Mate (of the chosen variety)
Lafuran: Soul mates (plural)
Li: Water
Lia: Rain
Lo: Language/to be of something

M

Mansa: War
Ma: You
Mar: Your
Me: String
Marlo: Day

N

Na: Death (the concept, not the creature)
Narlasha: Special instrument in Tyrladan. Strings made of light that change with the time of day. Not playable at night. Brightness and tone of the strings rise and fall with the setting sun or sun(s), depending on where it is played in Tyrladan.
Neylka: Nothing (the nothingness between the worlds in the Afterlife)

P

Penda: North

R

Ralun: Minor Mansalo god of darkness (accomplice to Terrence)
Rashia: Squirrel

S

Sel: Music
Selben: Gods
Selbena: God
Selbeno: Goddess
Selyento: Tree of music Sira: Fire
Siralto: Goddess of Light

T

Thma: Gift
Toines: (Comparable to dollars—currency)
Tye: Paper
Tyrladan: Afterlife
Tryta: Darkness (the God)

U

Uht: Place

V

Velyasa: Window/portal

Y

Ya: To
Yehta: Limbo/purgatory

ACKNOWLEDGMENTS

This book is a labor of love that has taken six years to craft. A speck of inspiration in high school has turned into a story far brighter and wonderful than I could have ever imagined. Death, Terrence, and Clarisse are all very near-and-dear to my heart.

Of course, it goes without saying that I am indebted to many people for their constant encouragement while I wrote this book.

Firstly, as in the dedication, I must thank my mother first. She has held my hand through literally everything and been my saving grace. To my dad, I owe him the bravery I was born with to do things on my own. Going indie is not for the faint of heart; my dad has always encouraged me to embrace my inner entrepreneur and take life by the horns.

I would like to thank my cover designer, Lily Dormishev, for bringing to life the artwork I could never hope to produce myself. A big thanks to my editor, Marissa Gramoll, for helping me fix my idiosyncratic tendencies, develop my plot, and become a better storyteller. To my proofreader, Beth Swicker, for helping me find the little grammar errors that still hid within my draft even after many rounds of professional editing and self-editing. I am also indebted to

Liz Steinworth for her amazing formatting abilities. Like how this book looks and reads on the inside? That's all Momma Rogue.

As odd as it is, I would like to thank my horse, Andy, for giving me wings and confidence I didn't know I had. This book really came to life after meeting him. His coat, ironically, is a color like fire. He sure ignited mine.

And lastly, thank you, dear readers. Thank you for coming along with me on this journey. I do hope you enjoyed it; if you did, I would be ever grateful if you'd come back around when it continues. And it *will* continue. This is not the last you've seen of my darlings, should you choose to return.

AUTHOR'S NOTE

Thank you again for taking the time to read *Remember the Stars*. If you liked what you read, I do hope you'll check out my social media accounts, my website, and maybe even sign up for my mailing list!

Also, if you don't mind and have the time, if you could leave me a review to let me know how I did and what you thought of my little world, I would love to hear your thoughts. Whether that review go on Amazon, Goodreads, your preferred social media platform, etc., I want to hear it. Be as honest as you like. My goal as an author is to provide you with stories that matter and that inspire. If I've done that, I'm happy. If not, I want to know how to improve. Without you, dear reader, this book would be for naught.

www.erismarriottauthor.com
facebook.com/ErisMarriottAuthor
instagram.com/erismarriott